RACE AGAINST DEATH

RILEY MALLOY THRILLER SERIES, BOOK 3

Judith A. Barrett

Wobbly Creek, LLC

RACE AGAINST DEATH

RILEY MALLOY THRILLER SERIES, BOOK 3

Published in the United States of America by Wobbly Creek, LLC

2021 Georgia

wobblycreek.com

Cover by Wobbly Creek, LLC

ISBN 978-1-953-87014-8 eBook

ISBN 978-1-953-87015-5 Paperback

Previously . . .

RILEY

My name is Riley Malloy, I'm a vet tech, and I understand animals, which must be why people call me a "dog whisperer." After the veterinary clinic where I worked in Pomeroy, Georgia, abruptly closed, I needed a job and a cheaper place to live that allowed dogs. I loaded my car with my belongings and Toby, a five-year-old black and brown mostly German Shepherd, who had been abandoned at the clinic. Toby and I headed to my grandma's cabin in Barton.

I was surprised when Marcy, my coworker from the clinic in Pomeroy, left a cat in a carrier on my doorstep, along with a note asking me to take care of her cat for a while. I was even more surprised to find that Princess was feral, so there's no way Marcy had any attachment to that sweet with a streak of cranky feline; however, Princess decided being a domestic cat wasn't too bad with its perks of regular food and a safe place to sleep.

I didn't realize it until later, but Marcy had left more than Princess in my care; she also left evidence that would expose a long-running illegal drug operation.

Marcy was out of her league, though, because she was murdered, and her killers came after me.

I was beaten, kidnapped, and left for dead when the thugs threw me into a cold river. I somehow made it to a riverbank even though I was badly injured, wet, and freezing. I was alone except for my friend, a Bob White quail, who encouraged me to keep going.

I'm certain I wouldn't have survived without Ben and Toby. Ben Carter is a lanky deputy with greenish hazel eyes and is super cute. In addition to being a stellar law enforcement officer, Ben is very knowledgeable about caring for animals because of the summers he worked with his uncle, a veterinarian. His uncle thinks Ben should become a veterinarian, and so do I.

After Ben and Toby rescued me, I needed time to recuperate from my injuries. Ben and I decided the killer must have had information only someone close to me would know, so Ben, Toby, Princess, and I left town to stay with Ben's folks, who are warm, kind-hearted people.

When I stopped the killer, Ben and I were relieved, but then my Aunt Millie warned me of a second killer who was even more relentless. With Princess's brilliant distraction, I was able to stop the second killer, too.

BEN

I still haven't recovered from how close Riley came to being murdered more than once; I'll fill in what she left out. Besides being brilliant and her remarkable talent to communicate with animals, she has fiery red hair and is the prettiest girl I've ever seen. Both of us applied to the University of Georgia Veterinary College with the offers of complete scholarships and the encouragement and prodding of friends and family.

UGA and the veterinary college accepted me, and Riley was accepted by UGA and placed on the waitlist for the veterinary college. I did not want to go to veterinary school without Riley, so I declined.

I had always wanted to be in law enforcement, and I liked working with and learning from Sheriff Dunn in Barton. Case closed, and I was happy to stay with Riley in Barton until Riley told me I had to accept and she'd attend UGA. I made my final decision, and we're going to UGA together in the fall.

Chapter One

While Claire and Riley reviewed the day's schedule, Zach joined them at the desk. When he glanced out the front window, his face paled. "A storm's blowing in. I'll clean my exam room again. Excuse the cliché, but better safe than sorry."

"What are you talking about, Zach?" Riley asked. "We cleaned the rooms before we left on Saturday, and the sky was clear when Toby and I came in earlier."

Zach hurried to the first exam room and closed the door.

"He might be right." Claire pointed to the front door.

When Pia stomped into the building, her dark eyes flashed, and she mumbled under her breath in Spanish until she reached Claire's desk. "It took me over thirty minutes to get here after I dropped off Jackson at school. It's a five-minute drive," she fumed. "I was stuck behind half the town by two police roadblocks on the way. I don't know what's going on, but no speeders were leaving the school; I can vouch for that. I made a blueberry-lemon pound cake, but it's probably stale by now, and all your cinnamon rolls are probably gone, Riley, and I'm certain nobody bothered to save one for me. When I asked Ben what was going on, he said to tell everyone 'Hi' for him. He's infuriating, Riley. We need to find you a new boyfriend."

As Pia rushed to the breakroom to put her lunch and the pound cake into the refrigerator, she bumped into Doc Thad, and he raised his eyebrows.

Claire waved her hands and shook her head; Doc Thad furrowed his brow and peered at Claire. He shrugged as he turned to Pia. "What's your rush, Pia? Trying to make up for coming in late?"

Pia growled, "You're probably the one who ate all the cinnamon rolls before I could get here to claim mine, and you need to find a new friend."

Pia bumped him with her arm as she stormed past him.

Claire sighed. "I was trying to warn you, Thad. Pia's on a tear because she was stopped at two police roadblocks on her way to work, and to make it worse, Ben was polite to her."

"Ben was nice, so I can't joke about being late to work? I think I'm missing something here." Doc Thad scratched his head; Claire rolled her eyes and then answered the ringing phone as Doc Thad skimmed through the folders before he left her desk.

After Claire hung up, she said, "Amanda was supposed to bring baby Zoey here this morning, but she heard about the traffic tie-up. Even though her mother offered to drive, Amanda was worried about being stuck in the car with three crying babies. She'll call tomorrow, and we'll try again. I'm dying to see that sweet cutie, even though I was positive Amanda's baby was a boy. Didn't three boys make sense to you? Amanda said her mother would stay another two weeks, and she's grateful for the help with her two older babies and the newborn; although little Sean is three years old, maybe I shouldn't call him a baby."

Doc Julie Rae hurried down the hallway from her office. "We need to have a quick staff meeting."

"I'll grab Zach. Where is he?" Doc Thad asked.

"Exam room one." Riley pointed.

"Pia," Claire shouted. "Staff meeting."

Pia glowered as she came out of the breakroom with a cinnamon roll wrapped in a napkin. "They left me two measly cinnamon rolls. I'll bet they were the smallest ones." She sulked as she leaned against the wall near the reception area and ate the pastry.

"The sheriff's dispatcher called me. It will be on the news shortly because the mayor called a press conference," Doc Julie Rae said. "Two men stole a van at the gas station while the driver filled her tank at the pump. Unfortunately, two children were still in the van: Caleb, the younger of the two boys who came with Albert, the guinea pig, and two-year-old Janelle, who Gracie saved from being hit by a car not long ago. Janelle's mother was taking Caleb to school because his older brother was sick."

"Oh, no." Pia headed to the front door. "I need to make sure Jackson's okay; I'll pick him up and bring him here."

"Wait, Pia, you can't; the school's on lockdown," Doc Julie Rae said. "There's more."

Doc Julie Rae leaned against the desk. "Remember Hector? The two-year-old pit bull mix? Janelle saw

Hector at the next pump and called him to their van. I guess Caleb opened the back door so Janelle could see Hector, and Hector leaped inside with the children as the men pushed over Janelle's mother and jumped into the van."

"Hector would want to protect the children," Riley said.

Doc Julie Rae bit her lip and nodded. "Not long after that, a parent who had dropped off a child at school found Hector in the middle of the street a block from the school. Hector's been shot. The sheriff and Ben are bringing Hector here."

"What about the children?" Pia's eyes widened.

"We don't know," Doc Julie Rae said.

Doc Thad, Riley, and Zach rushed to the trauma room. "We'll get the room ready," Doc Thad said.

"I'll meet them outside with our trauma cart." Riley grabbed the cart and ran with it to the front door.

The sheriff slammed his cruiser to a stop and jumped out. He and Ben lifted Hector onto the cart, and Riley covered the pittie with a warm, soft blanket before she rolled the cart to the building.

Ben bent over Hector as they went inside. "I told you Riley would be waiting outside for you."

Hector whimpered, and Riley stopped the cart. Hector whined.

"I'm right here. Where is that?" she asked.

Hector whimpered, then whined again, and Riley said, "Thanks. Doc Thad and Zach are waiting for you. Zach will take some x-rays, and Doc Thad will check your wounds. I'll be close. If you need me, they'll let me know."

While Riley and Ben continued to the exam room, Ben asked, "What did Hector say?"

"When the two bad guys stopped and opened the car door to pull out Hector because he was attacking them, Hector and the children jumped out and ran. The children ran to a dumpster behind the grocery store and may have found a way to climb inside the dumpster." Riley's voice had a catch in it. "Hector and Caleb planned it. Hector kept the bad guys busy so Caleb could escape with Janelle and hide."

Ben kissed Riley's cheek before he ran for the front door and shouted as he left, "You're awesome."

When Riley and Hector reached the trauma room, Riley leaned close to Hector. "Where did they shoot you?"

Hector whined.

"Doc, Hector was shot in his right shoulder." Riley pointed to a wound on Hector's neck that had soaked a trauma dressing. "They knifed him too. This is his worst wound other than the gunshot."

"We've got you, Hector," Doc Thad said. "We'll grab some x-rays; Zach is fast. After your x-rays, Riley and I will take care of your wounds. We'll make you as comfortable as we can while I stitch you up."

Hector licked Doc Thad's hand, and Doc Thad put his hand over his heart. "Thank you, Hector. That means a lot to me."

Zach took over the cart and rolled Hector into the x-ray room. "I'm not only fast; I'm good."

Doc Thad reviewed the x-rays while Zach returned Hector to the trauma room. When they arrived, Riley bent close, stroked Hector's muzzle, and hummed a tune to him before she removed the trauma dressing.

"Good news, Hector. The knife didn't nick an artery." She cleaned the wound and covered it as Doc Thad returned.

"We've got a bullet we need to get out of you, Hector," Doc Thad said. "Zach, would you ask Doc Julie Rae to join us?"

Doc Thad and Doc Julie Rae gowned while Riley rolled Hector into their surgery room.

"They'll take good care of you," Riley whispered.

After Hector's surgery, Zach said, "I'll stay with Hector."

Doc Julie Rae nodded. "Thanks, Zach. I'll call George to let him know that Hector will be here tonight."

"If Mr. George can't make it, I'll stay," Zach said. "Hector is my new hero."

Riley's phone buzzed with a text from Ben. "Tell Hector we found kids thanks to him."

She showed the text to Zach.

"Thanks, Riley," Zach said. "I'll tell Hector as soon as he stirs."

Riley cleaned the trauma room while Doc Thad cleaned the surgery room, and Doc Julie Rae left to examine their scheduled patient, who was in exam room one with Pia.

A young man with long black hair and tattoos on his neck and his arms from his wrists to his elbows rushed into the building. "How's Hector? I heard the sheriff brought him here."

"He's resting," Riley said. "He was shot and knifed while he distracted the kidnappers so the children could run away. He's a true hero. Doc Thad and Doc Julie Rae removed the bullet and stitched his neck wound. He'll need to stay a day or two, but he'll bounce back soon. You can see him if you like. He's still asleep from the anesthesia, and you can speak to him, but don't expect him to respond. It might relax him, though, to hear your voice."

The young man exhaled. "Thank you, Riley. We've got a song he likes to hear."

"Zach's with him. I'll show you where they are." Riley led the young man to the kennel.

"Hey, Zach. How's my buddy doing?" the young man asked.

Zach rose from the floor beside Hector's crate, and the two young men shook hands and bumped shoulders.

"How ya been, Mitch?" Zach asked. "Haven't seen you in a while. Hector's resting after his surgery."

"He loves kids," Mitch said. "I wasn't surprised that he trotted over to talk to the little girl when she called him, but it sure shocked me when those..." He glanced at Riley and then continued, "Jerks drove off with him and the kids."

"This is third-hand, but I'll tell you what I know." Zach sat on the floor opposite the young man, and Riley headed back to the reception area.

"How's Hector?" Claire asked.

"Resting and well-guarded," Riley said.

"I'd be right there with them if you'd take over the desk." Claire smiled.

Riley's phone buzzed with a text from Ben. She smiled and then showed the text to Claire.

Ben: "How's Hector?"

"I like Ben; he's a good man, Riley," Claire said. "Let's keep him around another week or two, at least."

"He's working out, so far." Riley smiled.

Riley replied to his text. "Doing fine. How are the kids?"

"Stink like week-old garbage but fine."

Claire giggled. "I guess they made it into the dumpster with no problem. Don't you think Caleb has a future as an undercover agent?"

After a busy morning, Zach left Hector with Mitch and joined Riley and Pia at Claire's desk. "I'll cover patients, so you can break for lunch, Riley."

"Thanks, Zach. I'll grab Doc Julie Rae, and then you can have lunch with Claire and Doc Thad," Riley said.

While they ate, Pia said, "It's funny I haven't heard anything from Tom because he'd want to know how Hector and the kids were. He calls me whenever he wants the inside info."

"Maybe he thinks you're busy, too," Riley said.

Pia snorted. "Never stopped him before." She picked up her phone and frowned. "I missed a text from him. It says, 'loco n,' and that's all. That's strange because I've never heard Tom call anything loco; it must have been a pocket text."

She shrugged and called him. "His phone rang to voice mail. He's probably in a big meeting, but he'll see I called."

"Charlie calls Claire if I miss his call. Is there someone you can call at the Distribution Center to tell you what's happening?" Doc Julie Rae asked.

Pia shook her head. "I can't think of anyone that wouldn't be busy if Tom's busy."

Pia picked up and tossed the trash while Riley cleaned and swept under the table; Doc Julie Rae set up the coffee for the next morning.

"I'll tell Zach that he can come to the breakroom or eat his lunch next to Hector if he prefers, then I'll let Doc Thad know we're back on duty," Doc Julie Rae said.

After Riley relieved Claire, she handed Pia the top patient folder from the stack of folders on Claire's desk.

"Looks like it's going to be a busy afternoon," Pia said as two cars pulled into the parking lot.

Riley peered at the cars. "The second one is the sheriff's cruiser."

When the client came inside with a cat carrier, Pia led the way to exam room one.

After the sheriff came inside, he smiled. "I expected to see Claire at the desk. It must be lunchtime. How's your arm doing?"

"It's doing great. I completed my physical therapy sessions, but I'm supposed to be careful with it for a while longer." Riley peered at the sheriff. *Is this a personal visit?*

The sheriff raised his eyebrows, and his eyes twinkled. "I understand you fired the physical therapist."

Riley shrugged. "Matter of semantics."

The sheriff chuckled. "Is Doc Julie Rae available?"

"I don't think she's gone into the exam room yet. Do you want to go to her office, or shall I tell her you're here?"

"I'll go to her office," he said.

Riley drummed the desk with her fingers. *He's here on business; something's up.*

As Riley hung up the phone after setting up an appointment for later in the week, Doc Julie Rae hurried to the desk.

"Please take over Pia's patient and send Pia to my office. I'll ask Claire to cut her break short," Doc Julie Rae said.

When Riley entered the exam room, Pia smiled.

"May I see you for a minute, Pia?" Riley asked.

After they were in the hallway, Riley said, "Doc Julie Rae wants you to go to her office. I don't know why."

Pia's face paled, then she gave Riley a quick summary of the tiny black kitten and hurried to Doc Julie Rae's office.

When Riley returned to the exam room, she said, "Doc Julie Rae will be here in just a minute. Pia told me that Ethel's eyes were red and had a discharge. Doc Julie Rae will examine her eyes and have the right medicine for her."

After Doc Julie Rae entered the room, she gently cleansed Ethel's eyes before examining her.

"There are no signs of any trauma, but both eyes have an infection." Doc Julie Rae applied eye drops and then left as the client listened while Riley explained how to rinse away the discharge and apply the drops.

"Claire will schedule Ethel's follow-up appointment for you, but give us a call or come in if you think Ethel's eyes haven't improved by Wednesday," Riley said.

Riley returned the kitten to the carrier and led the client to Claire's desk. As Riley glanced at the cars on the road, Pia sped away from the animal hospital; Riley frowned. *Where is Pia going?*

When the reception area cleared of clients and patients, Claire asked, "Did you see Pia tear out of here? What's going on?"

"I have no idea. The last I saw of her, she went to Doc Julie Rae's office to talk to the sheriff."

"The sheriff left right before you came out of the exam room. He told me to be safe when he left, but he says that all the time," Claire said. "I'll bet Doc Julie Rae knows."

"You might be right, but if she wants us to know, she would have said something. She must not think we need to know."

"Well, she's wrong," Claire said. "Do you think Tamara might know something? Her husband works at the Distribution Center. If it were something at the school, I would have heard something by now."

"I'd hate to put Tamara on the spot," Riley said.

"I know. That's how you are. Go clean your exam room or whatever it is that you vet techs do to hide from me." Claire chuckled.

"I can take a hint." Riley tossed her hair. "Pretend I'm gone; what are you going to do?"

Claire snorted. "Call Tamara."

"Are you sure about that?" Riley held up her hands when Claire glared at her. "I've got an exam room to clean."

After Riley cleaned the exam room, she strolled to the kennels and smiled. *Those two are certainly keeping an eye on Hector.*

As she turned to leave, Zach asked, "Did you need me, Riley?"

"Pia left for a bit. This is just a heads-up for you. I'll take the next patient, but we'll need you to take the patient after that."

Hector whimpered, and Riley smiled. "Hector wants to hear his song again."

Zach rose from the floor and followed Riley while Mitch sang to Hector.

After they went into the exam room that Riley needed to clean, Zach said, "Mitch was always a kind-hearted guy when we were in school. He was one of my few friends. He works at the Distribution Center in the technology department."

"Really? But he wouldn't know if anything happened this morning because he's been here, right? I think there's something because Pia suddenly left after the sheriff talked to her."

"I'll ask him." Zach left the room, and Riley finished cleaning. *Wonder if Claire will be mad that I found an alternate source for information.*

Zach opened the door. "Mitch called a buddy at work. You'll have to hear it for yourself."

When they reached the kennels, Mitch said, "My friend didn't know much, Riley, but the rumor going around work is that our Finance Manager disappeared along with a huge sum of cash. Of course, the gossips refused to think of any reason Tom Grant would suddenly disappear unless he was guilty of something. I know Mr. Grant, and he'd never take a penny that wasn't his. Someone said that Mrs. Grant came to the center, but a deputy talked to her before she came inside, and she left."

"That means Pia is coming back," Zach said. "I'm staying here with Hector and Mitch unless I have a patient."

Riley's eyes twinkled. "You might have a lot of company back here, Mitch."

Hector whined, then grinned, and Riley laughed. "I'm glad you're feeling better, Hector, but I promise you no visitors allowed."

Zach and Mitch stared at Riley. "What did Hector say?" Zach asked.

"He said his kennel might get crowded. That's why I told him 'no visitors.'"

Zach chuckled. "I'll make you a sign, Hector, and we'll tell everyone it's Riley's order."

Hector yipped, and Riley said, "Hector agrees with you, Zach."

Mitch cocked his head. "They call me eccentric at work. I feel like I found my tribe."

Hector relaxed on his pad in the kennel and closed his eyes.

"I have a sign to make." Zach hurried to Claire's desk.

"He'll probably sleep for the rest of the afternoon," Riley said. "You can leave if you like and come back later."

"I have some things at work that I'd like to complete today." Mitch pulled back his hair and raised his head to look at Riley. "Are you sure?"

"I'm positive, and we'll check on him regularly," Riley said.

Mitch stroked the sleeping dog's head. "I'll be back soon, buddy. Zach will call me if you need me."

After Mitch left, Pia came in the back door and joined Riley and Claire at the front desk.

"Tom's not at work, and nobody knows when he left or where he went. One of his staff told me in the parking lot that a rumor was going around about inventory shortages and missing cash. The sheriff asked to search our home, but I told him he needed a search warrant. I want to know why the investigators aren't focused on finding Tom; if they thought he'd gone home, they could have knocked on the door, and he would have opened it to let them in. I didn't know what to do, so I went home. I guess I thought I'd wait for him there, but that didn't make any sense."

Claire rose and put her arm around Pia. "Let's go to the breakroom; you need to sit down."

Pia nodded, and Riley said, "I'm coming too."

On the way, Claire shouted, "Zach, would you take over the front desk for me?"

Zach's eyes widened when he saw Pia, but he continued with his head down to Claire's desk.

"Thanks, Zach," Claire said. "Let me know when you have a patient, and I'll take over."

After reaching the breakroom, Riley poured Pia a cup of coffee and joined Claire and Pia at the table.

Pia gulped down her coffee. "That helped. I checked Tom's notebook, which he's kept for years. He lists the projects he needs to do around the house and a maintenance record. I found some notes and calculations that made no sense to me." She pulled out her phone. "I left the notebook at home because I was afraid I'd make things worse if it wasn't there when they showed up with their search warrant, but I took pictures of the pages from this month because his notes weren't anything like what he usually records. I have to find Tom, and I thought you two might help me."

Claire furrowed her brow. "The professional investigators will be looking for Tom; won't we be duplicating what they're already doing?"

"They won't be looking for Tom," Pia's voice cracked. "They'll be trying to find a crook. That's different."

She picked up her phone and sent a text, and Riley's phone buzzed.

"I sent you the pages because I thought you might see something I can't see, Riley," Pia said.

Claire nodded. "The investigators won't look at Tom's notes like Riley would." Claire rose. "I'll relieve Zach. I think staffing the desk makes him nervous because he feels stuck."

"I need to work to keep from thinking the worst. Dogs, cats, and guinea pigs help me to relax." Pia rinsed her cup.

Riley glanced at the text from Pia before she left the breakroom. *I'll look at this later.*

Toward the end of the workday, Riley's phone buzzed with a text from Ben. "I'll be working late. Don't wait up. Sorry."

Riley went into exam room two while Pia was cleaning it. "What are you doing for dinner tonight? Ben will be late."

Pia smiled. "Come home with me. I'll cook while Jackson finishes his homework, and you can read. Jordy wouldn't mind a Toby visit."

"I'll run home, check the mail, and feed Toby, then we'll come to your house. Anything I can pick up at the grocery store?"

"Ice cream. I need ice cream to get through the rest of the day."

After George arrived and everyone had finished their tasks for the day, Zach said, "I'm going to stick around until Mitch shows up. See you in the morning."

On the way home, Riley said, "Pia may be right. The investigators seem to be focused on unearthing an unknown crime at the Distribution Center and ignoring a missing man, but maybe another team is looking for Tom. If there is, they should have let Pia know."

Toby yipped, and Riley nodded. "I'm sure someone is looking for Tom too."

After they were home, Riley sorted through the mail while Toby ate and then tossed the junk mail before they returned. While Toby cruised the backyard, Riley stared at her phone. *I wonder if Tom meant to send Pia a text and was interrupted.*

Riley stopped at the grocery store for ice cream before she continued to Pia's house. As she parked in front of the house in one of the newer neighborhoods, Riley smiled at the wide sidewalks, neatly mowed and trimmed lawns, rose bushes, and bicycles and tricycles parked on the front porches. *This is definitely a neighborhood of young families.*

Jackson threw open the door, and Jordy, their black lab, rushed out to greet his friend, Toby. Jackson was lean, had dark skin and hazel eyes like his father, and was almost as tall as Pia. *Everybody towers over me except Doc Julie Rae.*

"Hi, Aunt Riley. Mama's cooking and she said you might bring dessert. Did you?"

"Of course I did. What's your favorite ice cream?"

"Cold," Jackson giggled, and Riley laughed.

"You are in luck, sir. That's exactly the kind I brought."

Jackson's eyes twinkled. "Can I carry it inside for you?"

Riley smiled as she handed the grocery sack to him. *Well played, Jackson.*

"Mom!" Jackson shouted as Jordy and Toby rushed into the house. "Aunt Riley's here, and she brought ice cream."

Jackson peeked into the sack. "Chocolate is my very favorite."

"I knew that." Riley followed him to the kitchen. Riley stopped in the doorway to inhale the heady aroma of spices mingled with chocolate that swirled through the air.

"We're not having anything fancy," Pia said. "Just chicken and vegetables over rice and a salad. Jackson requested brownies to go with his chocolate ice cream.

You and I will be in sugar-shock, and Jackson will bounce off the walls."

Riley giggled. "Dinner and a show."

Riley sat at the breakfast bar while Jackson set the table, and Pia stirred the chicken and then pulled the brownies from the oven.

After they ate dinner, Jackson cleared the table while Pia loaded their dishwasher. When Jackson sat at the table and opened his homework notebook, Pia placed two hot brownies in a bowl and scooped two generous servings of ice cream on top of them. As the ice cream melted, it oozed over the sides of the brownies, and Jackson set aside his homework and dug in.

"This is my favorite dessert." Jackson scooped up another large bite of brownie and dripping ice cream.

"Let's take our dessert out back to the screened-in porch," Pia said. "We won't have to worry about mosquitos, and it's chilly, not hot, so it's tolerable."

Riley stopped Pia from putting a second scoop of ice cream on her brownie. "Tolerable sounds great."

After they were outside, Riley pulled out her sweatshirt from her backpack. "I thought I'd want this out here."

Pia nodded. "Especially since we're eating ice cream. When we finish our dessert, I'll have to go inside to supervise homework."

She pulled a bound maroon book out of her sweatshirt pocket. "This is Tom's journal. I'd like for you to read it from the beginning. That will help you get a feel for Tom's typical entries."

"I hope you don't have your hopes set too high, Pia." Riley frowned as she dropped the journal into her backpack.

Pia sighed. "I probably do, but I'm grasping at straws here. Tom's assistant called me; she was really upset. She saw Tom park this morning, and then two men approached him. She didn't think she recognized them, but her eyesight had been failing for a while. She started walking closer to them because she was very nosy, but she claimed Tom might have wanted her to take notes while they talked. Tom told her to go inside and cancel his meeting with Dylan. She hurried to her desk because she was upset that she'd forgotten about the meeting and was surprised when she called Dylan because he didn't know about any meeting either."

"That's odd." Riley furrowed her brow.

Pia nodded. "She told the sheriff what she saw, but she said she was flustered and maybe got a few details wrong. I'm sure she did. She's really good at her job as long as her routine isn't changed. When Tom didn't come to his office, she assumed he'd gone straight to Dylan's office."

Riley cocked her head. "Then who called the sheriff?"

"I called Tamara and asked if she knew anything, and she called one of the supervisors who told her that the new security guard saw the men approach Tom then get into his car after they briefly talked. When the guard saluted Tom as he passed the gate, Tom frowned and shook his head. The guard called the sheriff's office because Tom always speaks to him and smiles."

Pia finished eating her dessert and then sighed. "That's Tom. I think the entire sheriff's department was tied up with the stolen van, but the young guard called again and insisted on talking to the sheriff. The sheriff and Ben went to see him after they dropped off Hector. To the sheriff and Ben's credit, they believed the guard. I guess Ben might be an okay boyfriend for you after all."

Jackson opened the back door. "Mom, there's a man here to talk to you. He told me he was with the GBI and showed me his badge and ID when I asked him for them. He's legit, but you might want to check his ID too. He's waiting on the porch."

"I'll bet this is your warrant. I'll go home unless you want me to stay," Riley said.

"No, this may take a while. Jackson and I will work on homework and stay out of the way, but thanks."

When they reached the front door, Marc smiled at Riley and handed Pia the warrant to read.

"Marc is with the GBI, Pia," Riley said. "He's a good guy and can take it, so be as tough as you like."

Marc chuckled. "Mrs. Grant, your son checked my ID and badge, but I'd be happy to have you examine them too."

"Jackson told me you were legit, and Riley just confirmed it, so I'm fine."

"Thanks for dinner," Riley said.

"Thanks for coming."

Riley frowned. "What about..."

Pia interrupted. "I'm not sure what time I'll be at work tomorrow. I'll need you to cover for me."

Riley nodded. *Got it.* "I can do that. Keep me posted, and call me if you need me."

Toby trotted to the car with Riley as Pia invited Marc inside while she read the warrant.

Riley shook her head. "I guess we're accomplices now. I hope we can help Tom and aren't hurting him. What's your take on all this?"

Toby yipped.

Riley rolled her eyes. "I don't plan to go to jail, but you couldn't go with me if I did, so yes, you'd stay with Ben."

Toby yipped and grinned.

"There's no guarantee that Ben would take you to the farm to be with Princess and the puppies." She glared in the rearview mirror. "Do you want me to ask him?"

Toby threw back his head and howled.

"Fine. I'll ask him."

After they were home, Riley let Toby out back while she heated water for a cup of tea. She sipped her tea while she read Tom's journal. She set the journal on the table next to the sofa and paced. "His journal has snippets of a story mixed with to-do lists and some calculations. I'm unsure if the numbers relate to the project costs or something else. The story appears to be about an Old West bank robber. I wonder if Pia has another notebook with the full story because I'd really love to read it."

Riley resumed reading, but when her eyelids drooped, and her head jerked, she rose and stretched.

"Let's take one last outside break, then we'll lock up and leave on the porch light and the light over the stove for Ben."

After they went inside, Riley headed to her bathroom and showered. When they returned to Barton after living in Carson with Ben's parents, they moved into one of the larger, two-bedroom houses their favorite real estate agent, Helen, owned; Ben insisted the larger bedroom with the bath was hers.

She put on her pajamas and climbed into bed while Toby flopped down on the rug that was between Riley's bed and the doorway.

Riley closed her eyes, rolled from her left to her right side, and tossed the quilt to the floor. *Now my feet are cold.* She sighed and leaned over to pull the quilt back over her. *I'm never going to be able to sleep tonight. I wonder where Tom is. Why isn't Ben home?*

Riley opened her eyes at the sound of a key scrape in the front door and glanced at the time. *Two o'clock. Ben's home.*

While Toby padded from her bedroom to the living room, she turned on her bedside light before she grabbed her robe and headed to the front door.

"Dang." Ben strode inside and hugged Riley. "I didn't mean to wake you. It's been a long day."

"I wasn't asleep." She shivered and then wrapped her arms around him. "I've been worried about Pia's husband. Is there any news?"

"I'll turn on the fireplace to take off the chill," Ben said, "then we can talk without freezing you."

While Riley sat on the sofa and pulled the afghan over her, Ben lit the gas fireplace. After unbuckling his utility belt and setting it on the dining table, Ben sat beside her and put his arm around her shoulders. "The sheriff is spearheading the search for Tom until a GBI team takes over while Marc focuses on the distribution center. I've been working for both of them, and they have run me ragged."

"Have you eaten? I can scramble some eggs and even make you a breakfast burrito." Riley snuggled against him.

"Sheriff bought sandwiches about nine, so I'm not hungry, but how about some hot tea? I'll cook." Ben squeezed Riley and then strode to turn on the burner under the teakettle.

While they sipped their tea, Ben said, "I needed to slow down before I could sleep. Sorry you had to get up, but thanks. So, what do you and Pia think?"

Riley told him about the text Pia got and the journal. "Pia had high hopes that there might be something in the journal to help find Tom, but there isn't. I think Tom was writing a book of Old West short stories. I will ask Pia about it the next time I talk to her because he had some short paragraphs in his journal, and I'd love to read more."

"Old West stories are our favorite, aren't they?"

"They certainly are, and his style is reminiscent of the old classics we enjoy reading."

Ben kicked off his boots, set his empty cup on the floor, and leaned back.

"Are you tired enough to go to sleep?" Riley asked.

"Yes, but I'm comfortable." Ben sighed. "What about you?"

"I'm fine." Riley yawned. "Maybe I am tired enough to go to sleep."

Ben rose and turned off the fireplace, then offered his hand to Riley.

"Pull me up," she moaned. "I'm finally too tired to stay awake."

As they strolled down the hallway with their arms around each other, Riley asked, "What time do you need to get up for work?"

"Sheriff Dunn said to sleep in, but Marc wants to meet at the sheriff's office at nine. I'll set my alarm for seven."

"I leave for work by six thirty. I'll have the coffee ready for you."

When they reached her doorway, Ben kissed her. "Good night, honey. See you in the morning."

Riley pulled up the covers, closed her eyes, and listened to Ben's even breathing. She rolled to her side, opened her eyes, and peered at the time. *Four o'clock. I think I know what Tom's text meant. I wonder if Pia's awake.*

Chapter Two

Riley slipped out of bed, dressed in jeans and a long-sleeved shirt, and pulled on a pair of warm socks. She stuck her phone in the back pocket of her jeans and carried her boots while she tiptoed to the living room, with Toby following her. She put on her sweatshirt and quietly opened the back door; after she and Toby went outside into the cold, she shivered. *I should have grabbed my warm jacket.*

She frowned at her phone. *Do I call or text?*

She sent Pia a text. "Call when you're awake. Not urgent."

She hugged herself and stamped her feet for warmth while her teeth chattered. After she strolled around the backyard with Toby under the clear night sky and the full moon's bright light, she smiled when Toby alerted her to the far-off sound of a yowling cat. The low, rhythmic rumbling of traffic on the nearby state road and an occasional hoot of an owl were the only other sounds until her phone rang.

"Not urgent, but is everything okay? I've been up all night. What about you?" Pia asked.

"I haven't been sleeping either, but I have a question. Do you and Tom have any of the family tracking apps on your phones?"

"I hadn't thought about that. Tom installed one on our phones a while ago, but I've never paid attention to it. Why?"

"I've been thinking about that text, 'loco n.' What if his message was supposed to read, 'loc on'?"

Pia groaned. "I don't know how to do any of this."

"I'll be right over. We'll figure it out," Riley said.

After she hung up, Riley said, "I'm going inside to write Ben a quick note and grab my backpack and car keys. I'll be right back out, then we'll go to Pia's house."

While inside, she picked up her backpack and keys and scribbled a quick note: "I'm at Pia's. She wanted to talk."

She listened to Ben's slow, even breathing, then left by the back door.

When she started her car, she held her breath and squinted at the dark house. "I don't think we woke up Ben, Toby."

She pulled into Pia's driveway, and Pia opened her front door. "Jackson's still asleep," she said, "I closed his door, but he's a sound sleeper, so we won't disturb him. I have coffee."

"Oh, good," Riley said. "Ben didn't get home until after two and fell asleep after we talked for a while, but I've been dozing off and on all night."

Pia set her phone on the dining table before she poured Riley's coffee. "Tom told me he installed some app on my phone so he could always see where I was and

I could check on him, but I never took the time to figure it out."

Riley sat and opened Pia's list of apps, scrolling through them. "This is it." She picked up her cup and sipped her coffee.

Riley opened the application and groaned. "The app has to update. I guess we wait."

Pia refilled their cups and then paced while Riley pretended not to notice.

"I've been reading Tom's journal; so far, I haven't found anything that might help us, but do you know where the stories he was writing are?"

Pia stopped pacing and smiled. "He mentioned his tales of the Old West. After Jackson went to bed, he'd relax by writing in his journal and then working on his stories. He told me once that his writing was true, but the names were changed to protect the guilty." Pia chuckled.

"I think he jotted down ideas and scenes as he thought of them. I'd really like to read his stories. They're on his computer?"

"Yes, but Marc took his computer. He told me I'd get it back in a week or so, but Tom kept backups of all his work on a flash drive. I'll give it to you to copy if you like."

"That would be great. I'll get the drive back to you today or tomorrow if I don't have time enough to copy it this morning." Riley glanced at Pia's phone. "It finally updated."

Pia gave Riley the flash drive and leaned over Riley's shoulder to peer at the screen.

Riley frowned as she scrolled. "I'm sorry I bothered you because, according to your app, Tom's phone is in the distribution center's parking lot. He must have turned off the phone or his location services before he left." Riley rubbed her forehead. "That makes no sense. Are you okay?"

Pia bit her quivering lip. "I'm really disappointed, but I'll be fine. I'll keep the app open in case anything changes." Pia yawned.

Riley stifled her yawn. "I think I can sleep a few hours before work."

On their way home, Riley said, "If we go in the back door, maybe we won't wake Ben. I need at least a power nap before work."

When Riley pulled into the driveway, the house was still dark. She and Toby strolled to the back and went inside. Riley set her alarm for six, removed her jeans and shirt, and crawled into bed.

She opened her eyes and blinked when her alarm went off. *That went fast.* She stretched, then quickly showered and dressed for work. When she left her bedroom, the welcoming aroma of coffee and bacon drifted down the hallway, and she smiled. *That sneak got up before I did.*

"I found your note. You must have changed your mind because you were sound asleep when I woke." Ben poured her a cup of coffee. "I wanted to have breakfast with you, so I set my alarm too."

Riley sipped her coffee. "I went to Pia's but didn't stay very long."

Ben nodded after Riley explained her interpretation of the text and what she had found on the family locator app. "Still, it scared me when I saw your note; I'm not quite over the Evy event."

Ben scrambled a large batch of eggs with green chile. He crumbled bacon onto two tortillas and divided the eggs between them. While he added grated cheese and rolled up the tortillas into burritos, he said, "I liked your locator app idea; it's too bad it didn't work out like you hoped."

"Pia and I were very disappointed." Riley refilled their coffee and pulled out salsa from the refrigerator while Ben removed their burritos from the oven and set their breakfast on the table.

"Wake me up next time, okay?" Ben asked.

Riley furrowed her brow. "I'll think about it."

Ben sighed. "I guess that's a start."

As they ate, Ben asked, "Did you say the app showed Tom's phone was still in the parking lot? I'll check that first thing when I go to work."

"Thank you," Riley said.

"I'll take care of the dishes so you can run off to the clinic." Ben smiled. "I'm not sorry I slowed you down; your lunch is in the refrigerator."

"Thanks." Riley grabbed her lunch and backpack, then kissed Ben before she and Toby headed to the door.

When she reached the parking lot, she said, "Toby, everybody beat us to work except for Pia. Feels strange."

Riley hurried to the breakroom, and Toby trotted to Claire's desk. Doc Julie Rae followed Riley into the breakroom.

"Is everything okay? I almost called you, then I decided you and Pia must have gone to look for Tom," Doc said.

Riley smiled. "We would have if we had a glimmer of a clue, but I can't blame Pia. I would have been here my usual time, except Ben trapped me with a breakfast burrito," Riley said.

"Dang. What can you do with a man who has such devious schemes?" Doc Julie Rae chuckled.

Riley grinned as she put her lunch into the refrigerator. "I know, right?"

When Riley joined Claire at the receptionist's desk, she picked up the stack of patient folders.

"So, what scheme did you and Pia hatch? Were you out all night looking for Tom? Next time, call me; I have fantastic night vision," Claire said.

Riley looked up from the patient record she was reading and raised one eyebrow. "The reason I'm late is because Ben got up before I did and made breakfast burritos. I felt sorry for him and was too polite to let him eat alone."

Claire snickered. "You're always thinking of others, so back to Tom." She raised her eyebrows.

"Doc Julie Rae asked me essentially the same thing. I'll let you know that I was awake all night stressing about Tom and Ben. I had this great idea, but it fizzled."

Claire shook her head. "I'm sorry to hear that. Let me know what I can do, and next time, don't leave me out."

Riley set the folders down and narrowed her eyes. "Ben said the same thing."

Claire laughed. "And yet, you don't take the hint."

"I'll take the first patient," Riley said.

While Riley cleaned the exam room, her phone buzzed with a text from Ben.

"Nothing in the parking lot. Sorry."

Riley stared at the message. *Tom's location must have been turned off in the parking lot.*

When Riley arrived at Claire's desk, Toby sat at the door with his chest out, and his head high as a new patient came into the door. Riley's eyes widened. *It's the white standard poodle with the rhinestones on her pink collar.*

"We'll take this one, Claire," Riley said.

Claire handed her the folder and frowned. "What's wrong with Toby?" she whispered.

"Shh. He's being manly."

"Oh." Claire covered her smile with her hand and nodded.

Riley glanced at the folder. *Regina, of course.*

"Is this a get acquainted checkup for Regina?" Riley asked as the client approached Claire's desk.

"It certainly is." The middle-aged woman's voice was pleasantly musical. "I'm Bethany, and we're new; Regina needs a good vet. Everyone recommended Doctor Sorenson and her team." She smiled at Toby. "And who is this stately gentleman?"

"This is Toby; he's on the staff," Claire said. "His specialty is calming our injured clients."

"I'm Riley." Riley smiled as she motioned toward the exam rooms. "Let's go to exam room two."

Toby led the way, and Regina followed him. Riley and the client followed Regina.

After Riley weighed Regina, Riley asked, "There is nothing in her medical records about any particular problems; is there any area of concern we should focus on today?"

"Is her weight okay? I've been worried that I might be underfeeding her because she looks thin to me. I carefully measure her food and even give her a little extra, just in case."

"Her weight is perfect, but Doc Julie Rae will check her. Have you been outdoors more than usual?"

Regina yipped, and Riley said, "Toby enjoys being outside in our backyard, too."

Bethany peered at Riley. "She has been running more than she did when we lived in the apartment in Atlanta, and she's drinking much more water than she ever did. I'm worried that she's dehydrated or diabetic."

"I'll let Doc Julie Rae know about her increased water consumption, too," Riley said.

Regina whimpered in a musical tone similar to Bethany's voice, and Toby yipped.

Riley smiled as she left to find Doc Julie Rae then explained Bethany's concerns to Doc.

"What do you think, Riley?" Doc asked.

"There's no change in Regina's weight, according to the records her previous vet sent us. I suspect Regina may have lost some fat and gained some muscle since she has frequent access to a fenced yard where she can run."

"Makes sense to me. More exercise also explains her increased water consumption."

"Oh, when I was leaving the room, Regina told Toby he was handsome," Riley said.

Doc Julie Rae smiled. "Maybe I'll suggest play dates at the new dog park for Regina."

"That would be an excellent idea. Toby needs a little more exercise, and I suspect he wouldn't mind more Regina time."

"Charlie would enjoy taking Chuck and Toby to the dog park. Chuck has put on a few pounds, too, and Charlie's mentioned a few times that he'd like to see some adults occasionally. He and the boys did join a homeschooling group, but the boys don't want to go anywhere without Chuck. I don't blame them, but some of the children, and by that, I mean the parents, are nervous around big dogs. Leave it to me. I'll see what I can arrange."

Riley followed Doc Julie Rae into the exam room. When Doc mentioned the dog park to the client, Regina fluttered her eyelashes at Toby, and Toby grinned.

"Does Regina have something in her eyes?" Bethany asked.

"I'm pretty sure she's flirting. Toby is a very handsome guy," Doc Julie Rae said.

Bethany stared at Doc Julie Rae. "He is, isn't he? I've just never seen her do that before." She tittered. "I was worried about the services that a small town would have, and my husband was worried about whether I could adjust to a slower pace. He will be happy to hear that we've found the perfect vet for Regina. He's the new General Manager for the Distribution Center."

"I didn't realize there was a new General Manager, but we don't get out much, do we, Riley?" Doc Julie Rae asked.

Riley shook her head and wiped down the scale with sanitizer to avoid giggling. *Doc Julie Rae is a riot sometimes.*

Bethany continued, "Ezra has been here for six weeks, and he comes home exhausted every night. The previous General Manager was promoted to Regional Manager a little over three months ago, and the company wanted Ezra here as soon as possible. Regina and I visited him a few times, then we moved our furniture this last week."

"Well, welcome. There actually is a lot to do in Barton, but not much after dark, especially on school nights or weekends." Doc Julie Rae smiled.

"I was really impressed with the school. I visited them because I'm trying to tell our daughter to come here with her three girls. Her husband works overseas as a contractor. I'm a homebody, and Ezra was always working, so we never went out."

"I'll talk to my husband, and one of us will call you to schedule a meeting at the dog park. He's a stay-at-home dad and would bring our boys and Toby."

"We'd love it."

Riley took the client to Claire's desk to schedule Regina's next checkup, and Regina and Toby trotted along together to the reception area.

While Riley was cleaning the exam room, Doc Julie Rae joined her. "Lindsey called and asked us to check her horses. They have been very skittish at night and are off their feed, and she's worried about a predator. I have a cooler, so we can take our lunches and picnic at Lindsey's."

"I would love that," Riley said.

"Good. Pia's here now, so we won't leave the office short-handed."

"I have to talk to Pia, then I'll be ready to go whenever you are."

"Come get me when you're ready, and don't forget to wear a warm jacket. If you don't have one here, I've got an extra one, or we could swing by your house."

"I have my sweatshirt, but I wouldn't mind picking up my warm coat," Riley said.

After Riley finished cleaning, Pia waited outside the exam room.

"Have you heard anything?" Pia asked.

"Ben texted me that he couldn't find anything in the parking lot."

Pia nodded as she headed toward the breakroom. "I'm glad Ben's looking; he won't quit."

Riley raised her eyebrows. "I was disappointed he didn't find anything, but you're right."

Pia smirked. "You look terrible."

Riley giggled. "I couldn't look nearly as bad as you."

Pia's dimples deepened as she laughed and hugged Riley. "Thank you for helping me through this."

Riley checked in with Claire. "Doc Julie Rae and I are going to Lindsey's farm to check the horses."

"Better you than me," Claire said. "The wind has picked up. We have a cold front blowing in. Be safe, and let Ben know where you're going. Is Toby going with you?"

"Probably."

"Toby, it's warm in here." Claire peered under her desk; Toby snuffled, rose from his comfortable position, and stretched.

"We'll be back sometime this afternoon. We'll have lunch there; Doc said we'd have a picnic, but I'll bet we eat in her truck."

Toby followed Riley to Doc Julie Rae's office; after Riley and Doc picked up their lunches, the three of them climbed into Doc Julie Rae's truck and went to Riley's house. Riley ran inside and grabbed her heavy coat. When Riley returned, Doc headed north on the highway toward Lindsey's farm.

Riley gazed at the rows of planted pine trees, the fields of cotton, and the farms as they rolled down the highway to the horse farm. When they passed a field of cows, Riley automatically said, "Cows."

When Doc Julie Rae chuckled, Riley furrowed her brow. "Why do we always say 'cows' when seeing them in a field?"

"My theory is that it's from the game we played in the car before electronics. It's ingrained in our brains to win the cow game," Doc Julie Rae said.

Toby barked sharply.

Riley's eyes widened. "Slow down, Doc. We need to turn around. Toby saw something in the ditch."

Doc Julie Rae slowed, then turned around on a dirt road and asked, "Which side of the road?"

Toby whined, and Riley said, "On our left, going this way."

As they crept along, the occasional trucks and cars easily passed them.

"Traveling so slowly is making me nervous. I'll find a place to turn back if we go past the point where Toby saw it."

As the truck crept along, Riley peered at the side of the road. When Toby yipped, Riley said, "Turn around."

Doc Julie Rae turned back and drove as slowly as she could, and three more cars and a large truck passed them.

"Drop off Toby and me here, and wait for us at the next dirt road," Riley said. "I think that would be a much easier way to search and much safer for us and for other drivers."

Doc nodded, then pulled over. Riley and Toby crossed the ditch, walked, and searched as she drove away.

When they reached Doc Julie Rae, Riley said, "Nothing, except I wish we had a trash sack; we could have picked up as we walked along the ditch. It was really irritating to see how thoughtless some people are."

Doc nodded. "See you at the next road."

Before they reached Doc's truck again, Toby darted into the ditch and raced almost out of Riley's sight. She heard him bark and jogged for a few yards, then slowed to catch her breath before she continued more comfortably until he was in sight. When Riley was closer, Toby grinned and wagged his tail.

Riley peered at the object near Toby's feet and squinted for a better look. "It's a phone."

She hurried to join Toby but stopped as she reached for the phone. *I don't want my fingerprints on it.*

She removed her warm gloves from her pocket and put them on before she picked up the phone. *My gloves feel good. I should have put them on when I got out of the truck.*

Riley dropped the phone into the large inside pocket of her coat as she hurried to the truck.

"We found a phone. I don't know whose it is, of course." Riley opened the door for Toby before she climbed in.

"Are you going to call Ben?" Doc asked as she pulled onto the highway and continued to Lindsey's farm.

"I'll text him and ask him to call me, but I'll tell him it's not urgent."

After she sent the text, she pulled the phone from her pocket and put it into the truck glove compartment.

"I don't want it to fall out of my pocket at the horse farm," she said.

"No kidding," Doc Julie Rae said as she turned on the road that led to Lindsey's farm.

When she turned at the gate around the farm, Doc said, "There's Lindsey; she has obviously been watching for us."

After Doc parked, the wizened, weather-beaten woman who wore a black bandana over escaping wisps of gray hair strode their way.

"Get ready to stretch your legs," Doc Julie Rae said. "Remember that old woman can walk faster than we can run."

Riley moaned. "You're right. We'll pay for this tomorrow."

Lindsey jerked open Toby's door, and he jumped out. "Hey there, Toby. How's the boy?" Lindsey rubbed Toby's ears, and he leaned against her.

"Let's go straight to the barn. We can talk there." Lindsey took off, and Toby trotted alongside her.

"Let's walk fast, but not super-fast," Doc whispered.

"Good. I have a feeling we'll need to conserve our energy," Riley said.

When they strolled into the barn, Lindsey stroked one of the older horses and cooed. Toby was whining with soft, calming sounds of encouragement to the other horses.

Riley scanned the barn. *All of the horses are wide-eyed and scared.* She hummed a calming tune as she approached one of the older horses. "What's wrong?"

The horse whinnied and snorted, then shook her head, and Riley clucked her tongue. "I'm so sorry. I'll tell Ms. Lindsey."

"What is it?" Lindsey asked.

"A wild boar near the pasture has been charging the horses, especially the younger ones. The older horses try to block it while the others run, but the pasture isn't big enough for them to get away, and the boar is fast. We'll need to check them for leg injuries."

"I thought something was bothering them at night, and I was worried about snakes. It didn't occur to me that they're spending the day avoiding a wild boar and then coming back to the barn exhausted and nervous," Lindsey said. "I've got a couple of good boar hunters. I'll have them hang out near the pasture for a few days; we'll keep the horses in the barn or the corral until they get that feral hog. Let me talk to my guys, then I'll be back; I want to record any injuries."

"That was awesome, Riley," Doc Julie Rae said. "I would have found any leg injuries, but it might have taken me a while to put the pieces together." Doc Julie Rae stroked the horse in the stall next to her. "Have you heard any more about your application to UGA?"

"I forgot to tell you, UGA accepted me and am on the wait list for the veterinary college; Ben was accepted into the university and the college, so we'll be going to UGA in the fall."

"That's great news. I'm sure you're at the top of the waitlist," Doc said.

"There are several required classes I can take while waiting, so I won't be that far behind Ben."

"I'll bet it took a little fancy footwork on your part to get him to agree to attend the veterinary college with you on their waitlist," Doc Julie Rae said.

"That's exactly right," Riley said.

When Lindsey returned, Doc said, "Tell Lindsey your news, Riley."

Riley told her about being accepted by UGA and on the waitlist; Lindsey whooped, and the horses whinnied.

"See, even the horses are excited." Lindsey grinned.

After they examined all the horses and Lindsey recorded the name of the horse and the location of injuries, Lindsey said, "We can take care of the cuts. I'm just glad it's not any worse. Ready for lunch? We've got hot soup and fresh warm bread in the dining hall, and I heard we're having peach cobbler for dessert."

"Sounds great," Doc Julie Rae said as she winked at Riley. "We have our sandwiches, but we'll save them for tomorrow. We never turn down a hot meal on a cold day."

On the way to the dining hall, Riley checked her phone. Doc Julie Rae raised her eyebrows, and Riley shook her head.

"He must be busy," Riley said.

Doc Julie Rae nodded. "We can stop by the sheriff's office before returning to work."

After they washed their hands, Lindsey led them to the dining room.

"You probably could have found your way here from all the chatter." Lindsey chuckled.

When Lindsey opened the dining hall door, the din of cheerful voices and the clink of silverware greeted them. Riley and Doc Julie Rae followed Lindsey to the serving line.

Lindsey leaned close to them and then spoke loudly enough for them to hear. "We're harvesting cotton and peanuts this week and have a full crew in addition to our nursery, horse, and cattle teams. We're hauling peanuts to the dryers, so we've got truck drivers here too, but it's always this loud."

The line moved quickly, and Lindsey spotted two seats next to each other with a seat across the table from them. "Stay with me," she shouted. "We're going to grab our seats."

She loped off ahead of them, took the single seat and set her bowl at the one place across from her and her dessert at the other. Riley and Doc Julie Rae weaved their way through the mass of people who were leaving and others who made their way with their food to sit with friends.

When they reached their seats, Lindsey chortled. "You two are creampuffs. You need to show up here more often to toughen up and get yourself a place to sit and eat."

After they ate, Lindsey picked up her plate, bowl, and silverware. "We bus our own dishes. Follow me, but keep up this time."

Lindsey jumped up from her seat and strode away, and Doc Julie Rae said, "Let's go, girlfriend. We can do this."

Doc Julie Rae weaved through the crowd to stay on Lindsey's heels, and Riley stayed alongside Doc. After they were outside, Lindsey said, "There's hope for you two yet. Thanks for coming, and show up whenever you need a hot meal or another lesson in maneuvering crowds."

As they strolled to the truck, Toby trotted from the horse barn to join them.

Lindsey said, "I appreciate your talents, Riley. You'll be a fantastic veterinarian."

On the way back to town, Ben called. "Sorry I didn't call sooner. Are you okay?"

"I'm fine. On our way to Lindsey's farm to check her horses, we found a cell phone in the ditch."

"Whose phone is it? Was it turned on?"

"I really don't know anything. I freaked over fingerprints and put on my gloves before I picked it up."

"Perfect. I'll come by the clinic and get it from you. Are you in town?"

"We're about ten minutes away."

"I'll see you there."

After Ben hung up, Riley jerked open the glove box and sighed with relief when she saw the cell phone. "I had a panic moment; I was suddenly afraid someone might have taken it."

Doc Julie Rae shook her head. "No one could have without breaking in. I locked the truck before we headed to the horse barn. I had my panic moment earlier than you when Lindsey opened Toby's door."

Toby yipped when they reached the parking lot behind the animal hospital building, and Doc Julie Rae smiled. "You're right, Toby; Ben is here and waiting for us."

After Doc parked, she jumped out and let Toby out of the truck while Ben opened Riley's door. Riley held the phone in her gloved hand and offered it to Ben, who wore gloves.

"Hi, honey." Ben took the phone. "Marc told the sheriff and me that if you weren't a dog whisperer and headed to veterinary college, he'd recruit you for the GBI."

Doc Julie Rae laughed. "He might have to fight Lindsey; Riley will have to tell you about her diagnosis of the skittish horses."

While Riley climbed out of the truck, Ben examined the phone. "It's missing the SIM card."

"Really? That's great news," Riley said.

"Why do you say that?" Ben hugged her. "I'm glad everything went well for a change."

"If Tom removed the card, he could insert it into another phone that uses the same service provider and same size SIM card and use the new one as his own. Why would the bad guys remove it when they could take away Tom's phone?"

Ben smiled. "Good point."

"Okay, you two are talking over my head. What's a what-you-said card?" Doc Julie Rae asked.

Riley smiled. "Sorry, Doc. A SIM card, which stands for Subscriber ID Module, is like a microchip that stores information about the phone. If a SIM card is removed and then placed in a different phone that is appropriately similar, the new phone has the same number and information as the old phone. The uncertainty is compatibility."

"Thanks," Doc Julie Rae said. "The technology boggles my mind, but at least I understand why you said it was good."

"Go inside, honey. You must be freezing," Ben said. "I'll see you after work. If anything comes up, I'll let you know."

Toby beat them to the door and whined to go in. On their way inside, Riley said, "Did you notice Pia's car wasn't here?"

Doc Thad met them as they went to the breakroom to hang up their coats. "I sent Pia home, which means Claire told Pia to go home because she was dead on her feet."

"I didn't expect her to last the day. I'll give her a call later," Doc Julie Rae said. "How's Zach doing?"

Doc Thad chuckled. "He's overcoming his drive to be a perfectionist and becoming more efficient. Pia had a talk with him before she left; I sure wish I could have listened in. I asked Zach what she said, and he told me Pia had a unique motivational style that was very effective."

Doc Julie Rae raised her eyebrows. "I suspect I don't want to know what she said, but I'm going to ask her anyway."

"If you'll excuse me," Riley said, "I have to go be more efficient."

Riley tossed her hair as she left the breakroom, and Doc Thad chuckled. When Riley reached the receptionist's desk, Toby was lying across Claire's feet.

"If you go out again this afternoon, Toby told me he's staying here to keep my feet warm," Claire said.

"I believe you. It's getting colder. I'm glad Doc Julie Rae told me to take a warm coat." Riley picked up the folders and scanned the patients' records. "Good. There's nothing complex."

Claire nodded. "That's what Zach said. Before she left, Pia lit a fire under him, and he's doing great."

"Do I have time to peek at Hector?"

"Go ahead. Mitch was called into work for some computer emergency but returned before Pia left. Janelle came to see Hector and squealed when she saw him, and he yipped. Janelle wanted to go into the crate to sit with Hector, but Zach convinced her that waiting until Hector was a little better would be better. It took everything I had to keep from laughing at her little quivering mouth."

"I'll bet Janelle planned all along to stay with Hector," Riley said.

"You may be right; she was really disappointed. Janelle's mom learned more about what happened from Caleb's mom. After Hector and Caleb decided on a plan to stop the bad guys, Caleb told Janelle he'd give her a piggyback ride if she could jump out of the van with him when the van stopped. He unbuckled her seatbelt, and Janelle slid next to him. When Hector attacked the bad guys, the kids jumped out. After Caleb rounded the corner and reached the dumpster, he told Janelle they'd hide until the bad men went away, but they'd have to be quiet so they would win the game. He dropped Janelle into the bin, hopped in behind her, and showed her how to cover her eyes to hide. Caleb's mom said that was how her boys played hide and seek. Wasn't that brilliant?"

"I'm in awe of Caleb's resourcefulness. Isn't it great that he hadn't outgrown his ability to understand animals?" Riley smiled.

"I remember talking to my cat, Whiskers when I was young," Claire said. "I've been practicing on Toby because I want to be like you and Caleb."

Toby yipped, and Claire said, "Thank you, Toby."

After Riley left Claire's desk and rounded the corner to the kennels, Mitch smiled, and Hector grinned.

"Feeling better, Hector?" she asked.

Hector growled a short, soft, throaty growl, and Riley smiled. "Of course, you're tough. You did an awesome job of protecting Caleb and Janelle."

"The guys at work heard about Hector." Mitch rose and stretched. "He's becoming a town legend. One of the guys told me that too often Pitties get a bad rap but not in Barton anymore, thanks to Hector."

Toward the end of the day, Pia texted Riley, "Call me after you get home."

After the last client paid and left, Claire locked the front door as Riley strode to the desk. "Riley, what did you plan for dinner, or do you and Ben take turns cooking?"

"We kind of take turns, but he made the hot tea last night, so I think it's my turn. I'm not sure what time he'll be home, so I could make grilled cheese sandwiches or heat a jar of pasta sauce and make spaghetti," Riley said.

"Spaghetti sounds good on a cold night. I always brown some hot sausage and add it to the sauce to make it fancy."

"Good idea; I'll grab a large, premade salad and some French bread since I'll need to stop at the grocery store anyway for the sausage. What did you plan?"

"I couldn't think of anything that sounded good, so I'm copying your spaghetti." Claire smirked.

Riley giggled. "I should have known it wasn't a casual question; now you owe me a menu idea next time."

Zach hurried to the desk from one of the exam rooms. "I cleaned my exam room. After work, I'll grab some takeout, bring it here, and stay here with Hector and Mr. George; Mitch agreed to go home if I stayed. Mr. Charlie will bring a rollaway bed for Doc Julie Rae's office. I told her I'd be fine with my sleeping bag, but she said Mr. Charlie bought the bed a while ago, in case Mr. George can't stay with an overnight patient, but she never remembered to bring it in."

"I never thought about that before: where does George sleep?" Claire asked.

Doc Julie Rae joined them. "George doesn't sleep. He talks with the patients until they fall asleep, then reads the rest of the night. He told me he power naps during the day, has always been a night owl, gets along better with animals than people, and loves to read."

"I didn't realize how staying with our patients was so absolutely perfect for him," Claire said.

Doc Julie Rae nodded. "I told him I was the same, except I'm a night owl until about nine-thirty when I turn into a pumpkin."

Claire and Riley giggled while Zach smiled.

Before she headed to the back, Doc said, "Zach, go ahead and collect your things that you want for tonight and in the morning and pick up your supper. We can close up."

"Thanks, Doc." Zach hurried to grab his coat from the breakroom before he left.

"So, when did you really buy the rollaway bed?" Claire raised an eyebrow.

"Today, as soon as Mary Ruth at the pawnshop calls Charlie to let him know she got it in. She's a magician, isn't she? I called her and asked for a cot, but she went one better. What makes you so smart?"

"I have a nose for a fancy prevarication from my years of teaching, and that was one of the best I've heard."

"Thank you; for a minute there, I thought you would accuse me of not telling the truth." Doc Julie Rae waggled her finger at Claire.

"You two are too much; I'll see you in the morning." Riley rolled her eyes. "Ready, Toby?"

Toby pulled himself to his feet and then stretched before he trotted to the back door.

While Riley examined the premade salads, Mrs. Smythe appeared beside her and pointed to Riley's shopping cart. "Mediterranean salad would be best if you're making spaghetti."

"Thank you. How did you know I'm making spaghetti?"

"An educated guess and the French bread and sausage gave it away. You're dressing up a jar of pasta sauce, aren't you?"

"Yes, ma'am."

Mrs. Smythe glanced around, then waited until the shoppers close to them moved away. "You and Pia are good friends. She needs to know that something unsavory is happening at the Distribution Center, but Pia's Tom is not involved. Tell Pia her instincts are good. She will need to hear that and needs a smart friend like you."

Mrs. Smythe wandered away and randomly picked up a butternut squash then seemed to absent-mindedly put it into a nearby shopper's cart before she wandered to the next aisle.

Good cover, Mrs. Smythe. It was amazing to watch you lean into the strength of a stereotypical, absent-minded elderly person.

On the way home, Riley said, "If I brown the sausage, I can put it in the refrigerator until I know Ben is on his way home, then add it to the sauce to warm up while I slice the French bread and toast it. Claire's a genius."

Toby yipped, and Riley smiled. "I like Claire too."

After they were inside, Riley fed Toby and called Pia.

"You're at home, right? Are you okay? Is everything okay at work?" Pia's voice was shrill and louder than usual.

"Everything's fine, and I'm at home. How are you doing?"

"My sister's coming tomorrow, and Jackson, Jordy, and I are going home with her to Miami until Tom returns," Pia sobbed.

"Pia?" A wave of dread ran up Riley's spine, and the tiny hairs on the back of her neck separated and stood upright.

"The sales manager, Angie, is missing too. She's young, attractive, and works hard. You wouldn't think someone who is an introvert and as quiet as she is would be drawn to sales, but she's an amazing listener, and her customers and staff love her. Tom told me once that her customers bought what she was selling so readily because they hoped her kindness would rub off on them. I learned that a rumor leaked from the corporate level claims that the two of them ran off together. The people at the Barton Center think corporate is nuts. In fact, when Angie's wife called me about the rumor to give me a heads up, she was livid."

"So, why are you and Jackson going to Miami?" Riley furrowed her brow.

"I don't want Jackson to hear any bad things about his father at school because I'm afraid he'd either get into a fight or completely withdraw from his friends."

"If you talked to Jackson about it first, he wouldn't be surprised at school. Jackson might not be as fragile as you think, but he's probably as scared as you are about Tom."

When Pia didn't say anything, Riley bit her lip. *Did I go too far?*

Pia sighed. "You're right. I'll call my sister and cancel. She told me it was a big mistake for me to take Jackson out of school, but I wasn't willing to listen to her. It's hard for me to be at work because I feel like I should be home in case Tom shows up, but when I'm home, it's worse because he's not there, and there's nothing I can do. I understand now exactly how Ben felt when you were abducted. I want to be like Ben, throw Jordy and Jackson in my car, and go find Tom."

"You'd have the right helpers along, wouldn't you?" Riley smiled.

"Inspector Jackson and his bloodhound, Jordy, would jump right in." Pia snuffled. "I panicked and forgot that Jackson's as strong as Tom. Thanks, Riley."

"Anytime. You'd do the same for me," Riley said.

"You bet I would." Pia's voice strengthened, and Riley smiled as they hung up.

"Crisis averted, Toby," Riley said, "but why did Angie disappear?"

After Riley fed Toby and let him out, she removed the sausage from the casing and browned it. Before she put the drained sausage into the refrigerator, Toby yipped, and Ben's truck pulled into the driveway. Riley hurried to let Toby inside as Ben strode into the house.

"Hi, honey, I'm home." He grinned as he strolled to Riley and hugged her. "I love saying that. What are you cooking?" He peered at the stove.

"I'm glad you didn't have to work late. We're having a fancy spaghetti dinner."

Ben released her and removed his coat. "Do we have any plans or obligations tonight?" He removed his utility belt and hung it on the hook he'd installed in the utility area.

"Nothing. Are you on call?"

"Not officially. What's new?"

After Riley added the sauce to the sausage, she brewed a cup of tea for Ben while she told him about Angie missing and the rumor.

Ben frowned. "Marc got a call from the Atlanta office to let him know the investigation to find Tom was on hold because Angie and Tom left together. I'll give him a call. Thanks for the tea."

Ben called and then hung up. "He didn't answer. I'll text him and Sheriff to let them know the rumor is unfounded."

After he sent his text, Ben said, "We wouldn't have heard this for quite a while if you and Pia hadn't talked." He rose and hugged her while she stood at the stove. "Marc told me once that I had an unfair advantage because I had an undercover operative." He nuzzled her neck, and she shivered. "Are you cold? Want me to get your sweatshirt?"

Riley turned and kissed him. "I'm not cold; you give me the shivers."

When Ben's eyes widened, she snickered. "Good shivers, not cold shivers."

He returned her kiss. "I learn something every day. How about a walk before dinner?"

"I'll turn off the burner, grab my coat, and tell you about our visit to Lindsey's farm."

As they strolled down the road, Ben asked, "How far do you want to walk?"

"Just a few blocks," Riley said.

After she told him about the skittish horses, feral hogs, and lunch, Ben said, "Now, this is why both of us should be veterinarians. I would have loved to have gone to lunch with you."

Riley laughed. "We could specialize in farm animals and make barn calls."

"Perfect." Ben chuckled. "I'd forgotten about all the times my uncle scheduled our appointments at certain farms at lunchtime. The food was great."

"Would we come back here or go to Carson?" Riley asked.

"Hadn't thought about that. We could do either, but there might be more of a need for us in Carson."

"We'd have to come back to Barton for barn calls at Lindsey's farm, though," Riley said.

Toby raced to the end of the block and treed a squirrel, then grinned when they reached him.

"Well done, Toby," Riley said.

After they'd walked another half block, Riley asked, "Does your uncle have an office, or does he specialize in the larger farm animals?"

"He has an office, but I always went with him on the farm visits, so I don't know how he arranges the office schedule. I think he has a partner who sees dogs, cats, and small mammals in the office, but I'm not sure. That would be a good question for him on our next visit to Carson."

"That's interesting. I'll have to ask Doc Julie Rae how she managed the office and farm visits before Doc Thad," Riley said.

"I suspect Amanda juggled her schedule for any equine emergencies. So, which would you prefer?" Ben asked.

"I was going to ask you the same question. I'd want to do both, but if I could do only one, it would be farm visits. What about you?"

"My ideal job would be for you and me to work together on farm visits. There are a number of large farms around Carson, and my uncle always told me it would be more efficient if we both could take patients, but he may have been using a subtle tactic to persuade me to go to veterinary school. Ready to head home?"

When they turned back, Toby raced past them, and Ben chuckled. "I think Toby's ready to go inside."

"I wonder if Helen owns any rental property in Athens," Riley said when they reached the house. "I'm concerned that we won't be able to afford anything there like we have here."

"I'll bet she has contacts."

While Riley set a pot of water on the stove to boil the spaghetti, Ben said, "I'll turn on the fireplace unless you think it would warm up the house too much."

"I think it will be a while before I complain of being too warm," Riley said.

After Riley tossed the spaghetti into the boiling water, Ben asked, "What are you doing next?"

"I'm going to divide the salad, slice about a third of the French bread, butter the slices, and toast the bread in the oven."

"If you do the salad, I'll take care of the French bread."

While Ben sliced the French bread, his phone rang. "It's Marc. If you finish up the bread, I'll take the call outside."

Riley nodded, and Ben answered his phone. He threw on his coat before he and Toby went out back.

Riley sprinkled parmesan cheese on the bread while it toasted, then dished up the spaghetti and sprinkled more cheese over the sauce. While she brewed two cups of tea, Ben and Toby came inside.

"That looks delicious." Ben hung up his coat and washed his hands.

"Thanks, honey. Let's eat."

Ben told Riley about his day as they ate; while they cleared the table, Ben said, "Marc was concerned that the entire investigation took a turn on the basis of a rumor. He's convinced now that both Tom and Angie were abducted, and there's a cover-up involved."

Riley frowned. "That doesn't sound good at all, does it? How could that be?"

"Marc said politicians apply pressure on an agency on behalf of their constituents all the time, and they don't always realize the impact or check the validity, but sometimes the politicians themselves have a vested interest in slowing or diverting an investigation."

"Care for a beer or a glass of wine while we watch the fire glow in the fireplace?" Riley asked.

"I'll declare myself off duty for the evening and have a beer. That's an excellent idea. What about you?"

"A glass of wine sounds good," she said.

"You cooked; I'll pour. Make yourself comfortable, and I'll bring your wine to you." Ben texted the sheriff, and the sheriff responded.

When Ben handed Riley her glass of wine and sat beside her, he said, "Sheriff Dunn said to relax and enjoy our evening."

"Sounds nice."

"Do you think UGA has coed dorms?" Ben mused as he stared at the condensation slipping down his bottle.

"I don't know, but I wouldn't be interested," Riley said. "Would you?"

"Not at all. I intend to be with you..."

When Ben didn't finish, she gazed at him. "I always want to be with you."

"That's what I wanted to say." He met her gaze, put his arm around her, and pulled her close. "I love you, Riley Erin."

"I know, and I love you too, Benjamin Jacob."

They leaned back, sipped on their drinks, and enjoyed the fire.

"I loved you first." Ben smiled.

"You are so competitive, but I knew I loved you before you knew I loved you," Riley said.

Ben shook his head. "I'm not exactly sure what you said, but you win."

"Yes, I did, and I'd jump up and dance, except I'm too tired. Lindsey ran our legs off at the horse farm. Do you ever run?"

"I haven't in a while; I ran every day until I moved to Barton. I need to get back into the routine; I'm getting out of shape."

Riley moaned. "I wonder if I can talk Claire or Doc Julie Rae into jogging fifteen minutes before we eat lunch."

"I'll run fifteen minutes in the morning with you, then run fifteen more. I'd rather run in the morning while it's cool." Ben shifted to kiss her, and she wrapped her arms around his neck and pulled him into a sweet kiss that intensified into a passionate longing.

After the kiss ended, Riley sighed as she gazed at his loving face. "Friends don't kiss like that."

Ben chuckled. "I know; isn't it great?"

Riley leaned back and tried to stifle her yawn. "Lindsey called Doc Julie Rae and me 'creampuffs.' I'm glad I had sense enough not to be insulted because I think she was right."

"I think both of us have a sleep deficit to repay." Ben kissed her and then helped her to her feet.

"Good night, honey." She hugged him, then pulled him close.

After they kissed with a shared passion, Ben sighed. "See you in the morning. I'll take Toby outside for a while."

Riley undressed and put on her pajamas but opened her bedroom door so Toby could join her. She turned off her light and slipped under the cover. Her eyelids were heavy as she relaxed and thought about Ben. *He's a good kisser.*

"Riley?" Ben tapped on her door.

"I'm awake. Come on in. What is it?"

"Sheriff called me. A hunter found Angie's body in the woods in Alabama earlier today."

"Any..."

"No, just Angie."

"I have to call Pia," Riley said, turning on her bedside lamp and swinging her feet to the floor.

Ben sat beside her on the bed. "No, you have to let Angie's wife have time to tell the rest of the family before the information reaches them through someone else."

"You're right."

"Do you want to get up and talk for a while? I didn't turn off the fireplace yet." Ben put his arm around her.

"I'd like that; my mind is going a million miles a minute."

"I'll heat water for our tea."

After they sipped their tea, Ben asked, "Do you think you could sleep now?"

"I don't know. Why don't we stay on the sofa and cuddle?"

Ben shook his head. "You'll sleep better in your bed. I'll see you in the morning."

Riley padded to bed while Ben turned off the fireplace and the lights. *Spoilsport.*

Chapter Three

Riley woke the next morning before her alarm went off. She closed her bedroom door, slipped into the shower, and dressed for work with a long-sleeved T-shirt under her scrub top. When she tiptoed toward the kitchen, she smelled coffee and smiled. *One of these days, I'll get up before he does and have coffee ready for him.*

"Good morning, honey," she said.

"You smell good; do you scrub with flowers?" He pointed to the table. "I poured your coffee."

Riley picked up her cup and held it with two hands. "Isn't it my turn to cook breakfast?"

"Nope." Ben dropped slices of bacon into the cast iron skillet on the stove. "I'm making pancakes this morning. I've never made pancakes before this; we need a waffle iron."

"Pancakes sound good. Has Toby had breakfast?"

"Not yet. I couldn't get him to come inside. Evidently, a new squirrel or cat is in the neighborhood because he's been on guard for the past twenty minutes. Maybe if you open the back door, he'll smell the bacon and take a hint."

Riley strolled to the back door and called Toby. He dashed to the door from the yard's far corner and howled when he came inside.

"I didn't hear anything." Riley turned to Ben. "Toby said there was a commotion two blocks away. Did you hear any sirens?"

"I'm kind of immune to the sound of sirens because of the deputy cars, so I wouldn't have heard them."

Riley fed Toby, then pulled out butter and strawberry jam from the refrigerator and set them on the table next to the syrup bottle. After she put forks and knives on the table, she refilled their cups.

"I'd ask what's on the agenda for today, but I don't want to know." Ben leaned to kiss Riley, and she turned up her face for a quick kiss, but he surprised her with a passionate good morning kiss.

"Wow," she said. "Nice kiss."

Ben tapped his brow with two fingers in a salute. "Thank ya, ma'am. Any ole time you get a hankerin' for a kiss, just let me know."

Riley giggled. "You must have slept as well as I did."

"I don't know if it was exhaustion or relief knowing you were safe, but I slept great."

Ben furrowed his brow as he peered at the pancakes on his griddle. "Looks like we've got bubbles."

He held his breath as he lifted the edge of the pancake with his turner, then exhaled. "It's ready to turn. Here goes nothing."

He cringed as he flipped the pancake, and it landed flat on the griddle without folding. "Only have to do that three more times," he mumbled.

He flipped the second pancake, and when it landed on the batter side as neatly as the first one, he danced a jig and waved his spatula while Riley giggled.

"You want one or two pancakes, honey?" he asked.

"I'll have one. I want two, but I could eat only one." Riley smiled.

"I already made one for the griddle. Mom always makes two. Toby didn't mind eating the practice pancake."

"Grandma did that too. She told me it was to check the temperature of the griddle, but I noticed they always came out perfect, and she fed them to her dogs or the barn cats."

Ben flipped the third and fourth ones. "Perfect again. I should quit while I'm ahead. Dad always took possession of the first small pancake and put whatever homemade jam Mom had on it then folded it like a taco. Mom said when I was four, I told her I needed a jammin' taco like Dad, which is why Mom makes two when I'm home."

"Why didn't you have a jammin' taco this morning?" Riley asked.

Ben stared at her. "We don't have any homemade jam."

Riley rolled her eyes. "Oh, of course. Silly me. So, when will we learn how to make homemade jam?"

Ben plated up the pancakes. "All we need to do is tell Mom we need homemade jam lessons, and she'll put aprons on us, or better yet, we can ask Mom for some homemade jam. One pancake for you, two for me, and one extra; you can have it, I can have it, we can split it, or freeze it. We have options."

Riley buttered her pancake and cut it into bite-sized portions. When she poured on the syrup, Ben stared.

"My grandmother used to cut her pancakes before she poured on any syrup," Ben said. "When I asked her why, she said only people with magical powers did that. I tried, but I ran out of patience and drowned my pancakes with syrup, then tore off bites that weren't in neat squares and ended up with a pool of syrup on my plate. When I asked Mom about it, she told me my grandmother was wired differently than other people."

"Unfortunately," Riley said, "I don't have magical powers, but I like my pancakes to get the full benefit of soaking up every drop of syrup. My grandmother said I had her sweet tooth."

Ben shrugged as he tore off a piece of his second pancake. "I'm still going with the magical powers. You understand animals, and you mesmerized me."

"You can keep that sweet talk coming, mister, as long as you want. I've got the sweet tooth, so evidently, I soak it up." Riley sopped up the last of the syrup with her last bite.

Ben grinned. "I've got to run."

"You cooked; I'll take care of the dishes. See you tonight."

Ben leaned over and kissed her. "Mmm. Sticky."

"Yep, and don't you forget it." Riley smiled as Ben grinned, waved, and dashed out the door with his lunch.

When Riley and Toby arrived at the animal hospital, Riley's phone buzzed a text. *Melissa? Why is Ben's mom texting me so early?*

She read the text: "Hi, it's Mom. How flexible is your boss? Could you get away for a few days?"

This is odd. Riley called Melissa. "Hi, Mom. What's up?"

"I didn't mean to bother you so early. Did I wake you?" Melissa asked.

"No, not at all. We've had breakfast, and Toby and I just pulled into the staff parking lot at work."

"Oh, good. I was just wondering how flexible your schedule is. Could you possibly...oh, I don't know...take some vacation or personal time maybe this afternoon through Sunday?"

"It's short notice, but I'll ask my boss and check the schedule. I'm sure my boss will say yes, but I'll need to make sure the clinic won't be slammed while I'm gone."

"See how nice you are? So, I'm planning that you will be here for supper, so don't worry about that; your bedroom is ready for you. Speaking of your bedroom, are you...oh, never mind; you'll tell me this weekend."

Riley frowned. "Is there something I need to know?"

"Other than you have a meddling Mom? No, I don't think so." Melissa laughed as she hung up.

"That was strange, Toby. Something's going on, and somehow, you and I are in the middle of a conspiracy."

Riley opened Toby's door, and then they rushed to the building and hurried inside.

Doc Julie Rae met them in the hallway. "Ready for coffee, Riley? It just finished."

"Thank you," Riley said as Toby trotted to the kennels to check on Hector. "How's everything?"

"George somehow managed to talk Zach into going home. I was relieved when George told me this morning because I was worried about whether Zach would sleep at all. Hector had a good night; he's downright chipper this morning. I plan to send him home today. Both he and Mitch will rest easier at home, and Mitch knows what to watch for."

"That's good news. I thought he might be here the rest of the week," Riley said.

"Ordinarily, I'd agree with you, but the special bond between Mitch and Hector is particularly healing. If Mitch is ever in the hospital, we'll have to designate Hector as a service dog to help Mitch recover more quickly. Actually, now that I've said it, I'll ask Claire to start the paperwork. There's no reason to scramble later."

"I need to check the rest of this week's schedule, but first, I wanted to talk to you. Ben's mom called me and asked if it would be possible for me to take off the rest of the week. She was very vague."

"You can do whatever you need, but you know that. What's up?" Doc Julie Rae asked.

"You know as much as I do. I'll check the schedule, just in case, but it was important to her that I left for Carson later today."

"If it's a big secret, hush-hush project, you'll still let me know what it is, right? Otherwise, Charlie, the boys, Chuck, and I will show up to check on you."

Riley giggled. "I'll let you know."

"Okay, you check the schedule, and I'll hold my breath all day to see what happens later. Metaphorically speaking." Doc Julie Rae laughed.

While Riley checked the schedule, Claire rushed to her side. "Anything big going on?"

"I was checking the schedule, and there's nothing unusual, but I didn't listen to any of the messages yet, so I don't have a good answer. I'd like to check on Hector before our morning gets into gear. Toby went straight to the kennel when we came in."

"Okay, I'll check the messages and let you know if we have anything that will add extra interest to our usual crazy mornings." Claire took over her desk and picked up the phone.

When Riley arrived at Hector's crate, Doc Julie Rae opened the door to examine Hector, and Toby yipped.

"I'm not surprised Hector is ready to go home," Riley said.

Hector grinned.

Doc Julie Rae sat with her legs crossed on the floor next to Hector's crate as she gently stroked his back. "You're doing great, Hector. I'll talk to Mitch about when you can go home, but you'll have to take it easy for a while: no running or chasing squirrels."

Hector barked.

"Yes, you can sit on the porch and bark at the squirrels," Riley said, "but if you leave the porch, you'd better be walking slowly, or you'll be restricted to the house."

Hector whined, then grinned.

Riley put her hands on her hips. "I am not a spoilsport, and we'll be checking with Mitch regularly to see how you're doing, so you better behave."

Hector licked Doc Julie Rae's hand.

"Thank you, Hector, but Riley is right; you must behave." Doc Julie Rae gracefully rose to her feet and winked at Riley before she headed to the breakroom.

Hector yipped, and Riley snorted. "I don't know how Doc Julie Rae stays so limber either. We should ask her sometime, except she might make us do limbering exercises with her; let's not ask."

After Riley sat on the floor with her legs to the side, she hummed and rubbed Hector's ears; Hector closed his eyes and relaxed.

Zach strolled to the crate and whispered, "Is Hector asleep?"

Hector opened his eyes.

Riley grabbed onto the crate and pulled herself up. "He was relaxing."

"I saw Doc Julie Rae in the breakroom. I'm glad you had a good night, Hector."

While Zach talked to Hector, Riley went to the breakroom and smiled when she spied Pia.

"Want that cup refilled?" Pia pointed to the empty cup that Riley carried.

"I sure do. How did you sleep?"

Pia refilled Riley's cup. "I slept great. My sister was happy to hear that I wasn't pulling Jackson out of school, and I told her that she didn't have to come here, either. Thanks for talking me down off that ledge."

"Any time, and I know you'd do the same for me."

"Sure would, but not quite so gracefully," Pia said.

Riley drank her coffee and then rinsed her cup. "I'm actually more comfortable, too, because Marc shifted the GBI investigation to finding Tom instead of assuming

Tom took off voluntarily. I'm more than ready to let the professionals take over their jobs so we can focus on our work here, which is much more fun."

"You are so right. I've got my hands full working and caring for Jackson and Jordy. I'm not ready to add investigative responsibilities to my daily tasks."

Pia rinsed her cup as Riley said, "I'm worried about my stamina. I haven't been getting as much exercise as I should and need to start jogging. What do you think about jogging with me for fifteen minutes on our lunch break before we eat?"

"Oh, man, you hit me where it hurts because I realized I need to get back to running this morning. There's nothing better to perk up my attitude, and I never would have spiraled down like I did if I'd still been running." Pia sighed. "Okay, I'm in. I suppose you want to start today." Pia frowned at Riley's feet. "Are you going to jog in your boots, or did you bring running shoes?"

"I didn't even think about running shoes," Riley said.

"We can run in our street shoes until we remember to bring in the proper footwear, but we might want to vary our pace with a walk and then a short jog today. I'm really out of shape."

Riley nodded. "Good idea. We might give up if we're in too much pain tomorrow."

"Come get me when it's time for lunch, and we'll go."

"Where are we going for lunch?" Doc Julie Rae strolled into the breakroom.

"We're going to start jogging before we eat. Would you like to join us?" Riley asked.

Doc Julie Rae furrowed her brow and stared at the ceiling. "I just remembered that conflicts with a meeting I have."

"Oh, really, and what meeting is that?" Pia put her hands on her hips and glared at Doc.

"My regular exercise avoidance meeting." Doc Julie Rae marched out, peeked around the corner into the breakroom, and smiled when Riley and Pia laughed.

"You're the best, Doc," Pia said.

"I know." Doc Julie Rae waved the princess wave as she left for Claire's desk.

"Do we drag Zach away from Hector's crate to take patients this morning?" Pia asked.

"No, the two of us can handle the patients. Hector deserves the special attention," Riley said.

"Okay, I'll take the first patient."

Toward the end of the morning, Riley was at the receptionist's desk when the phone rang.

"Okay, bring her right in. We'll be ready," Claire said before she hung up. "Riley, we have a puppy coming in that was run over by a bicycle. The ten-year-old bike rider is on the way to the hospital with a broken arm and possible head injury even though he wore a helmet, and the puppy is bleeding from the mouth, has a distended belly, and is having trouble breathing."

"I'll see which doc is available, then grab Zach for x-rays before I set up the trauma room."

Riley dashed to the docs' offices and found Doc Thad. "We've got a puppy coming in that was hit by a bicycle. See Claire for details, and I'll grab Zach."

Riley raced to Hector's crate. "We have a puppy on the way that was hit by a bicycle, so we'll need x-rays. Do you want to x-ray or tech with Doc Thad?"

"I'll do either, but you'll understand the puppy better than I would and zero in on the injuries. Nobody is as fast with the x-rays as I am," Zach said.

Riley furrowed her brow. *Time to shake Zach out of his comfort zone.* "Why don't you take the lead? I'll back you up after the x-rays for the finer details."

Zach exhaled. "Okay, Riley. You're making me stretch, but I'll do it."

On their way to the trauma room, Riley asked, "Am I that transparent?"

"You tromped on me like a T-rex. I wouldn't call that transparent." Zach snickered.

Riley flipped her hair. "I have my own unique style."

Riley turned on the x-ray machine, and Zach readied their patient's room before the two hurried to Claire's desk. A red-faced man rushed into the clinic with a puppy wrapped in a small blanket.

The puppy whined and wiggled, and Zach furrowed his brow and side-glanced at Riley.

"The puppy's complaining about being confined by the blanket," she whispered, and Zach nodded.

"I'll take the puppy," Zach said.

Claire hurried to the man's side. "Come sit in the waiting area, and I'll get you a glass of water. What's the puppy's name?"

As the man walked with Claire, he said, "Rosie."

"I've got you, Rosie," Zach said softly, and the puppy quieted and snuggled against his chest.

After reaching the trauma room, Doc Thad waited until Zach set Rosie on the exam table, unwrapped the blanket, and examined her.

"Her right front leg is deformed, and her paw is bleeding," Doc said.

Rosie licked her paw, and Doc Thad examined inside her mouth. "No mouth or jaw injuries that I can see. The blood on the lower part of her muzzle may be from licking her paw."

He lightly palpated her belly, and she rolled to her back. Doc Thad chuckled. "Her abdomen is soft and full. She may have just eaten, but I'll ask. Rosie's all yours, Riley. We'll wait for the x-rays, but all I've found is her leg."

Riley rolled Rosie to the x-ray room. "Rosie, I will put a strap around you to keep you from falling off the table. Do you think you can be really still when I say 'stay'?"

Rosie yelped, and Riley said, "Thank you. I'll do my best to be quick."

After the x-rays, Riley rolled Rosie back to the trauma room while she loosened the strap. "Does that feel better? Doc Thad will study your x-rays, and then we'll put a nice splint on your leg."

Rosie yipped and rolled to her back when she saw Doc Thad, and he smiled. "Right after I look at those x-rays, you'll get another belly rub."

While Doc Thad peered at the x-rays, Zach returned from the waiting area. "Rosie had breakfast about thirty minutes before she went outside. Can the family come in now, Doc? The mom and two girls are here too."

"Let's have them come in for a quick peek, so they'll know she's okay; then they will have to leave because there isn't enough room in here for them. Too bad we don't have an observation room or something. I'll discuss it with Doc Julie Rae to see what she thinks."

"I'll talk to the family," Zach said.

While Riley set up the splint and other supplies, Doc Thad rubbed Rosie's belly. When the little girls came into the room, Rosie flipped her tail.

"Look, mama. Rosie knew it was us." The girls pushed close to the exam table, and Rosie wiggled to see them. Doc Thad picked up Rosie, and the girls stroked and cooed at the puppy.

"See? Mr. Zach was right. Rosie's fine. Let's go back to the waiting room so Doc Thad can put a splint on her leg. Will she go home with us, Doc Thad?" the mother asked.

Doc Thad smiled. "She certainly will. Zach will go over a few things with you, and Claire will set up a follow-up appointment. You all can go home together."

"Not together," the older girl said. "We came in Mama's car. Daddy will have to go home alone, but he can meet us there."

The man smiled. "Some of us are sticklers for detail, Doc Thad."

"I understand. I have one of those at my house, too." Doc Thad chuckled.

After the family returned to the waiting room, Doc Thad and Riley stabilized Rosie's leg while Zach left to pick up the instructions for Rosie's home care and to talk to the family.

When Zach returned, he tapped on the trauma room door. "Ready for us?"

"Yes, we are," Doc Thad said; the girls and their parents spilled into the room.

"We decided I'd carry Rosie to my car, and everyone would ride home with me. A neighbor will drop me off later to pick up our other car," the man said.

"Well done," Doc Thad said, and the man smiled.

After Rosie and her family left, Riley and Zach sanitized the trauma room and replenished the supplies.

"How was being the lead tech?" Riley asked.

"Not nearly as awful as I imagined, thanks. I was comfortable when I was solo, but it's different when there are two people. I've always stepped back to learn."

Riley smiled. "You stayed focused on the team, didn't you? Most new folks try to do everything themselves. Delegation is a skill that usually takes a while to learn."

"Thanks." Zach blushed. "I was surprised you had only one strap across Rosie when you came out of the x-ray room. Why did you do that?"

"I told Rosie the strap was to keep her from falling off the table and asked her if she could be very still for me, and she agreed."

"Do you think that would work for me?"

"I don't see why not, as long as you pay attention to the answer. If Rosie had told me no, or she didn't want to be still, I would have gone our standard route and used two more straps."

Zach frowned. "Do you do that every time?"

"It depends. Remember when the man brought Rosie in and had her tightly bundled in the blanket? If she had been comfortable, I would have wrapped her with straps and not asked. Your instincts were good when you took her from the man and held her firmly enough for her to feel comforted but not so tightly that she would be confined."

Zach snickered. "Stickler for detail is my new professional goal."

Riley smiled. "You know what's funny about what Doc Thad said? Claire might focus on details, but so does he."

As they left the trauma room for Claire's desk, Riley's phone buzzed a text from Ben that said, "Call at your convenience."

She headed to the hallway. "I have a call to make. I won't be long."

She went to the breakroom and called Ben.

"I didn't interrupt anything, did I?" Ben asked.

"No, I had just finished cleaning the exam room. What's up?"

"I have to go to Carson today to help my cousin's friend. Is that okay?"

Is this what Mom wanted me to be ready for?

"Of course, it's okay. Who's the friend? Anyone I know?"

Ben cleared his throat. "No, you don't know her. She's an old friend from high school."

"Friend or someone you used to date?"

"It's complicated." Ben exhaled. "Pamela Suzanne."

Ah ha. Mom is brilliant.

"Of course, we can help your old friend. I'll clear taking some time off with Doc Julie Rae. What time do you want me to be ready?"

"What? Really? You'll go too? That's a great idea. Do you think we could pack and eat lunch, then leave?"

"Absolutely. Are we going to a wedding or anything fancy tonight? We might need to leave a little earlier so I can find something to wear in Carson."

"No, nothing fancy that I know about."

Shoot. I was hoping Pamela Suzanne was getting married.

"That's good; I'll let you know if it's a problem for me to take off the time on such short notice, but otherwise, I'll see you at home a little before lunch."

"You're going home for lunch?" Pia stood in the doorway as Riley hung up. "I have a reprieve?"

Riley smiled. "We both do. Ben has a friend in Carson who needs his help, and we'll leave right after lunch. I'll need time to pack, then we'll eat and leave. I have to check with Doc Julie Rae first."

Pia raised her eyebrows. "You invited yourself along because the ex-girlfriend needs help, right?"

Riley giggled. "You're right."

Pia strutted into the breakroom. "Of course, I'm right. Well played; you're smart to offer to help out that poor thing. Let me know if Jackson, Jordy, and I can help sneer at her or anything like that. We could show up on Saturday. I'll bet she's tall, skinny, and a natural blond. We totally dislike her already."

"There's no way I could leave here if I thought there was something more I could do to help Tom," Riley said.

"If you hadn't told me that Marc redirected the investigation, I'd be in a panic, but I trust Marc. You were right when you said he is a good guy."

"I'm available by phone anytime, and I'll be only an hour away. We'll drop ole Pamela Suzanne in a heartbeat if you need me, but I couldn't leave you if Marc weren't here. You have his cell number, right?"

Pia nodded. "He gave me his card then waited while I put his cell number in my contacts, and the sheriff gave me his cell number too, and of course, there's Claire and Doc Thad, Doc Julie Rae and Charlie, Zach, and Hector and Mitch, and Tom's staff, so I've got a posse to fill in for you while you're gone. I can coach Jackson to call Ben 'daddy' if you need a spare kid. Just let us know."

"I'll keep that in mind," Riley laughed.

Riley hurried to Doc Julie Rae's office. "Ready to hear the super-secret project?"

"Oh, good. I haven't been able to concentrate on paperwork because I've been thinking of all the possibilities. What is it?"

Riley sat on the visitor's chair. "Ben's ex-girlfriend called him with a desperate plea for help."

"I didn't even think of the ex-girlfriend. Of course! What is it they used to say in the old detective novels? *Cherchez la femme?* I absolutely love your future mother-in-law. She's got your back, girlfriend. What a keeper. Wonder how she found out? Doesn't matter; I'm sure she'll tell you later, but I need to know too, but please don't tell me I need a life. I'm barely able to survive through yours. When are you leaving?" Doc Julie Rae picked up an envelope from her desk and fanned her face. "I can't believe how delighted I am to hear surprising news that's good for a change."

Riley smiled. "I'm really glad Mom called me. I'd be in a big snit, otherwise, over Ben dropping everything and running off at the whim of his old ex-girlfriend. Ben told me about Pamela Suzanne earlier, and it's a good thing, or I would have been totally blindsided." Riley furrowed her brow. "I do need to remember to get in a dig about his ex-fiancée because I promised him I'd never let him forget it."

"Were they really engaged?" Doc Julie Rae's eyes widened.

"Only in her mind." Riley wiggled her eyebrows, and Doc Julie Rae laughed.

"This is so good, and I'm such a terrible person. Does Pia know? Claire?"

"Pia does because she walked in at just the right time on my phone conversation. I need to tell Claire before I leave."

"You certainly do; then you can leave whenever you like so you can pack. Do you think you'll be back on Monday?"

"That's what I think; if anything changes, I'll let you know."

When Riley reached Claire's desk, Pia said, "Claire, you need a break. I'll watch the desk for you until you get back."

"What do you mean? I'm fine, and I have a lot of work to do," Claire grumbled.

"Believe me; you need a break," Pia said.

Riley giggled. "You can argue a while if you like, Claire, but you'll be angry later if you don't take a break now."

"You people are nuts." Claire pushed back from her desk. "Okay, I'm on a break."

Pia crossed her arms and narrowed her eyes. "You'll be left out if you don't go to the breakroom now."

Claire huffed and stomped to the breakroom. Pia raised her hand for a high-five, and Riley smacked it before she and Toby followed Claire to the breakroom.

Claire leaned against a table and scowled. "What's this all about? This better be good."

Riley told her about Melissa's call and Ben's urgent call for help from Pamela Suzanne.

"You're going, right? I wonder what conniving scheme that little snake has up her sleeve." Claire frowned. "How could a snake have a sleeve? Ignore that. You have to let me know what's going on. Do Doc Julie Rae and Pia know? Of course, they do or will before you leave. Let one of us know what's going on, and we'll fill in the other two."

"That's a really good idea, Claire. I don't know what Miss Ex-GF told Ben or how Mom got wind of it, but I'm sure I will later. I did ask Ben if we were going to a wedding tonight, and he said no."

Claire snort-laughed. "You are so bad."

Riley grinned. "I try. I've got to go now and pretend it takes me thirty minutes to toss my clothes into a duffel bag and throw my toiletries into a plastic bag."

Claire hugged her and then hurried to her desk.

After Riley pulled out her lunch and put on her coat, she hurried to the back door, and Toby stood in the hallway and watched. "You might want to go along, Toby; we'll see Mom, Dad, Princess, Duffy, and Finn."

When Riley opened the door, Toby raced outside and danced next to Riley's car as she hurried to open the door for him.

On their way home, she said, "I'm excited to see everyone in Carson, too. Seems like it's been ages, doesn't it? I wonder how much the puppies have grown. I really love Barton, and we have great friends, but doesn't Carson feel more like home?"

Toby yipped.

Riley peered at their driveway when she turned the corner to the house. "Ben's already home. He must be as excited as we are."

Riley and Toby dashed to the front door after she parked. "Hi, honey; we're home," she called out when they went inside.

Ben strode from his bedroom. "I thought I'd be finished packing before you got here. I'm really excited that you're going too. We'll talk on the way. Is there anything you need for me to do?"

"I'll let you know if I think of anything," Riley said.

Riley put her duffel bag on her bed and pulled out the empty plastic bag she used for toiletries. She quickly rolled all her clothes and placed her shirts and pants in neat rows; after she packed the rest of her clothes and a spare jacket, she hurried to her bathroom and dropped all her toiletries into the bag. When she returned to her bedroom, she placed her toiletries on top of her jacket and then narrowed her eyes as she scanned her bedroom. After she stuffed her favorite pillow in the space next to her jacket, she checked the bathroom. *If I've missed anything, Mom will probably have a replacement.*

She dragged her heavy duffel bag down the hallway, and Ben said, "What are you doing? That's too heavy for you to be lifting."

"That's why I'm dragging it."

"Told you to let me know what I could do," Ben grumbled as he strode to her duffel bag. When he bent over to pick it up, Riley ambushed him with a quick kiss on the cheek.

He smiled. "What if I apologize for being a jerk?"

Riley rolled her eyes and leaned in for a hot, sloppy kiss. He then wrapped his arms around her and returned her kiss.

He nibbled on her neck when they broke for air, and she giggled.

"Why don't we run away to the beach?" His eyes twinkled, and his mouth broke into a wicked grin.

"Whenever you say, honey." Riley gave him a quick kiss. "I need two minutes to pack up my laptop and chargers."

"Charger." Ben broke away. "I forgot my charger."

After Ben loaded their duffel bags into the truck, he returned to the house.

"Shall we eat here or on the road?" he asked.

"Let's eat here. It wouldn't hurt to have a minute or two to think of what we might have missed."

While they ate, Ben asked, "What about Toby's food and bowls?"

"Mom has all of that."

"I wouldn't mind taking my deer rifle. Hunting season for firearms opened this past weekend. Mom would love to have some venison in the freezer, and Dad has always wanted me to go with him; this might be a perfect opportunity."

Riley raised her eyebrows. "What about Pamela Sue? Won't we be busy all weekend with her?"

Ben smirked as he finished his lunch. "I doubt it."

After Ben loaded the truck, Toby jumped up on the backseat, Riley climbed into the passenger's seat, and Ben slid into the driver's seat and headed to the highway.

Riley leaned back and gazed at the passing farms. "There's still some cotton to be picked, but not much, and I don't see any peanuts at all. I guess the farmers have already harvested them. So, what are we doing for Pamela Suzanne?"

"Her boss in Atlanta has some information about a company in Barton, and she couldn't think of anyone except me to tell and didn't want to talk about it over the phone. That's about all I know, except she was dramatic, as usual. It's probably nothing, but with everything going on in Barton and as frantic as she was, I decided to hear what she had to say."

"It's still nice of you to be willing to listen to her. When are we going to meet with her?"

"I'll call her after we get to Mom's, then we can meet her in town somewhere; I thought the coffee shop would be the best place. We can have coffee while we listen to her, then leave whenever we like."

"That's a good idea," Riley said. "Toby and I are looking forward to seeing everyone. So, tell me about hunting; where would you go?"

"Dad bought some land a while ago that had been leased for years to hunters. The property had a well, but that was all, and the land suffered from a lack of maintenance. Dad has cleared a lot of brush, and he and his brother built a small hunting cabin so they'd have a place to warm up or rest. He's worked hard to make it a private wildlife refuge; Mom calls it his outside man cave. He and his brother have hunted on it a few times in the past, but in the last several years, Dad's gone alone because his brother hasn't been able to clear his schedule. I know Dad would enjoy it if we left in the morning."

While Ben talked, Riley leaned back and closed her eyes as she soaked in the comforting sound of his voice.

"Riley, we're here," Ben said.

"I didn't know I'd dozed off." Riley yawned as she sat up.

Toby whined when Ben turned at his parents' driveway. While Ben parked his truck and opened the door for Toby, Jake and the puppies rushed out of the barn. Duffy and Finn bounded to the truck, and Toby barked before he led them on a run around the barn, then up the driveway and back.

"I didn't realize how much Toby missed being where he can run," Riley said.

"He definitely loves it, doesn't he? Welcome back." Jake hugged her. "We missed you."

"I'll bring in our things," Ben said.

Princess strolled out of the barn and meowed at Riley. "I missed you too, Princess." Riley sat on the ground; Princess jumped onto her lap, and Riley stroked the barn cat's back.

When Riley shivered, Princess hopped off Riley's lap. Riley smiled as Princess marched to the barn with her tail high in the air. After Riley struggled and rose from the cold ground, she grabbed her backpack and jacket before she hurried to the house with her teeth chattering.

Melissa met her at the door. "It's getting colder; aren't you freezing? Why are you carrying your coat?"

"I didn't think about putting it on until I reached the house," Riley said.

Melissa shook her head. "I'll brew some tea, or would you rather have coffee?"

"Tea sounds perfect," Riley said.

"There's a fire in the fireplace if you want to take your tea there to warm your hands."

Riley sat at the table. "Feels good in here; the kitchen's warm and smells good too. What's cooking?"

"I'm stewing a chicken with carrots and celery for one of Ben's favorites: chicken and dumplings, and I just put a peach pie in the oven."

Ben brought in their duffel bags and large backpacks and set them by the back door before he hugged his mom.

"I'll put our things in our rooms, then help Dad," he said.

After Ben left, Riley asked, "What did Pamela Suzanne say when she called you?"

Melissa joined her at the table. "She told me she's called Ben several times, but her calls went straight to voicemail. I think he blocked her ages ago and forgot about it, but I didn't tell her that. She said she had to see Ben, and it was a matter of life or death, but that's her standard phrase for anything, so I didn't think much of it. I called him to give him a heads-up before I texted you. I knew he'd tell you he had to come to Carson, but not why. I was sure your feelings would be hurt because mine would have been."

"I definitely would have been shocked if he told me he had to leave right away for Carson. He didn't want to tell me why, so you know he was worried about what I would think. I would have been hurt that he didn't trust me enough to tell me, but he told me after I insisted."

Melissa chuckled. "Good. I knew you'd deal with it just fine. When are you two going to talk to Pamela Suzanne?"

"He was going to call her as soon as we got here so we could talk to her before supper." Riley rose, put on her warm coat, and then pulled on her gloves.

Melissa smiled. "You and Ben are perfect together."

When Riley opened the door to go outside, the three dogs rushed in, and Riley smiled when Toby yipped.

Riley said, "Toby said I should stay inside because it's cold."

"Smart dog," Melissa said. "Be safe, and call if you need me."

Ben was standing outside the barn while he talked on his phone. When he saw Riley, he motioned for her to join him. After he disconnected, he said, "Ready to meet

Pamela Suzanne? She still insists she has to talk to me in person."

"Let's go," Riley said.

Ben put his arm around her shoulders while they strolled together to the truck. He hugged her and lightly stroked her cheek before opening her door. "This is exactly why I love you; you're amazing."

Riley gazed at his worried expression before her eyes twinkled, and her mouth quivered as she tried not to giggle. "I love you more; I'm going to see your ex-girlfriend with you."

Ben grinned as he met her gaze. "I'll have to get back to you on that."

After he helped her into the truck, they headed to town. "This is actually a good excuse to go to the coffee shop," Ben said.

Ben parked in front of a boutique shop, and then they strolled to the coffee shop. Riley smiled at the sign that hung over the sidewalk.

"I love the name, Big Mug Coffee Shop," she said.

"It's great, isn't it? Everybody calls the owner Mugsy. I never knew her real name until the sheriff told me that one of her relatives went into the shop and asked for Alice, and the staff told her they didn't know anyone named Alice."

"Is that a bookstore next door?" Riley asked.

"Sure is. We can visit it before we go home if Pamela Suzanne isn't long-winded."

When they entered the shop, a woman in her forties with pale skin, dimpled cheeks, and black hair with streaks of silver grinned. She wore a flowing teal top and a white apron with dancing coffee cups on the bib.

"Ben Carter, I haven't seen you in ages, and this must be the elusive Riley I've heard so much about. You're smart, Deputy Ben, to keep her hidden from the riff-raff in this town. Riley, I'm Mugsy, and it's so nice to meet you."

Riley held out her hand to shake hands, and Mugsy shook her hand.

When an old cocker spaniel padded to Riley and whined. Riley smiled and rubbed the cocker's face, then rose and asked, "A hugger? Really?"

The cocker yipped, and Riley hugged Mugsy.

Mugsy laughed. "Melissa told me you were a dog whisperer. I guess Cookie told you I'm a hugger, didn't she?"

"Yes, ma'am, she did." Riley knelt next to Cookie and rubbed her belly. "You're a wonderful coach, Cookie. Thank you."

"Two coffees?" Mugsy asked.

"Yes, ma'am," Ben said.

Mugsy poured two large mugs of coffee. "Enjoy your coffee. Feel free to wander around, find a comfortable table, and sit a while."

"We're supposed to meet Pamela Suzanne here. I don't suppose you've seen her," Ben said.

Cookie growled low, and Riley bit her lip.

Mugsy furrowed her brow. "What did Cookie say, Riley?"

"She's not one of Suzanne's fans," Riley said.

Mugsy snort-laughed. "That's an understatement. She'll go to the storeroom if Pamela Suzanne enters the shop because Cookie is not allowed to bite or growl at the customers. Are you, sweet girl?"

Cookie yipped, then trotted to the back of the shop. A tall, slender blond opened the shop door and stuck her head inside. "Where's your dog, Mugsy?"

Chapter Four

Mugsy smirked. "She's on her way to the storeroom for her afternoon nap, Pamela Suzanne. You can come inside."

Pamela Suzanne breezed into the shop with the style of a runway model. She flashed a flirty smile at Ben, then narrowed her eyes at Riley and gritted her teeth. "Ben, I'd like to speak to you privately."

"You can go right ahead and talk to Ben, Pamela Sue," Mugsy said. "I won't eavesdrop. Coffee? Or just a private conversation?"

"It's Pamela Suzanne, and I don't want any coffee," she hissed.

"No charge for private conversations." Mugsy smiled.

Pamela Suzanne crossed her arms and grumbled, "You should have come to my house, like I said, Ben."

Cookie barked from the back room; Riley said, "Excuse the interruption, but our time is limited. I'll check Cookie now, Ms. Mugsy."

"Thank you," Mugsy said. "I wasn't sure if I'd be rushing you if I asked."

Mugsy linked her arm with Riley's, and the two of them strolled together to the back of the shop. "What are we doing?" Mugsy whispered.

"Cookie said Pamela Suzanne was about to bolt. We're giving her some space," Riley whispered. "Is there somewhere I could stand and hear them but not be seen?"

"Dang, you're smart. I've got the perfect spot."

Mugsy led Riley to a far corner and pointed to a three-panel room divider. When Riley peeked around the screen, she raised her eyes at a comfortable chair, a small table with a lamp, and a stack of books next to the chair. "I take a break here when I don't have any customers. I have my privacy but can still hear the front door open."

Riley smiled. "Thank you. Can they hear us?"

"No, but I'll be quiet, so you can listen."

"Ben, I've missed you. I'm sure you've been on the rebound with other people, so I want you to know I understand and forgive you," Pamela Suzanne said.

Riley rolled her eyes and glanced at Mugsy. Mugsy stuck out her tongue and mimed gagging.

"If that's what you wanted to talk about, I'll help with Cookie," Ben growled.

"Oh, you." Pamela Suzanne giggled.

Riley listened to Ben's footsteps as he headed toward the aisle that led to the back.

"Wait, Ben." Pamela Suzanne sighed, and Mugsy mimed a long, dramatic sigh, then placed the back of her hand on her forehead; Riley pressed her hand over her mouth to stifle her snicker.

"I have a very high-level position at a prestigious Fortune 500 consulting company; in fact, my friends tell me I'm the reason our group is so highly regarded, and

I'm on the fast track to supervisor. My boss told me about some fancy accounting with cash accounts and inventory that he said inflated the value of one of our client company's stock." She giggled. "Of course, I didn't have any clue what he was talking about because it wasn't my department, so I can't give you any details."

She lowered her voice. "But when he showed me what he said was the evidence, I made some copies as soon as he left his office. Imagine my shock when his secretary called a staff meeting to tell everyone that he was killed in a terrible crash. Not everyone attended the staff meeting because she had no authority to call it. I didn't go, of course, but we heard the details later from the few that went."

"Write down his name and any details you can remember," Ben said. "Do you have the copies you made?"

"Of course, but I didn't bring them with me; they're at my aunt's house."

Mugsy mimed strangling an invisible person, and Riley nodded.

"Drop them off at the sheriff's office, and I'll talk to the sheriff," Ben said.

"Oh, no, I couldn't do that," Pamela Suzanne said. "My boss said that there were corrupt officials involved. I wouldn't want the information to fall into the wrong hands because I'd be in danger."

"So, what do you want to do? And don't say I'd have to go to your aunt's house because that's off the table," Ben said.

"Fine; then I'll bring them here." Pamela Suzanne sneered. "Would that be okay with your precious redhead Riley? She certainly has a tight leash on you, doesn't she? I don't know what you see in her. She's chubby, short, and..."

"Hey, honey," Ben interrupted her. "Pamela Suzanne says you're short, and she's jealous of your chest."

The front door slammed, and Riley and Mugsy giggled.

"He's a keeper, Short-stuff," Mugsy said as they strolled together to the front of the store.

"How much did you hear?" Ben asked.

"We had a ringside seat and heard everything," Mugsy said.

"That's excellent. If she does bring any papers here before you close, Mugsy, text me immediately, and we'll drop everything to pick them up."

"If she doesn't bring them until tomorrow, your mom and I could pick them up," Riley said.

"Perfect," Ben said. "I didn't think about that."

"That works for me; I love a good conspiracy." Mugsy pulled out her phone from her pocket. "Cell phone numbers, please, and coffee's on me. I don't think I've ever had this much fun with my..."

Cookie barked as she trotted to the front of the store, and Riley laughed.

Mugsy scowled. "...young friends in ages. Are you happy now, Cookie?"

Cookie flopped down at her spot and grinned.

When they were on our way home, Ben asked, "Cookie told you what Mugsy was going to say, didn't she?"

Riley giggled. "She certainly did. I think Cookie thought it wasn't appropriate in mixed company. Cocker spaniels are known for being modest and even a little old-fashioned."

"I didn't know that, so what was Mugsy going to say?"

"You asked." Riley snickered. "According to Cookie, Mugsy was going to say she couldn't remember having this much fun with her clothes on."

Ben laughed. "That's hilarious."

When they reached the driveway, Riley said, "I'm ready to spend a quiet evening with you."

"We could even have a glass of wine in front of the fireplace. How does that sound?" Ben asked.

"Romantic," Riley said.

"Exactly the mood I had in mind. Do you suppose Mom and Dad would mind spending the evening in the barn?

Riley stared at him. "Why ever would you want them to do that?"

"Oh, you know, so we could have a little privacy."

"We'll have plenty of time for privacy after we return to Barton," Riley said.

Ben exhaled and then grumbled. "But that's not tonight."

Riley smiled as Ben parked the truck. "It'll work out."

Ben grunted.

As they walked into the house, Ben's phone buzzed with a text: "Pamela Suzanne is here. She claims she has documents."

Ben called Mugsy. "What do you think?" he asked.

"She has a folder, but that's all I've seen."

"I'll come to town if she gives you the folder; otherwise, you can close the shop at your regular time."

"I'll get back to you," Mugsy said.

"Did Pamela Suzanne give you the papers that she was in such a rush for you to have?" Melissa asked.

"She claimed the papers were at her aunt's, so we left. Mugsy said Pamela Suzanne has returned to the coffee shop with a folder, but I'm not returning until after Mugsy sees the documents. We're waiting for Mugsy to call me back."

Ben's phone rang. He listened, then said, "We'll be right there."

After he hung up, he said, "Mugsy has looked through the documents and said they appear to be what Pamela Suzanne claimed."

"I'll plan on dinner an hour later," Melissa said.

"I'm sorry, Mom," Ben said.

"Thank you, but don't worry about it. Chicken and dumplings are flexible; we'll be fine."

On the way to the coffee shop, Ben said, "I'm really mad at Pamela Suzanne; not only did she waste our time and inconvenience Mom, but she also caused us to waste gas driving back and forth." Ben slammed his palm on the steering wheel. "What makes me even madder is that her aunt lives over forty minutes from Carson. There's no way she went to her aunt's home and then back to the coffee shop in less than thirty minutes. I don't know what game she thinks she's playing, but I'm over it. Riley, I want you to look at the documents for me because you catch details others miss."

When he parked, he said, "Pamela Suzanne better be playing this straight, or I'll walk out."

"Don't leave without me," Riley said.

Ben exhaled and then kissed her. "Never."

He reached to open his door. "That might be the best way to manage her. I'll be at the bookstore, and if she does or says anything cute, she can deal with you or go to the sheriff."

While Ben helped Riley out of the truck, she said, "I've got your back."

He kissed her; then they went into the coffee shop.

Mugsy raised her eyebrows when she glanced at Ben's face as they walked into the shop, and Cookie barked from the back of the store. Pamela Suzanne sat at a table near the front window and scowled when she saw Riley, and Ben crossed his arms and glared at Pamela Suzanne.

Mugsy came out from behind the counter and held out the folder to Ben. Ben motioned his head toward Riley, and Mugsy smiled as she handed off the folder.

"What are you doing? I never agreed to allow her into the shop," Pamela Suzanne said.

Mugsy's voice was hard. "Excuse me, Pamela Suzanne; this is my shop. You may certainly come and go as you please, but Riley is a highly-regarded celebrity in our town, and I'm more than honored to welcome her to my shop."

Riley opened the folder and sat at the table nearest to Pamela Suzanne. After ten minutes of silence, while she reviewed each page and took notes, Riley said, "There are holes, but I see some links."

She slipped all the papers back into the folder before she rose, gave the folder to Ben, and turned to Pamela Suzanne. "Where are the rest of the pages?"

Pamela Suzanne sputtered. "What are you talking about?"

Riley hummed as she stepped closer to Pamela Suzanne. "I don't blame you for the pages you kept. They felt like insurance, didn't they? But believe me, they aren't. These people are not nice; they're deadly."

Pamela Suzanne dropped into her seat, and in her peripheral vision, Riley caught Mugsy as she tugged on Ben's sleeve and then heard them leave for the back of the store. *They're going to Mugsy's listening spot.*

Riley continued, "They've kidnapped my best friend's husband, and she's frantic because she's so afraid they've killed him, and I believe they caused the crash that killed your boss."

Pamela Suzanne sobbed. "I'm so scared. My boss told me he was afraid he was being followed, and I should be careful. When he told me higher-up authorities were involved, I couldn't think of anyone to tell except Ben. Ben and I had a falling out, but we were good friends once."

"I know. He told me how much fun y'all had when you were kids. I'm kind of jealous because I never had a good friend when I was growing up."

"Really? I'm sorry, but it's their loss," Pamela Suzanne said. "You were right; I have the rest of the pages in my purse." She pulled out a thick packet of folded papers from her purse, placed it on the table, and slid it toward Riley. "Here. You'll know what to do with the papers."

"Thank you," Riley said. "I know all of this is hard."

Pamela Susanne's eyes filled with tears. "What can I do to be safe?"

"Can you leave Atlanta and maybe stay with your aunt, or better yet, is there somewhere else you could stay?"

Pamela Suzanne snuffled. "My dad and his wife are in Florida at their place on the beach for the winter. They've been after me to join them; his wife has always been nice to me. Mom doesn't like her, but Mom's not a happy person; that's not uncommon after a messy divorce, is it?"

Riley opened the folded packet of papers and glanced through them before she put the papers into her backpack. "It happens, but I'm not sure people always think about the impact of their anger about old wounds on other family members."

"That's exactly right. Mom got so upset when I was a kid and told her I wanted to see my dad; I felt disloyal to her, but I hurt Dad by staying away."

"Did you bring enough clothes with you so you could leave first thing in the morning?" Riley asked.

"I have enough for a few days, but Dad's wife has always been good to me. She keeps telling me to come stay with them, and we can go shopping for Florida clothes." Pamela Suzanne giggled.

Riley smiled. "My dad's sister was like that too. My mother didn't like her at all, but she made a difference in my life."

Pamela Suzanne smiled as she rose. "We're much more alike than I ever thought we'd be." She held out her hand, and Riley shook it.

"Be safe," Riley said as Pamela Suzanne hurried to the front door. Pamela Suzanne smiled and waved as she left.

Mugsy and Ben strode to the front door.

"You are awesome." Mugsy hugged Riley.

"No kidding," Ben said. After Mugsy released Riley, Ben lifted up Riley into a hug and kissed her square on the mouth. "How on earth did you figure her out?"

Riley shrugged. "She reminded me of a skittish stray, so I spoke calmly, listened to her, and gave her time to adjust to me."

"What was that tune you hummed? It was very relaxing," Mugsy said.

"I've heard you hum that before," Ben said. "Where did you learn that?"

"My grandmother taught it to me; she hummed to injured deer and other wildlife, her barn cats, and even injured birds. It's always worked for me too."

"Do you want to look at the papers first?" Ben asked.

"I was concerned that she had given me blank sheets of paper, so I looked at them in front of her. I think she gave me everything she had."

"Is Pamela Suzanne changed now?" Mugsy asked.

Riley snorted. "Not at all. According to Grandma, a wild animal is a wild animal."

Mugsy chuckled. "So, that's why you were trying to find somewhere not so close for her to go."

"Dang, honey. You're not only brilliant, you're devious, but in a good way." Ben grinned.

"Gotta love ya, Riley; you are truly brilliant. Don't you love it, Ben?" Mugsy's eyes twinkled.

"Actually, I do. Ready to go, honey?" Ben asked.

"I'm ready and starving," she said.

"Y'all be safe and have all your meetings here from now on, especially if they're confidential." Mugsy chuckled as they left.

On their way home, Ben asked, "What would you have done if you couldn't have turned Pamela Suzanne around?"

Riley frowned. "It didn't occur to me that I wouldn't be successful. I was certain she felt cornered and was bluffing like a hissing raccoon. I guess if it didn't work, I would have continued distracting her while Mugsy threw a net over her."

Ben guffawed. "I'm kind of sorry I didn't get to see that."

After they arrived at the Carters', Toby, Duffy, and Finn rushed to greet them. The puppies yipped and jumped up on Ben while Toby howled at Riley, and she laughed. "Okay, Toby, we'll hurry into the house where it's warm."

When Riley, Ben, and the dogs entered the house, Melissa said, "Perfect. Give me ten minutes to warm the rolls, and I'll have supper on the table."

"Did you get what you needed from Pamela Suzanne?" Jake asked.

"Riley did." Ben told his parents about Riley, Pamela Suzanne, the papers, and how Riley learned her skills.

Jake shook his head. "Ben told me you understood animals, but I never considered how that might translate to a person in pain, Riley."

"I like your catch and release program, especially the part where you sent Pamela Suzanne far away into her natural environment of the wilds of the Florida beaches," Melissa said.

While Riley and Ben cleared the dishes and Jake loaded them into the dishwasher, Melissa covered the leftovers and placed them into the refrigerator.

After she turned off the oven she had left on a low temperature, Melissa asked, "Who's ready for peach pie and ice cream?"

While they ate dessert, Ben and Jake planned their morning hunting trip.

"We'll need to leave about four so we can be in place and quiet before sunrise," Jake said. "You might want to pull together your gear and load it into my truck so we can slip out and make a fast getaway in the morning, or is that the wrong thing to say to my son, the deputy?"

When Ben chuckled, Jake beamed.

"What about coffee and sandwiches?" Melissa asked.

"Thanks, honey. If we have lunch at the hunting cabin, we can stay until sundown," Jake said.

While Riley helped Melissa with the dessert dishes and the pots and pans, Ben gathered his hunting gear, then he and Jake loaded the truck and took the dogs out for a run. Riley watched through the window and giggled while the puppies tried to catch up with Toby.

"Do you have any candles, Mom? Ben hoped we could have a romantic evening for a change instead of chasing down bad guys."

"What a good idea. I have four or five hurricane globes that I've used with candles in the past when we've lost power, and somewhere, I have several boxes of candles. I think they're in the storage shed, but it won't take us long to find them. I wouldn't mind having candles in the living room permanently; it's much more convenient when we lose power if we have them in easy reach."

After they brought in five hurricane globes, Riley carried two of them to the living room as Ben came in with an armload of firewood.

"What are those for?" Ben asked.

"Candles to add to the romantic atmosphere. Mom's getting the candles. There are three more globes in the kitchen."

"I'll get them while you decide where to put them." Ben stacked the firewood next to the hearth and started the fire in the fireplace before he hurried to the kitchen and returned with the globes.

Melissa brought the candles to the living room and put her hands on her hips while she scanned the room. "Fire's nice, and I like where you've placed the globes for the candles. What else do you need? We have some excellent wines for you to choose from. Dad and I like to keep our favorite wines on hand for special occasions."

"I bought two bottles a few weeks ago," Ben said.

"Come see what I have, and you can decide."

Ben brought two bottles of wine, a corkscrew, and two wine glasses to the living room while Riley lit the candles. After Ben stoked the fire and opened a bottle of wine, Riley found a radio station that played classical music.

"We're going old school with some relaxing music." Riley lit the candles before she turned off the lights.

After Ben poured wine into two glasses, he joined Riley on the sofa and put his arm around her. Riley kicked off her boots and curled up as she relaxed against him.

"I'm afraid to say that this is nice because Pamela Suzanne might decide to stop by to tell her new best friend goodbye," Ben said.

Riley giggled. "She's social; she'll find a friend in Florida."

"Good." Ben placed his glass on the table next to the sofa, kissed her, and stroked her hair and cheek. Riley handed him her glass, and after he set her glass next to his, she traced his mouth with her finger.

After a deep, lingering kiss, Ben leaned back and gazed at the fire. "This is what it's supposed to be like."

Riley snuggled closer. "What?"

He kissed the top of her head. "Us. You and me together."

"Always," she murmured.

When Ben rose to add another log to the fire, Riley said, "Mugsy and I heard Pamela Suzanne tell you I was chubby and short; what on earth possessed you to announce she was jealous of my chest? Mugsy and I laughed so hard, we had to lean on each other to keep from falling down."

Ben raised his eyebrows. "It's simple, although I don't see what might be funny about your chest because I stare at it constantly." He smirked as he peered down the front of her shirt, then leered. "Yep. All the time."

Riley felt her face grow warm, and she touched her cheek. "Ben, I think you made me blush."

Riley heard the quiet click of the living room door closing, and she snickered as she whispered, "Mom just closed the door so we can have privacy."

Ben's cheeks reddened; he whispered, "I think Mom made me blush. I'll throw another log on the fire."

After he returned to the sofa, he picked up their wine glasses and smiled. "Dad and I decided we'd go hunting first thing in the morning. We'll be back after sundown."

While they sipped their wine, Riley said, "I keep thinking about Tom. It seems like I've forgotten something, and the cell phone in the ditch is still nagging me."

"He may have worried his cell phone could still be traced even with the SIM card gone, but I think you forgot we're having a relaxing, romantic evening," Ben said.

Riley smiled. "You're right. We've got wine, a fire, and candles."

She leaned against Ben. "What is the wood that is burning in the fireplace? It smells wonderful."

"Hickory," Ben said. "A tornado went through the hunting property last year and knocked down a stand of hickory trees. Dad and I spent a weekend clearing the road, then the following weekend, we brought the logs here."

"Can we take back some hickory firewood for the cabin?"

"That's an excellent idea. Hickory can be our romantic firewood."

Riley pulled him close for a kiss; he kissed her and moaned when she returned the intensity of his kiss.

After their long, passionate kiss ended, Riley sighed, leaned against Ben, and closed her eyes.

She woke when Ben swept her hair away from her face. "Honey, the candles burned down, and the fire's out. Let's go to bed."

Riley yawned and stretched. "I didn't know I'd fallen asleep. Who knew romantic evenings were so relaxing?"

Ben chuckled as he helped her to her feet and guided her to her bedroom.

"Good night, honey." He kissed her and then went to his room upstairs.

After Riley dropped her clothes on the floor, she put on her pajamas and slipped under her covers.

Riley woke at sunrise. She stretched as she sat up and breathed in the enticing aroma of coffee and cinnamon wafting from the kitchen. She dressed and hurried to join Melissa.

"Good morning, Riley," Melissa said when Riley reached the doorway. "I knew you were stirring because the dogs went on alert and have been watching the hallway."

Toby, Duffy, and Finn rushed Riley, and she knelt and rubbed Toby's ears and Duffy's and Finn's round bellies.

Melissa poured a cup of coffee for Riley. "Fried or scrambled egg with your cinnamon roll?"

"Whatever's easier." Riley sipped her coffee. "What time did Ben and Dad leave?"

"Four-thirty. I made sandwiches, and Jake packed enough food for tonight and tomorrow, but I didn't expect them to spend the night there because the beds were too uncomfortable. I'll make an omelet, and we can split it."

While Riley and Melissa ate, Melissa said, "Tell me about Pamela Suzanne. I was dying to ask you last night because Ben reported all the facts the same way he must fill out a police report, but Jake told me I was too nosy."

Riley grinned and told her about Mugsy's listening corner.

"That's absolutely delicious. I'll bet Mugsy hears some really juicy tidbits. The good townspeople of Carson are lucky she keeps everything to herself. So, what did Pamela Suzanne really say?"

"She was irate that I was there and told Ben she didn't know what he saw in me because I was chubby and short. Ben cut her off and shouted that Pamela Suzanne said I was short and that she was jealous of my chest. Mugsy and I cracked up."

Melissa laughed. "Your chest? He said she was jealous of your chest? What did Pamela Suzanne say?"

Riley giggled. "She stormed out of the coffee shop."

"Poor, skinny Pamela Suzanne." Melissa laughed even harder, and Riley laughed with her.

"I think I have a new nickname as far as Mugsy's concerned because she called me short-stuff."

"Well, I think it's great that Pamela Suzanne told Ben you were short because I doubt he'd have ever noticed otherwise." Melissa snickered.

Riley furrowed her brow. "My mother really hounded me about my weight. When I was three, her favorite word for me was 'pudgy.' She always introduced me after that by saying, 'This is my husband's pudgy daughter,' and was always putting me on the latest fad diet because she said boys didn't like fat girls."

"That is just so wrong to tell a child," Melissa growled.

"Dad walked into the kitchen once and heard her lecture me about my weight when I was eight, and he blew up. I ran to my room and cried because I really was the problem that my mother accused me of being. I often wondered where my real mother was and when she was coming to get me. When I asked Grandma where my real mother was, she cried and held me. She told me it wasn't my fault that my mother was broken, and she and Dad loved how I looked because I was the spitting image of my great-grandmother, a remarkable healer. She said I would always be surrounded and protected by love because the animals and birds would always be with me."

"What an excellent way to explain a troubled mother to a child," Melissa said. "Your grandmother was brilliant. Where is your mother now?"

"I have no idea. She left Dad and me when I was in high school, and we never heard from her again. Dad divorced her before I graduated, and Grandma worked hard to help me have a healthy body image, and I eventually developed a thick skin when it came to name-calling."

"I'm so glad you had your grandmother, who was such a positive influence when you were young." Melissa brushed away the tears on her cheeks, shook her head, and rose to clear the table. "What's your plan for today?"

Riley helped wipe down the table. "I don't have anything special planned, but I would like to take the dogs on a long walk and then maybe relax with a book."

Melissa nodded. "There's an easy trail through the trees behind our house that loops to the road; you could walk alongside the road to return to our house or backtrack through the woods. The woods might be safer than the road for Duffy and Finn."

"Toby would keep Duffy and Finn from going too close to the road, but I wouldn't mind letting Toby have a day off, too," Riley said.

"Dress in layers and take your phone," Melissa said. "It's cold now, but it'll warm up soon."

"I'm always cold these days." Riley smiled.

"You have your phone in your pocket, don't you?" Melissa sighed. "Thank you for letting me hover."

Toby and the puppies scrambled to the door when Riley grabbed her coat. After they were outside, Riley inhaled the cold air, and Toby yipped.

"We're taking the trail in the woods to the road, then we'll turn around and come back through the woods."

Toby and the puppies raced to the trail and waited for Riley; when she joined them, Toby led Duffy and Finn in a run along the path.

Riley jogged a few feet, then slowed to a more comfortable pace. While she walked along the path, she smiled at the loud crunch of dried leaves under her feet and the raucous calls of the crows warning of a nearby hawk. When a shadow slid over her, she shaded her eyes and peered overhead, but no hawk was in sight. *I heard the warning but never saw the danger.* Riley shivered and then exhaled. *Drama worthy of Pamela Suzanne. Shake it off.*

When the trail curved, Duffy and Finn lay across the path in a sunny spot, and Toby stood guard as he sniffed the air in the direction of the path ahead. Riley sat next to the puppies on a fallen log, and Toby trotted to her. Riley wrapped her arms around his neck and snuggled him. After she released him, Toby loped away, and Duffy and Finn scrambled to catch up with him.

Her phone buzzed a text, and she raised her eyebrows. *Eli Reeves? I thought he wasn't supposed to contact me.*

She frowned as she read the text: "Be careful who you trust."

Should I call him and ask what that means?

She continued on the trail while she pondered the text.

When Duffy and Finn raced to her and circled her before they dashed away, she narrowed her eyes and sent Eli a text: "Call to talk?"

His reply was immediate: "Can't."

She stared at her phone. "You can't talk to me? What are you warning me..." *Whose shadow is over me?*

Riley continued on the path, deep in thought. Toby and the puppies waited for her on the road.

"Going home by the road would be faster, or we could return on the trail. What do you think, Toby?"

Toby barked, then ran a few yards in the ditch alongside the road before he returned to Riley.

"Do you think Duffy and Finn would stay off the road?" she asked.

Toby grinned, then ran on the ditch bank that was farther from the road, and Duffy and Finn followed him. Riley abandoned her thoughtful stroll and quickened her pace on the shoulder to catch up with Toby as she hurried to the Carters' house.

Riley jogged down the driveway to the back door with the dogs trotting along in front of her; when they reached the house, they burst inside. Riley stopped in the middle of the kitchen to bend over and put her hands on her knees to catch her breath.

"Are you okay?" Melissa asked.

Riley nodded as she maintained her tripoding position and breathed heavily; the dogs rushed to the water bowl.

After Riley caught her breath, she said, "I jogged from the road to the house. I thought I was going to die, but it felt great."

"I understand exactly what you mean." Melissa chuckled as she poured coffee into two cups, and Riley sat at the table while Melissa started the dishwasher.

"I got a strange call on our house phone while you were gone," Melissa said. "We rarely use the phone; we have the telephone landline for our internet because that's all that was available when we first moved here. I keep threatening to disconnect it, but Jake's buddies told him their satellite internet goes down when it's stormy."

Melissa refilled the dogs' drinking water and then joined Riley at the table. "A man called and said he was with the GBI and asked for you. I told him you weren't here, and then he asked me where you were. Something in his tone got my hackles up, and I said, 'Excuse me?' in my sternest voice, and he hung up."

Riley frowned. "I can't imagine who that might be. Anyone from GBI who would ask for me by name would already have my cell phone number, so whoever called didn't know my cell phone number but knew about Ben and me and must have looked up your number on the internet. I can't make any sense of it."

"I can't either, but I didn't like his attitude." Melissa drank the rest of her coffee. "I'm going to attack the laundry before I sweep and mop the kitchen. Do you have anything for the washer?"

"I don't want to add to your work. I'll take care of it later," Riley said.

"Your few miniature pieces of clothing won't even be noticeable in the giants' pile of laundry." Melissa side-glanced Riley.

Riley giggled. "Have you been itching to work in a short joke?"

Melissa smirked. "Pretty much. Add your things to the laundry basket, and then, weren't you going to read?"

After Riley collected her clothes from the previous day and dropped them into the basket, she wandered to the living room and searched the bookshelves for a book to read. She smacked her forehead when she spotted a collection of stories about the Old West. *I have Tom's story on my computer.*

She hurried to her room, turned on her laptop, and sat on her overstuffed chair to read. *Wow. This is one hundred twenty-five pages; it's almost a novel.*

Riley kicked off her boots, put up her feet, and read. Halfway through the story, Melissa came into her bedroom.

"You must have found something interesting. You haven't twitched since you sat down with your computer. Ready for some lunch?" Melissa asked.

Riley glanced at the clock as she closed her laptop. "I completely lost track of time. I'm reading an Old West story. It's so good that I feel like I know the characters."

She giggled when her stomach rumbled. "I guess I'm ready for lunch."

On their way to the kitchen, Melissa said, "I heated up a jar of home-canned vegetable soup and whipped up a batch of biscuits for us. After I pull out the biscuits from the oven, I'll put the leftover peach pie in the oven to warm up. Would you like hot tea?"

"I'd love it. I'm always cold; I don't know why I can't get warm. Wouldn't you think I'd be over my short dip in the river by now?"

"I think that's normal. My mother told me that her family lived in Montana on a ranch for a few years when she was a child. She became lost in an unexpected blizzard while she was walking home from school when she was nine. A ranch hand who was looking for a lost calf found her curled up in a snow bank near a fence. He saw her bright red hat and thought the calf was injured and bleeding. He took her to the nearest ranch, and they nursed her for two weeks until she could tell them her name. She said the memory of the cold was in her bones for a long time."

Melissa ladled soup into bowls while Riley brewed their tea. While they ate, Melissa said, "Tell me about the story you're reading."

"It's about three cattle rustlers, except they present themselves as cattle drivers, who show up in a small town with a sad story about their crew being hit by a terrible sickness, and they were the only survivors. They claim they have a large herd to take to Kansas City to sell, but it's more than what the three of them can manage. They visit three different ranches, show them all the cattle they have, and ask for a ridiculously low price for all the cattle. The ranchers are a little greedy and see a great bargain, so they pay cash on the spot before the three guys can change their minds. The cattle rustlers leave town immediately, and the next day, the cattle return home, and the ranchers discover the herds they bought were actually their own free-ranging cows."

Melissa chuckled. "My first hint that the deal was not as good as the ranchers thought was when you said they were a little greedy. If it sounds too good to be true, it most likely isn't a good deal at all, is it?"

Riley smiled. "That's it. I haven't finished reading, though. What's your plan for this afternoon?"

"I'm going to clean the bathrooms, then get some pizza dough rising."

"Homemade pizza sounds great. Grandma used to make pizzas for the two of us. I'm spoiled; I can't eat a reheated frozen pizza, and I'm really particular about pizza parlors."

Melissa nodded. "Jake offers to take me out to dinner, but there are only a few places I'll go. After I remember I'll have to change my clothes and brush my hair, we stay home, and I cook."

Riley and Melissa's phones buzzed with texts. Riley looked at hers and asked, "What did Dad say?"

Melissa read her text: "Nothing."

Riley grinned. "Mine says, 'Saw squirrels.'"

Melissa chuckled. "Sounds like their typical hunt. Jake shows me deer photos from his game cameras: some of the pictures are selfies of deer checking out the camera, but the deer must have a calendar because they disappear the first day of hunting."

"I need to finish reading the story unless I could help you clean," Riley said.

"I'm taking a break. I was inspired by your walk today, so I'm taking the dogs outside."

Riley's eyes widened.

Melissa shook her head. "We'll walk part of the trail, then turn back. I love being in the woods, but I'm not running."

Melissa grabbed her coat and headed toward the back door, and Toby trotted behind her while the puppies scrambled, slid across the floor, and bounced off the door.

"I need to be as smart as Mom," Riley mumbled as she headed to her room to read.

Riley opened her laptop and made herself comfortable in her chair before she picked up the story where she left off.

After an hour of reading, Riley stared at the last page. "No!" she cried out, and Melissa ran to Riley's room.

Melissa's face was pale as she held onto the bed's footboard and caught her breath. "What's wrong? What can I do?"

Riley wailed. "Tom didn't finish the story. I don't know how it ends."

Melissa put her hand on her chest. "Is it a cliffhanger?"

Riley sighed. "No, it's worse; he stopped in the middle of a paragraph."

"We have to find him," Melissa growled. "He has to finish his story."

Riley furrowed her brow. "The owner of the general store has a dog named Loco. I think I need to read the story again."

Chapter Five

Riley stared at the story's title, 'Phantom Cattle'. *Is the title a clue to Tom's disappearance, or am I reading too much into a great story?*

Riley read the first page, reread it, took notes, and frowned at her full page of hand-written notes. *I need to find another way because I'm copying Tom's writing.*

She read chapter one, jotting down names as she read, and then wrote a summary of the first chapter. *This works. Names are the hardest for me to remember, and I can go back to the chapter if I need more detail later.* She quickly scrolled through the story. *Eight chapters; I can do this.*

After Riley finished her notes for the third chapter, Melissa entered her room with a cup of hot tea and three chocolate chip cookies.

"I've cleaned the entire house and made cookies for brain food. What else can I do? Would it help if I read the story, too?" Melissa asked.

"That's a good idea because we can brainstorm," Riley said. "I'll email it to you."

"Here's my email address," Melissa said. "I'm really excited to be helping instead of just fretting. I'll read in the kitchen because it's where I think best. Let me know if you need any more brain food."

After Riley sent the manuscript, she returned to chapter four.

While she read chapter six, her phone rang, and she answered it immediately.

"Are you okay, Pia?" she asked.

"I'm okay. I'm on a break, but I couldn't remember whether I'm allowed to call you or not, so I thought I'd ask," Pia said.

Riley giggled. "I've forgotten, too. What's going on?"

"Jackson and I talked, and you were right. He's his father's son because he was worried about me. He'd heard the nasty comments at school and was trying to shield me from them."

"What an awesome kid. I'm really glad you two have each other."

"Me too. I have some information, but I'm not sure what to do with it," Pia said.

"Hand it off to me," Riley said.

"I was hoping you'd say that. First, Eli Reeves called here and talked to Claire. He told her he was ordered to stay away from you because he'd crossed a line, and he understood that, but he had important information for you. Claire and I decided it must be important because the sheriff had asked Marc to make sure Eli didn't contact you at all after Eli first let his ego get in the way when he decided you had a crush on him and then spread the false rumors about Ben and the so-called wedding. You know Claire, she asked him what the information was."

"Did he tell her?" Riley asked.

"He said it was too dangerous, and she told him we all wished him well. He thanked her, told her he needed to think and hung up. I realize that doesn't tell you much."

"It's actually quite a bit. He trusts Claire; we'll wait to see what he decides."

"Do you think he really has information for you?" Pia asked.

"I think he does, but we'll have to see if he calls Claire back."

"Tamara stopped by without Mini-me yesterday and told Claire that Mini-me's dad had a few things to tell Mini-me's friend. Claire asked how she could help, and Tamara told her the dad would like to talk to the friend. What do you think?"

"No Mini-me? That alone is shocking, and because Tamara didn't use any names, it's definitely important. I trust Mini-me's dad. It's okay with me if Claire gives Tamara my cell number, if you and Claire think it's a good idea."

Pia chuckled. "I'm not surprised you know we discussed it in depth, and we agree with you."

"What about Thad and Zach? If they know, Ben knows."

"Claire and I voted to leave them out of the discussion," Pia said.

"Just needed to know; what else is going on?"

"Marc checks in regularly with us; he's still hopeful the GBI team will find Tom soon. He asked whether you'd found anything, and Claire told him we hadn't heard from you at all. Marc told her to let him know if we hear from you, and just for your information, this call never happened."

Riley frowned. "Are you concerned about Marc?"

"No, but Jackson told me he had a feeling that we need to stay under the radar. That boy reads way too much and has a wild imagination, just like his father, but Claire and I decided it was smart to keep things to ourselves until Tom came home. Have you had a chance to read the story Tom wrote? What do you think?"

"It's an awesome story, and Tom is remarkably talented at bringing the characters to life. One of the two main characters owns a general store, and her name is Novalee. It struck me as perfectly appropriate for her fiery personality, but I don't know why."

"Really? Novalee is one of the main characters?" Pia squealed. "That's my middle name. I never used it because I was teased so much about it when I was growing up. I can't tell you how many times I was called 'Novocain' in school. Who's the other main character? Is it a man named Blair?"

"Are you sure you haven't read the story?" Riley asked.

Pia giggled. "Blair is Tom's middle name. He always hated it because there was a girl in school named Blaire; even though she spelled her name with an 'e' at the end, Tom was still teased."

After they hung up, Riley furrowed her brow. *This puts a new spin on the story.* Riley resumed reading, but Melissa tapped on the doorjamb before she finished the last chapter. "Our hunters will be here for supper. Jake told me Ben missed you, which I interpreted to mean that Jake decided he couldn't sleep on one of the small, uncomfortable beds in the cabin after all. I don't blame the man for wanting to preserve a bit of his dignity."

Riley smiled. "I only have a few pages of the last chapter left. What did you think about the story?"

"I loved it. I've never read Jake's Old West books, but now I think I might enjoy Old West stories after all. Finish your last chapter, then come to the kitchen, and we can talk; I have loads of questions. I'm going to roast a chicken with my special rub."

As Riley walked into the kitchen, her phone rang.

"Hi, Mugsy."

"Is Ben with you?" Mugsy asked.

"No, I'm in the kitchen with Mom."

"Put me on speakerphone. She'll be interested in hearing this too," Mugsy said.

Riley shrugged. "Mom, Mugsy wants you to hear what she says."

Riley and Melissa sat at the table together, and then Riley said, "Okay, Mugsy."

"I got a call from Pamela Suzanne. She told me she must have lost Riley's number because she couldn't find it on her phone. If you just rolled your eyes, that's exactly what I did." Mugsy snorted. "She said something must be wrong with Ben's phone because it immediately rang to voice mail."

"I'm pretty sure he blocked her," Melissa said.

"Ha! Thought so. She asked for Riley's number, but after I told her I didn't have it, she asked if I could give Riley a message the next time I saw her. I was really growing weary of Miss Pamela Suzanne, but I persevered."

"Very admirable, Mugsy. You took one for the team," Melissa said.

"Thanks. She wanted Riley to know she made it safely to Miami, and I refrained from saying she should tell someone who cares. If there's anything important you think Pamela Suzanne can tell you, Riley, she sounded like she may cooperate."

"Good to know. Would you text me her number?"

"Are you sure? Of course, you are." Mugsy sighed. "Will do. So, when are you two coming to town for coffee?"

"Sounds like a great idea," Melissa said. "Do we need reservations?"

"Absolutely." Mugsy cackled. "I run a classy joint. Send me a text when you're on your way, and I'll clear your table by tossing out the riff-raff."

"You are so funny, Mugsy," Melissa said. "Please don't tell me you're kidding because I love it."

After Riley hung up, her phone buzzed with a text from Mugsy.

Riley read it. "Mugsy sent me Pamela Suzanne's phone number."

Melissa rose to load the dishwasher. "I don't understand why you would want her number."

Riley bit her lip. "I got the feeling Pamela Suzanne knew more than she said; I'm waiting for her to feel safe enough to tell me."

"I'm not sure I understand, but I trust your judgment." Melissa smiled.

Riley snickered. "I think I'm nuts too."

"I never meant..." Melissa laughed. "Okay, maybe I did."

Melissa's phone buzzed. "Saved by the bell." She grinned and read her text. "Oh, my goodness. Jake actually harvested the buck he's been eyeing for three years. His brother will be so jealous, but it serves him right for bailing. Jake and Ben are on their way to the processors."

"That's awesome," Riley said.

Melissa smiled. "We'll have to scramble and make a pumpkin pie. That's Jake's requested reward for his eight-point buck. Thank goodness I have a double-oven stove."

Melissa rolled out the pie dough. "Do me a favor. Don't call Pamela Suzanne. Ever. Everybody knows she's toxic."

"You may be right, Mom," Riley said. *Why did Mom say that?*

"Pull out a can of pumpkin from the pantry for our pie, please," Melissa said.

Riley opened the pantry door. "Got it."

Riley gathered ingredients from the pantry while Melissa pulsed the ingredients for the dough in her food processor.

Melissa wrapped the dough in plastic before she put it in the refrigerator. While the dough chilled, Melissa mixed the pumpkin with eggs, sweetened condensed milk, and spices. After Melissa rolled out the crust and placed it in the pie pan, she poured in the pumpkin mixture and popped the pie into the oven.

"I can't believe how quickly you made the pumpkin pie," Riley said.

"I've been training for this for three years." Melissa raised her arms in triumph and snickered. "My goal is to pull out the pie from the oven before Jake struts into the house."

Toby, Duffy, and Finn trotted to the back door, and Riley grabbed her coat. "I'll go outside with you."

Toby led the puppies to the driveway, and Riley followed them. After they dashed ahead, she sped up to a fast walk. They were waiting for her at the end of the driveway, and Toby barked when she stopped.

"You win; here goes nothing." She jogged slowly to the barn, and Toby trotted alongside her while Duffy and Finn explored the trees and brush alongside the driveway.

Princess waited for them at the barn's entrance. Riley picked up her pace to the barn for her grand finish. Riley kneeled next to Princess as she stroked her back and rubbed her ears. Princess purred and leaned against Riley.

"I'm glad you're happy and doing such an awesome job of keeping the barn clear of mice."

A sudden gust of wind blew from the north; Toby and the puppies raced toward the house, and Princess meowed before she dashed into the barn. Riley shivered as she pulled up her jacket's hood to protect the back of her neck. "I'm going inside too."

Riley hurried into the house and inhaled as she closed the door. "The house smells amazing. The hot pumpkin, cinnamon, cloves, and nutmeg, and chicken with garlic, rosemary, and thyme, and the vegetables smell like Thanksgiving dinner."

Riley hung up her coat and shivered. "The wind has shifted, and it's getting colder."

"I could feel the sudden drop in temperature when I let in the dogs and knew you'd be coming inside soon," Melissa said. "I brewed tea for both of us."

Melissa handed Riley her cup, and Riley wrapped her hands around her cup for warmth as she sat at the table.

Melissa set a plate of cookies in the middle of the table as she joined Riley with her tea. "When the dogs came inside, I gave them their treat, and I could feel the cold air around them; my teeth almost chattered. I can imagine what it's like out there. I lit the kindling in the fireplace shortly after you and the dogs went outside, so they're in the living room now, soaking up the heat. Did you stop by the barn? I was initially worried about Princess being away from you, but she's a marvelous barn cat."

"She told me how much she loves it here, and she's really proud of keeping the mice out of the barn," Riley said. "Why did you say Pamela Suzanne is toxic?"

Melissa finished her tea, rose from the table, opened the oven door, and pulled out the pumpkin pie. After she set it on the wire rack to cool, she set a pot of freshly peeled and quartered potatoes on the stove and turned on the burner for the water to boil. "Did I say that?"

Riley raised her eyebrows. "Yes."

When Melissa turned, her knitted brow and downturned mouth revealed deep sadness. She sat at the table, and tears welled up and spilled over her cheeks.

"Ruth and I were best friends and inseparable all through school from kindergarten until..."

Melissa swallowed hard before she continued, "When we were in the tenth grade, Darlene, Pamela Suzanne's mother, decided that Ruth was her favorite target, and she and her gang kept Ruth in tears with relentless taunting and bullying, but back then, it was called teasing. I was sent home time after time, then finally suspended for two weeks for fighting. That's when the attacks on Ruth intensified, and others joined in to torture Ruth. One afternoon, while I was still suspended and not allowed to have contact with anyone at school, Ruth put on her best Sunday dress and hung herself." Melissa sobbed as she left the kitchen.

Riley bit her lip as a tear slipped down her cheek. *That's horrible and so tragic.*

When Melissa returned, Riley hugged her, and after they sat at the table, Riley put her hand over Melissa's hand, and Melissa smiled. "You're a kind-hearted soul, Riley. Darlene left for Atlanta immediately after we graduated from high school. Pamela Suzanne looks like her mother and has some of her mannerisms. I doubt she's the bully her mother was, but I've still never trusted her. I was anxious every holiday because of the family's remarks about Ben and Pamela Suzanne. I hated the mean teasing Pamela Suzanne encouraged, and Ben tried to laugh it off, but it was bullying, not good-natured teasing, despite what they claimed when I called them out on it. The family toned it down after I reminded them of my thug reputation."

"Does Ben know?" Riley asked.

Melissa shook her head and started a pot of coffee. "Darlene and Pamela Suzanne were friends of the family, and nobody's left who remembers sweet Ruth except for Ruth's sister and me."

Riley's eyes widened. "Mugsy."

Melissa took in a sharp breath as she stared at Riley. "How did you know?"

"I just had a feeling."

"You're really uncanny sometimes, so back to Tom's story..."

The dogs interrupted Melissa as they barked and barreled down the hallway to the back door, and Riley laughed when she peeked outside and then opened the door for the dogs. "Dad's truck just pulled in. Do you think they'll come straight to the house?"

"Probably," Melissa said. "There are any number of noncritical things they would ordinarily do, but I'll bet they'll be ready for something hot to drink and a snack. Don't stand between the door and the cookies. You might get trampled."

Riley giggled. "Justifiably so." She narrowed her eyes at the plate. "Did we leave them enough?"

"Good thought." Melissa opened a cupboard and shook out more cookies from a cookie jar.

Ben strode inside, and Jake strutted in behind him. Ben hugged Riley and kissed her.

"Mmm. You're warm," he said as he held her tighter, and she snuggled against his chest and wrapped her arms around him.

Jake grabbed Melissa into his arms, and she squealed when he leaned her backward. Jake planted his mouth on her open mouth and kissed her thoroughly. When he returned her to an upright position, Melissa brushed away her hair from her face.

"Jake," she scolded. "Not in front of the children."

Jake snorted. "All Ben could see was Riley, and I'll bet Riley closed her eyes. Your secret's safe." Jake patted her bottom, and Melissa giggled and smacked his arm. "You need a shower, smelly man. After you aren't so stinky, we can have dinner, and maybe you can have dessert if you can behave."

Jake hurried to their bathroom to shower.

"Am I a smelly man?" Ben whispered into Riley's ear.

"You smell like Ben," she said.

"Achhh! I'll shower immediately." Ben released Riley and clutched his chest, and Riley giggled as he winked and then staggered to the stairs.

"They're really very much alike, aren't they? What can I do?" Riley asked.

"Always have been," Melissa said. "You can see if Princess wants to come inside, feed the dogs, and set the table."

Riley threw on her coat and headed to the barn, but Princess met her on the way. "Ready to come inside for supper?"

Princess dashed past Riley to the front door and waited. After they were inside, Riley fed the dogs while Princess explored the downstairs and upstairs. When Princess returned, she meowed, and Riley set down Princess's food for her and then washed her hands so she could set the table.

Melissa pulled out the chicken and tented it before she started making gravy. "Thanks for checking, Princess."

"How did you know what she said?" Riley stared at Melissa before she pulled out the silverware.

"She has been inspecting the house every time she comes in since it turned cold; I finally figured out she was checking for mice and then giving me a report. I really appreciate it, too. After you set the table, would you mash the potatoes?"

Jake entered the kitchen and slipped up behind Melissa to wrap his arms around her waist while she stirred the gravy.

He buried his face in her hair and then nuzzled her neck. "You smell like pumpkin pie. Shall I pour drinks, or is it too early?"

"You smell clean," Melissa continued to stir. "I need a little space to make this gravy, though, so if you'd take care of the drinks, that would give me a little elbow room. Hot tea for Riley and me."

Ben strode into the kitchen. "You want iced tea, Dad? I'll take care of the cold drinks."

While they ate, Jake and Ben discussed the improvements they needed to make to their stands, the cabin, and the property after hunting season.

Riley listened and ate a few bites, then moved her food around her plate with her fork while she was lost in thought. I guess it's not unusual that Tom would name the hero after himself and the story's female lead after Pia, but it definitely puts a different light on the story.

"Riley?" Melissa whispered and patted Riley's arm. "Are you okay?"

"Oh." Riley glanced at Ben, but he and his dad were still in deep conversation; she frowned at her plate. "I'm actually starving, but I got lost in the Old West story."

She cut a bite of chicken then, swirled it in the gravy, and picked up a taste of mashed potatoes on one corner of the chicken before she popped it all into her mouth. "Mmm. This is delicious."

"Can we talk about the book?" Melissa asked.

Riley nodded because her mouth was full.

"I have a feeling this conversation will go on the rest of the night. They'll disappear after dessert, then we can talk," Melissa said.

"Perfect." Riley took one last bite, including a tiny morsel of everything on her plate.

When Melissa served Jake his large slice of pumpkin pie with a mound of fresh whipped cream that was the size of a softball, Ben held up his iced tea glass. "A toast to the just desserts for the hunter."

Jake snort-laughed, then wiped his eyes. "I accept the honor, fleeting as it is."

After Jake and Ben polished off their desserts, Jake said, "I need to clean my gun and muddy boots. Care to go with me to the barn, Ben?"

After the two men left the house, Melissa said, "Told you," as she and Riley finished their pie.

While Riley cleared the table and wrapped up the leftovers for the refrigerator, Melissa loaded the dishwasher and then scrubbed pots and pants. "I don't understand why Novalee told Blair she didn't trust the

Ranger after the Ranger took off to find the rustlers when the ranchers discovered they'd been duped. Seemed to me that he was definitely on the ranchers' side and wanted to bring the hustling rustlers to justice."

"Hustling rustlers." Riley giggled. "Maybe Novalee heard something in her store that will come out later in the story."

"We really need the rest of the story. Do you think Pia has it? Could it have been on Tom's computer? Do you think Pia has a backup?" Melissa asked.

Riley's eyes widened, and she smacked her forehead. "I'd completely forgotten. Pia gave me the flash drive that was the backup to Tom's computer. I need to find it."

Riley raced to her room and searched through all the pockets in her backpack, and Melissa hurried to Riley's room. "Did you find it?"

Riley dug deep into the main compartment and then exhaled. "Found it."

After she inserted the flash drive into the slot on her computer, she frowned as she scrolled through the long list of folders and files, and Melissa peered over her shoulder.

"It will take you forever to go through all those files," Melissa said.

"I'll save this to my computer and sort the files by date so I can start with the newest files first."

"Why don't you go to the living room and put your feet up? I'll get the fire going, so you'll have inspiration," Melissa said.

Riley smiled. "Thanks, but I need to focus while I sit at my desk and take notes."

Four hours later, Ben tapped on her door. "Honey, Mom told me I couldn't interrupt you when we came inside, but it's late, and Mom and Dad have already called it a night. What do you think about getting a fresh start in the morning?"

Riley stretched. "I'm almost at the end of this document. I'll finish it, then go to bed."

Ben strode to the chair in her room and sat. "I can't sleep as long as you're awake. I'll sit here until you turn off your computer."

Riley glared at him. "Isn't that blackmail?"

"Call it what you like." Ben grinned.

After she finished reading the document and taking her final notes, Riley powered down her computer and flipped through her notes.

"Did you find anything?"

"Nothing; I have a ton of notes, but I still don't see anything. I think a fresh start is exactly what I need."

When she rose from her chair, Ben strode to her, held her, and kissed her gently. "Good night, honey."

"Good night."

After Ben climbed the stairs, Riley got ready for bed, slipped under her covers, and turned off her bedside lamp. *There has to be a better way. Maybe Tom's journal will help. I haven't looked at it in a while.* She tiptoed to her door and closed it, then turned on her bedroom light. As she hurried to find the journal, she glanced at her window. *Ben can see the light from my window from his room.*

She hurried back to her bedside table, turned off her light, and pulled out her flashlight. Toby nosed open her door and flopped on the floor next to her bed. Riley snorted and climbed back into bed. *It's a conspiracy.*

The aroma of coffee woke her. When she opened her eyes, Melissa smiled as she brought a cup of steaming coffee into her room, and Riley turned on her bedside lamp.

"I know it's awfully early, but Ben and Jake slipped out to go hunting," Melissa said. "Ben made a point to tell me that you needed your sleep, so I waited until they were on the road, then gave them an extra ten minutes in case they forgot something so we wouldn't get busted."

When Melissa handed her the coffee, Riley smiled and swung her feet to the floor. "I'll have our breakfast ready by the time you're dressed. We'll have a quiet morning, so you can focus on Tom's files or walk the dogs, although you may want to wait until ten or so when it starts to warm up a bit before you go outside."

Riley drained her coffee, made her bed, and dressed for the cold morning. When she carried her empty cup into the kitchen, Melissa said, "Perfect timing. Let's fill that cup. Your breakfast this morning is strawberry and whipped cream crepes and a soft-boiled egg."

Riley gasped at the lacy tablecloth and the delicate plates and eggcups. "It's beautiful. My grandma had egg cups on her shelf but never used them."

"I went fancy except for our coffee cups. I would never mess with our coffee." Melissa chuckled.

While they ate, Melissa's phone buzzed a text, and she frowned. "That's odd. Jake said they were on their way home. Nothing about a deer."

Riley picked up her phone as it buzzed, and she read her text. "Ben said, 'Be home in ten.' That's vague."

After she took her last bite, Riley said, "Something's up. I have to pull my things together just in case."

"I don't understand, but I trust your instincts. While you're packing, I'll fry some bacon, and then by the time I cook their eggs, they'll be here," Melissa said.

Riley packed her clothes and toiletries in her duffel bag, secured her computer and chargers in her computer bag, and then returned to the kitchen.

"I have bread in the toaster," Melissa said. "I'm ready for whatever's going on."

Ben rushed inside the house. "Dad brought me back; I need to leave for Barton as soon as I can get packed."

As Ben rushed toward the stairs to go to his room, Riley asked, "How much time do I have until we leave?"

Ben stopped and then returned to the kitchen. "You aren't going."

"Really? Why is that?" Riley said in a calm voice.

"I'm going alone." Ben narrowed his eyes and tightened his jaw.

"Oh, really?" Riley raised her eyebrows and gazed at Ben. "You want to be alone? Are you sure?"

"Um, Ben..." Jake said.

Melissa put her hand on Jake's arm, and Jake leaned back in his chair, shook his head, and sipped his coffee.

Ben jutted out his jaw and met Riley's gaze. "I'm leaving in ten minutes. I'm doing this alone."

Riley narrowed her eyes, and her tone turned to steel. "Your choice is to be alone. Fine."

He turned and stomped down the hall and up the stairs to his room, and Riley dashed to her room. She returned with her large duffel bag, backpack, and computer bag. She joined Jake at the table, and Jake stared at her while his breakfast grew cold.

After ten minutes, Ben came downstairs with this duffel bag and backpack. He carried his bags outside and then returned. "You can't go, Riley. Someone shot Sheriff Dunn last night. I have to go back on duty."

"Shot?" Riley growled. "The sheriff was shot? When were you going to tell me?"

"I'm telling you now; he's in surgery." Ben raised his voice. "I have to go back."

"Without me?" Riley raised her eyebrows as she spoke in a quiet voice.

"Ben." Jake's eyes narrowed, and he tightened his mouth as he shook his head.

Ben glanced at his dad and then clenched his teeth. "I have to leave for Barton immediately; we can continue our discussion on the road." Ben picked up Riley's duffel bag and stormed out the door.

Jake exhaled. "Your son isn't nearly as...what's the word?"

"Obtuse? Pigheaded? Shortsighted? Clueless?" Melissa asked.

Riley rolled her eyes and then hugged Jake. "Thanks for the support, Dad."

Melissa handed Riley a sack. "Here's Ben's breakfast sandwich. Let me know what we can do to help you."

Riley hugged Melissa. "Thanks, Mom, and I vote for 'clueless'; it has a nice ring."

Riley grabbed her backpack, computer bag, and breakfast sack before she and Toby raced out the door. "I hope we don't have to run up the driveway to catch Ben," Riley said, and Toby dashed ahead, jumped into the truck's open driver's door, then leaped over the seat to the back.

Riley slowed her pace to a fast walk and climbed into the truck as Ben closed his door.

"Thanks for saving my spot, Toby." Riley clicked her seatbelt, pulled her sunglasses from her backpack, and leaned back.

Ben started the engine, drove to the end of the driveway, and turned onto the road. After they reached the highway, Ben said, "I don't want to be without you."

"We belong together," Riley said. "If you went to Barton without me, you wouldn't be able to work because you'd worry about me in Carson, but I would find a way to get to Barton, and you'd worry. See how much worry I'm saving you?"

Ben nodded. "I think that's what Dad was trying to tell me, and I'm grateful you're so stubborn."

Riley cleared her throat. "Determined."

Ben chuckled. "What are you going to do when we get to Barton?"

"Go to work." Riley pulled out her phone and called the veterinary hospital.

When Claire answered the phone, she asked, "How can I help?"

"Ben and I are returning to Barton, and Toby and I will return to work before lunch," Riley said.

"You know about the sheriff, right?"

"Yes; that's why Ben has to return. Do you have any details?" Riley asked.

"Yes, ma'am, we are swamped. Thank you for calling." Claire hung up.

"What did Claire say?" Ben asked.

"She was busy, but something's wrong besides the sheriff."

"Keep me up to date," Ben said.

"Always do," Riley said.

Toby whined, and Ben raised his eyebrows. "Always?"

"Eventually," Riley said.

Ben snorted, and Toby sneezed.

Riley smiled as she leaned forward and gazed at the familiar landscape.

Ben cleared his throat. "Riley, when I told Dad on our way back from hunting that I wanted you to stay with him and Mom, he said you'd be going with me to Barton, and when I argued with him, he told me I was arguing with the wrong person, and if I was serious, I needed a logical reason."

Ben side-glanced at Riley. "Evidently, I missed the logic of what Dad told me. I don't have a logical reason, but when I heard Sheriff Dunn was in the hospital fighting for his life, it scared me almost as badly as I was scared when you disappeared."

"It would scare me if you disappeared, and it scared me when you told me Sheriff Dunn had been shot, but logically, we're stronger when we're together," Riley said.

"Right, and that's why I finally paid attention to Dad. Thanks for coming with me, Riley."

"I love you, Ben."

Ben patted his chest. "You own my heart; I love you too."

When Ben pulled into their driveway and parked, Toby barked.

Riley grinned as she jumped out and then opened Toby's door. Toby explored the front yard while Riley grabbed her backpack and computer bag and opened the front door. Toby pushed past her and dashed into the house. Riley dropped her backpack and computer on the kitchen table, then hurried outside to help Ben, who had already set her duffel bag on the front porch. Riley dragged her bag to her room, and when she returned to the living room, Toby stood at the back door. Riley hurried to the kitchen and opened the back door for Toby.

Ben carried his duffel bag and backpack to his room, and Riley stepped out onto the back porch and texted Melissa to let her know they had arrived safely. While Toby inspected his yard, Riley rocked and listened to the birds, the nearby traffic, and the familiar neighborhood sounds of cats, dogs, and children.

When Ben joined her on the porch, he had changed to his uniform. "Honey, your lunch is in the refrigerator. I have no idea when I'll be home; can you take care of the grocery shopping and dinner after work?"

"Sure can. Thanks for lunch." Riley jumped up from the rocker, hugged Ben, and kissed him. "Be safe, sweetheart," she said.

Ben stroked her hair, then returned her kiss. "You too, honey."

Riley checked the cupboard and refrigerator, wrote down her shopping list, and then called Toby. "Ready to go to work?"

Toby dashed inside, and Riley grabbed her phone and keys. After Toby had jumped into her car, she headed to the veterinary hospital.

"I'm excited about returning to work, but I hate that we cut our vacation short, Toby."

After she turned at the employee lot, she scanned the cars as she parked. *Are we one car short?*

Riley and Toby rushed inside, and Toby dashed to the front while Riley headed to the breakroom and put her lunch in the refrigerator.

Claire squealed, "Toby!"

When Riley turned to leave the breakroom, Doc Thad grinned as he stopped in the doorway. "You're late."

Riley smiled. "I'll get my excused tardy slip from Claire."

Doc Thad chuckled as he continued down the hallway to the exam rooms, and Riley hurried to Claire's desk.

"It's great to see you." Claire rose from her chair and hugged Riley. "We're backed up because Zach's not here, and I apologize for being so short with you on the phone earlier. I didn't want you to feel pressured to return because we were short-handed, and I panicked."

Riley smiled. "It was weird. I thought you were talking code at first."

Claire snickered. "It was terrible, wasn't it?" She handed Riley a folder. "Exam room three."

Riley glanced through the file and smiled at the old collie, who waited for Riley to speak to her.

Riley knelt. "Hello, Francine, how are you doing?"

Francine's man released her leash, and Francine padded to Riley for a face rub. While Riley cooed, Francine whimpered, and the man joined them. "We're here for her annual exam, but she's having trouble sleeping at night, and it's hard for her to get to her feet sometimes."

"Let's go to exam room three, Francine, and Doc Thad will check you to see what's going on."

As Francine walked in front of her, Riley said, "You're doing a great job with your weight."

"Thanks, we're walking a mile twice a day. It's good for both of us to get outside; I'm glad she's still enjoying it. We couldn't walk a quarter mile when we first started, but we've persevered, haven't we, girl?"

Francine yipped, and Riley nodded.

Francine stepped up on the scale and grinned at Riley.

"You should be proud; your weight is perfect."

"That's good news," the client said.

Doc Thad walked into the exam room and glanced at Francine's file. "Your weight is excellent, Francine. You're getting your exercise, aren't you? What's going on?"

"Francine's having trouble sleeping at night, and it's hard for her to get up after she's been lying down for a while," Riley said.

"I'm worried about whether we should be walking so much every day," the man added.

Doc Thad listened to Francine's heart and lungs. "Heart and lungs are fine." As he checked her, Francine flinched and whined when he touched her knees. "Her joints are tender and feel inflamed; an anti-inflammatory will help. Is the pain keeping you from sleeping, Francine?"

Francine yipped, and Riley said, "That's it, Doc."

Doc Thad nodded. "I'd like to see her again in a week to be sure the inflammation is down."

"Should we stop taking our walks?" the client asked.

Francine whined.

"No, twice a day is great; let Francine set the pace and the distance."

Riley walked with the client and Francine to the desk, then hurried to the exam room to clean it for their next patient.

Doc Thad joined her. "I don't know if anyone has had a chance to tell you, but Zach didn't come to work today. Claire called Amanda to see if she knew where he was, but Amanda didn't answer because she and the baby were at the pediatrician's office. Did Zach contact you, by any chance?"

Riley frowned. "No, I haven't heard from him."

After she finished cleaning the room, Riley hurried to Claire's desk, but Claire was on the phone, so Riley pulled Hector's file for Mitch's phone number and sent Mitch a text.

"This is Riley. Have you heard from Zach?"

Claire handed Riley a folder, and Riley greeted her next patient, a newly adopted kitten.

After the kitten and the client left, Doc Julie Rae returned to the exam room. "We still haven't heard anything from Zach."

Pia joined them in the exam room. She had pulled back her long, black hair into a low ponytail. "Claire just talked to Amanda. Amanda said she'll call Zach's mother."

"I sent Mitch a text because he and Zach are old friends, but I haven't heard back from Mitch yet," Riley said.

"Ordinarily, I'd call the sheriff's office for a wellness check, but I think I'll ask Charlie if he and the boys could go by Zach's apartment instead," Doc Julie Rae said.

Riley's phone buzzed a text, and after she read it, she said, "We need to stop trying to find Zach. This text is from Mitch."

She read the text aloud. "Zach & I are okay. Need to be under the radar. Cover us. More later."

"What do you think?" Pia asked.

"We need to cover them." Doc Julie Rae headed out the door. "I'll tell Claire to call back the neighbor because Zach showed up at work, but I'll still ask Charlie to cruise past Zach's apartment to see if his car is there."

"Do you think this has anything to do with Tom?" Pia asked after Doc Julie Rae left.

"It must, but I don't see the connection," Riley said.

"We're not backed up anymore, but my patient is here, so I have to get busy. You'll tell me why you suddenly appeared when we eat lunch, right?" Pia asked.

Riley smiled. "Of course."

After the last patient on the morning schedule left, Riley finished cleaning the exam room and then hurried to check in with Claire.

"Pia and Doc Julie Rae are in the breakroom waiting for you," Claire said. "I'll give a shout if we get a walk-in."

When Riley reached the breakroom, Doc Julie Rae pointed to the table. "Pia pulled out your lunch to save time. Sit, eat, talk."

Chapter Six

Riley poured a cup of coffee while she told them about Pamela Suzanne, Mugsy, and the call Ben received.

"Let me guess," Doc Julie Rae said, "Ben told you to stay with his parents. Am I right?"

Riley's eyes widened.

"You nailed it, Doc." Pia chuckled. "Riley, Doc had Charlie and the boys on standby in case you called to say you needed a ride to Barton. Jackson overheard me talking to Doc on the phone and was sad when I took him to school. He asked why he couldn't be homeschooled and save Aunt Riley, too."

"He's got a point." Riley giggled and then unwrapped her sandwich to eat.

"Charlie drove past Zach's apartment, and Zach's car is gone, so I guess that wherever Zach and Mitch went, they took Zach's car," Doc Julie Rae said.

"Zach, Mitch, and Hector," Riley said. "Mitch wouldn't have left Hector."

"That's true; I should have thought of that," Doc said.

Pia frowned. "This has to be related to Tom's disappearance, but how? What would Mitch or Zach know about Tom's disappearance that we wouldn't?"

"Mitch works at the distribution center; maybe he uncovered whatever Tom found," Riley said. "I still think the answer is in the second half of Tom's story."

"What story?" Doc Julie Rae asked.

Riley told them Tom's Old West story.

"I need to hear more. What's the rest of it?" Doc Julie Rae asked.

"That's it. I'm searching for the second half, but it's slow-going."

"That's why you asked me about a hard copy," Pia said. "That has to be a first draft or something. I couldn't find anything, but I'll keep searching."

"What if we give Charlie the task of searching the files? He might have some app that can do the searching for us. He could search for 'Novalee.' It's unusual enough that there shouldn't be any problems with a false match."

"I should have thought of that. Ask him if he knows of an app, and I'll install it and run it this evening," Riley said.

"That would be better because Riley would know when she found the complete story rather than just another copy," Pia said.

"I'll have the name of an app by the end of the day. Let's return to work so Claire and Doc Thad can eat lunch."

"I'll take the desk, Pia," Riley said.

"Is it your turn?" Pia asked as they straightened the breakroom.

"It must be; I haven't been around for two days." Riley headed toward the receptionist's desk.

"That's right. You're the slacker." Pia giggled as she followed her.

"Next patient in ten minutes," Claire said. "I'm glad you're back, Riley."

Claire rose, and then Toby followed her to the breakroom.

"Why didn't Toby stay at the receptionist's desk?" Pia asked.

"Lunch break," Riley said. "I'm sure he's on the payroll."

"Doc Thad will take Toby outside, won't he?"

"I suspect he will. Doc Thad knows the cold gets to me and how much Toby enjoys the chance to go outside." Riley sat at Claire's desk and reviewed the first three files on top of the stack.

Pia picked up the top file. "Archie for another annual?"

"Check Claire's note," Riley said. "Mrs. Hartway insisted it was time for Archie's annual, and her daughter called Doc Julie Rae, who decided Mrs. Hartway would be less agitated if Archie had a checkup. I suspect it won't be long until Mrs. Hartway doesn't remember Archie anymore."

"That's sad," Pia said.

"I agree, but I think it's sweet that Doc Julie Rae and the daughter want Mrs. Hartway to be comforted, knowing she always took good care of Archie." Riley brushed away a tear.

Pia sniffled. "I'll give Archie the royal treatment."

The phone rang after Pia led Mrs. Hartway, her daughter, and Archie to exam room one.

When Riley answered, Eli Reeves said, "May I speak with Claire Faraday?"

"She's at lunch; may I take a message?" Riley bit her lip.

"Is this..."

"I'm authorized to take messages." Riley interrupted him.

"Right. Please tell Mrs. Faraday that her suspicions are confirmed regarding our mutual friend, and the person in question has possession of a computer. She or her friend can contact me anytime, and I will be happy to intercede however I can." Eli hung up.

Riley shook her head. *Eli can be so pompous sometimes.*

Riley frowned at the neat stack of files for the afternoon's appointments. *I'm bored. Claire didn't leave any work for me.* She sent Ben a text: "Lunch was great. Thanks."

She stared at her phone and willed Ben to return her text.

When Claire returned to her desk, Riley sighed and put her phone into her pocket.

"Eli called and asked for you. I told him I was authorized to take messages and took notes." Riley handed Claire the notepad.

After Claire read Riley's notes, she wrinkled her nose. "He said earlier that the information was dangerous; evidently, it's also obscure. I didn't know I had suspicions, but I suppose you would be the mutual friend."

Claire read it again, then squinted at Riley. "You don't look all that suspicious to me, but I guess I'm too naïve."

"That's it, and you have a computer. Do we need an intervention?" Riley giggled, and Claire laughed.

When Claire regained her composure, she asked, "What do you think, really?"

"Eli's not very good at subtle messages," Riley said.

Claire nodded. "Other than the obvious, what do you think he's trying to say?"

"I have no clue," Riley said. "I'd call him and ask for details, but his drama annoys me; I'll have to think about it."

When the next client and patient came inside, Riley's phone buzzed a text. *Ben.*

"Surgery went well. Drs are hopeful."

Riley sighed in relief. She set her phone on Claire's desk so Claire could read the message as Riley greeted her patient.

Later in the afternoon, Riley finished cleaning exam room two after her latest patient, then hurried to Claire's desk.

"Mini-me's dad called a few minutes ago. He's waiting to talk to you in our parking lot," Claire said.

"Ready for a break, Toby?" Riley grabbed her coat from the breakroom and met Toby at the back door. A blast of cold wind sent shivers down her back when they went outside. Dylan stepped out of his car and waved. "I've got the engine running."

Riley glanced at the back seat before she jumped in. *I'm getting a bad case of nerves.*

"I'm taking my family to my brother's; we'll pick up his trailer and take a little vacation. I'm the operations manager at the center, and I noticed some inventory discrepancies on a report. Mitch is the smartest IT guy I know, so I asked him to check the report for me, even though reporting wasn't his area of expertise. Mitch found what he called 'coding irregularities' and told me to do what I could to protect my family."

"Do you have any idea who is behind the inventory discrepancies?"

Dylan shook his head. "My report is one I created myself, and Mitch said the data I pulled with my report was correct. The Atlanta office generated the official reports that hid the inventory shortages that my report revealed. Mitch and I know the Atlanta office is the source of the false reports, but we don't know who is behind it. Mitch and I think it's at a high level."

Dylan cleared his throat. "Our new general manager, Ezra Buchanan, is from Atlanta."

"Do you have concerns about him?" Riley asked.

"When it comes to my family, I have concerns about everyone except you and Ben," Dylan narrowed his eyes.

Understandable.

"What do you plan to do with your findings?"

"Mitch recreated my reports and sent the results to somebody. I don't know who, but Mitch would have only sent them to someone he trusted."

Toby whined, and Riley gazed at Dylan. "Toby said..." Riley stopped as she coughed.

After she cleared her throat, she asked, "What do you have for me?"

Dylan reached under his seat and pulled out a thick folder. "Tom was writing a story, but when he realized he was being closely monitored, he wrote a page at a time, then printed and deleted it from his laptop without saving it. He brought me fifteen pages every morning for two weeks before he disappeared. He told me if I ever thought my family was in danger to burn the pages. I haven't read it, but I couldn't burn it. Tom put a lot of work into his story."

Dylan exhaled. "After GBI took Tom's home computer, I understood why Tom was so cautious because Mitch said there had to be a cover-up, but we didn't know how far the Atlanta tentacles reached. Riley, be wary of anyone involved in the investigation of Tom's disappearance."

"Do you think Tom left voluntarily?" Riley asked.

Dylan rubbed his forehead. "I'm not sure. I wasn't surprised when he didn't show up at work because it seemed like he had been planning something for a while, but after I heard he left in his car with two men and without his family, I was worried." Dylan narrowed his eyes at a car that traveled slowly on the road in front of the animal hospital. When he turned his attention back to Riley, he said, "Sorry. I thought I recognized the driver."

"Do you know where Tom was planning to go?" Riley asked.

"He mentioned a buddy's hunting cabin once, but I don't know where it is. I assumed it wasn't that far away, but that's only from the impression I got when Tom talked about going hunting."

Dylan handed the folder to Riley. "We packed last night and will leave as soon as I get home. We won't have phones, but we may pick one up later."

Riley took the folder. "Be safe."

Dylan smiled. "Thanks, we will, but you're a fine one to talk."

Riley returned his smile as she climbed out and opened Toby's door. After they went inside, Riley hung up her coat and slipped the folder into her backpack.

Claire peered at Riley when she approached the desk.

"Everything okay?" Claire asked.

"Yes. Dylan is taking his family on their planned vacation; with all the goings on, he didn't want us to worry about Mini-me."

Claire raised one eyebrow. "I see. So, what else..."

The office phone rang and interrupted Claire, and Riley snatched up the folder as the next client carried in a small cat carrier with a protesting kitten inside it.

Riley quickly glanced at the folder. *One kitten; two labs.*

"What's the problem, Jazzy?" Riley asked.

The kitten mewed, and Riley giggled; the client smiled. "She's been terrorizing my poor old labs with her meowing, especially at night, all night. I don't know if she is suffering with pain or if she's being a pain."

"Let's go to room one, and Doc Julie Rae will examine her. If Doc doesn't find anything, Jazzy may just be complaining because she wants to be out of her carrier with her new friends."

The client stopped and tilted her head. "Really? I thought she would be afraid of the dogs because she's so small, so I've kept her in her carrier. If the dogs want her out, too, then that explains why the dogs are howling. I thought her ruckus was hurting their ears. The three of them carry on late into the night, and I've been waking up with a migraine. Maybe Doc Julie Rae can save me a visit to my doctor for my headaches," the client said.

"No promises. We'll see what Doc says."

When Riley lifted the orange kitten out of the carrier, Jazzy purred.

"I'll weigh you first; Doc Julie Rae will be right in."

"How are we doing?" Doc asked as she strolled into the exam room.

The client filled in Doc on the details of the yowling kitten and Riley's theory that the kitten and dogs wanted to be together.

Doc examined Jazzy quickly and thoroughly. "She's not in pain; let her out of her carrier when you get home. If she's comfortable and doesn't seem fearful of the dogs, then you should have a happy, quiet home this evening. Give us a call tomorrow to let us know how it went. If you have a problem tonight, leave a message, and we'll see you first thing in the morning."

Jazzy purred as the client carried her to Claire's desk, and then Riley returned to the exam room. After Riley wiped down the exam table and cleaned the equipment, Pia met her in the hallway.

"There's a bit of a lull, and I thought I'd check on you," Pia said. "Claire heard back from Amanda. She said she didn't hear back from Zach's mother, so she's thinking something came up with the family. It's been a busy day, hasn't it? I'm glad you were here."

"So am I."

"I brought cookies but forgot to offer you one. Want a reward for showing up?"

"Absolutely." Riley grinned.

On their way to the breakroom, Pia said, "I was complaining about my weight to Tom once while I made cookies..." she giggled. "Doesn't make any sense, does it? He said he'd miss my dimples if I quit baking, so I keep making cookies."

As they stood beside the table and munched on cookies, Riley asked, "Have you ever had venison?"

"It is the best; I love it. What about you?"

"I think I have, but I'm not sure because it was so long ago. Ben's dad got a deer while we were there, and I'm looking forward to trying it. Ben's mom is an awesome cook."

"Tom goes hunting with a buddy of his whose family has property they bought years ago at an auction. They have turned it into a wonderful wildlife refuge. We've been to their hunting cabin a few times in the off-season. It's so peaceful."

"Really? Where is it?"

"It's in Worth County. Easy to find."

"Ben and I thought we'd go for a drive tomorrow afternoon if he doesn't have to work, and he's been talking about taking the back roads to Worth County. He said there's a place that looks interesting for lunch."

"That's so funny. There's an awesome diner near the hunting cabin; I'll bet that's what he has in mind. I'll give you directions." Pia explained how to get to the diner and then how to get to the property from the diner.

"It almost sounds like you could walk to the diner from the cabin," Riley said.

Pia snorted. "Maybe you could, but not me. It's three miles away."

Riley chuckled. "It sounds really nice; I'll bet many of Tom's friends go there to hunt."

Pia's eyes widened. "Oh, no. Tom's mom told me once that hunters are more jealous of their hunting spots than their wives. They might brag about the size of a big buck, but the conversation and banter turn to absolute silence if anyone asks where they bagged the deer."

"So, who goes hunting with Tom?"

"His friend, Brock, and Brock's brother, and occasionally Brock's dad. They consider Tom a part of their family."

"Do they know he's disappeared?"

Pia's face paled. "I haven't thought of letting Brock know, and Tom always told me that Brock would always drop everything for me and Jackson. I'll do that right now."

Pia picked up her phone and sent a text.

"Thanks, Riley. You just saved me from being disowned by my extended family."

"I think somebody's here. I'll take the patient." Riley hurried to the reception area, and Claire handed her a file. After the patient left and Riley cleaned the exam room, Pia joined her.

"I received a sweet reply from Brock." Pia showed Riley her phone.

Riley read the text. "We're here for you if you need us. Don't worry."

"Very comforting," Riley said.

Pia nodded as she brushed away a tear before she left the room.

Riley followed her to Claire's desk but stopped in the hallway when her phone buzzed a text. *Ben, finally.*

She smiled as she read. "I'm Sgt and officially hate desk work. Might be a little late."

When Riley reached the receptionist's desk, Pia and Claire were looking at the Saturday schedule, and Doc Julie Rae joined them.

"I heard from Zach. He apologized for not letting us know he had a family emergency, but he'll be here tomorrow," Doc Julie Rae said. "What does tomorrow look like?"

"Our schedule is slammed tomorrow morning," Pia said.

"We need to fire our scheduler," Claire added.

"I have seniority," Doc Julie Rae said. "If anyone gets to be fired, I've got dibs. What about the rest of the afternoon?"

"Only four more patients," Claire said.

Riley glanced at the clock. "Pia, if you'll take the next patient, I'll take the rest so you can scoot out a little early."

"Are you sure?" Pia asked. "I wouldn't mind surprising Jackson by picking him up early. There's a horror movie on TV he's been waiting all week to watch, and we could make cookies, order a pizza, and pop some popcorn before the movie starts."

"I'm positive. Ben will be working late, so I'm in no rush for a change, and pizza, cookies, popcorn, and a movie sounds like a perfect night for you and Jackson," Riley said.

"Thanks, Riley," Pia said as the next client and patient approached the door.

At the end of the day, Riley, Claire, and Toby headed to the breakroom.

"I have no idea what to pick up for supper. Do you have any suggestions?" Riley asked.

"I actually am planning to make my chicken enchilada casserole with homemade red enchilada sauce. It's really easy and super yummy. Would you like the recipe?" Claire asked.

"Homemade sauce? I don't know," Riley said.

"I'll send it to your email, and we can review it together if you have any questions. I also added a recipe for southwest slaw, but you can make a tossed green salad instead."

Claire pulled out her phone, found her recipe, and sent it to Riley. Riley opened her email and read the recipe.

"I don't see anything I can't do. This is great, and I love that you have a shopping list for the ingredients at the bottom of the recipe. Is this your private recipe?"

"Kind of, but that's only because I've tweaked it over time. Call me if you have any questions, but you'll be fine."

Claire sat at the breakroom table to wait for Doc Thad while Riley put on her coat, and then Riley and Toby left.

After Riley parked and climbed out of her car, Toby hopped in front to sit in the driver's seat, and Riley smiled as she went inside to shop. *Not everyone has a seat warmer.*

She rolled a grocery cart inside the store and headed toward the produce section first. *If I can find shredded cabbage, I'll try the slaw.*

After she found a mixture of green and red shredded cabbage, Riley stared at the bin of ears of corn. *Claire's recipe says to roast two fresh ears of sweet corn, but couldn't I substitute a can of corn?*

"Ah, roasted ears of corn; you're making an enchilada casserole, aren't you?" Mrs. Smythe, a legend in Barton for her peanut butter and jelly hors d'oeuvres when she was a newlywed long ago, stood at Riley's elbow. Her cane, thinning gray hair, and vague look in her eyes hid her sharp mind and keen wit.

Riley smiled. "You're right. Claire gave me a recipe that includes roasted corn, but the recipe doesn't explain how to choose fresh corn."

"First, the husk should have a slinky, bright green dress that wrapped tightly around the body, or ear, as some say; next, our voluptuous vixen should have brown, slightly sticky hair, some people call it tassels. If her hair is black and dry, she's seen better days."

"That's easy to remember." Riley picked out two ears.

"Well done," Mrs. Smythe said. "That young man is a marvelous writer, isn't he? It's amazing how he draws a picture with words that pull you into the story, and it's such a marvelous way to chronicle current events."

Does Mrs. Smythe know about Tom? Riley nodded.

"I would pay particular attention to the secretive ranger." She lowered her voice to a whisper so soft that Riley leaned closer. "He's not a stranger to these parts, and that young deputy is in harm's way."

Riley frowned. *There isn't a deputy in the story, at least that I've read so far.*

"I think the author might need a little collaboration; he appears to have written himself into a corner that could become a cliché trap." Mrs. Smythe's eyes brightened. "Oh, look; they are bringing out fresh flowers."

Riley followed Mrs. Smythe, and Mrs. Smythe pointed to a small vase with yellow and orange rose buds.

"Yellow for friendship, and orange for irresistible. My dear husband was my sexy best friend, too." Mrs. Smythe bowed her head briefly at the mention of her husband, and Riley automatically followed suit.

Riley felt her face grow warm. *I never thought of Ben as my sexy best friend, but she's right.*

Mrs. Smythe's eyes twinkled, and she winked before she wandered away while she hummed, "The Yellow Rose of Texas."

Riley hummed the yellow rose tune while she loaded the rest of the ingredients into her cart, including a few items not on Claire's list, before she wheeled to an open cashier station and checked out.

As she headed to her car, Toby barked when he saw her. She snatched her groceries out of the cart and raced to her car. She tossed her sacks into the car and hopped in as Toby barked and then jumped to the back. She turned on the engine and accelerated as a whack hit the side of her car. Toby barked again, and as she dialed nine-one-one, her rear window shattered, and Toby yelped.

"This is Riley Malloy. Someone shot at me in the grocery parking lot."

She sped down the street. "I've left the parking lot and am on the way to the sheriff's department. No one seems to be following me." Toby whimpered, and Riley glanced in the rear-view mirror at the blood on the seat and pushed the accelerator to the floor with all her strength.

When she reached the well-lit parking lot, her tires screeched as she slammed on the brakes; two deputy cruisers with strobing lights and piercing sirens passed her and headed toward the grocery store, and Ben raced to her car.

When he jerked open her door, she said, "I'm fine. Toby was hit. I'll call Doc to meet us at the clinic."

"Get in back with Toby; I'll drive," Ben said.

Riley climbed out, jumped into the backseat with Toby, and grabbed at the door to close it as Ben sped out of the parking lot. When he took the hard turn to the clinic, the door slammed shut, and Riley called Doc Julie Rae while she hummed to Toby; Toby whimpered.

"Are your keys to the clinic on your keyring?" Ben asked as he sped down the street.

"Yes," Riley said.

"I'll give you the keys to unlock the door and bring Toby inside."

"Doc called Doc Thad. We'll have lots of help," Riley said.

When Ben parked, Riley dashed to the door as Doc Julie Rae and Doc Thad tore into the lot. Doc Thad raced to the door and went inside with Riley. Riley flipped on the lights, and Doc Thad ran to the trauma room. Riley sprinted to the x-ray and turned on the machine.

Riley hurried down the hallway toward the back door and met Doc Julie Rae and Ben, who carried Toby. She walked alongside Toby and hummed.

"How is he, Riley?" Doc Thad asked when they reached the trauma room.

"He has a neck wound and a bullet in his shoulder."

"Put him on the cart; I want x-rays first, then we'll do our examination," Doc Thad said.

After Ben placed Toby on the cart, Riley rushed Toby to the x-ray room and opened her mouth in surprise when she saw Zach.

Zach said, "I've got this, Riley."

Riley grinned. "You're the best."

"I know." Zach wheeled Toby into the x-ray room.

Riley rushed back to the trauma room. "Zach's here. He's doing Toby's x-rays."

"I called him," Doc Thad said. "This was critical."

Riley's eyes narrowed. "You knew? You knew where Zach was and never said a word?"

Doc Thad shrugged. "Nobody asked me, and whatever you want to call me, Claire already did. I was invited to stay here tonight."

Doc Julie Rae's voice was ice. "I don't feel sorry for you."

"I do, man, and I appreciate that you stood by your friend," Ben said.

Riley narrowed her eyes at Ben, and he strode to her and hugged her. "Whatever's going on was important, but Zach dropped everything to be here for Toby. I think that's admirable."

Riley sniffled as she buried her face in Ben's chest. "You're awesome, but that's a terrible argument because it's not fair to be right."

Ben held her tighter, whispering, "Toby will be okay."

George came into the room. "Just letting you know I'm here."

Zach rolled Toby into the trauma room. "Come see the x-rays, Doc."

Doc Thad rushed out of the room while Doc Julie Rae examined Toby. Ben assisted Doc Julie Rae while Riley stroked Toby's back and hummed.

When Doc Thad returned, he said, "There's a bullet lodged in his shoulder, but there are no broken bones. His neck wound is clean and close to the surface, so there's no internal bleeding. We'll prepare for surgery."

Pia stepped into the trauma room. "I'm your surgical tech. I'll get the room ready."

"Where did Pia come from? What about Jackson?" Riley asked.

"Claire is with Jackson," Doc Thad said. "It was her idea, but just to let you know what a trooper she is, Claire hates scary movies."

"I'm a good surgical tech, too," Ben said. "I'll scrub up and help Pia get the room ready."

Zach joined Riley when Ben wheeled Toby into surgery.

"He'll be fine, Riley," Zach said. "He's got the best with him."

Riley nodded. "You cut your hair."

Zach ran his hand over his head. "Think the chicks will like it?"

Riley giggled. "You know they will, but won't your girlfriend complain?"

Zach's face reddened. "It was her idea."

"Smart," Riley said. "Anybody I know?"

"Is this how your world-renowned interrogation skills work?" Zach asked.

Riley giggled. "Too subtle?"

"A lot is going on, Riley," Zach said. "I wish you weren't in the middle of it, but you are."

"I can help," she said.

"We'll talk later. Let's get this room clean," Zach said.

Riley and Zach cleaned up the blood and scrubbed the floor, exam table, and utility cart. After they finished, Riley stood back with her hands on her hips. "Should we wash the walls?"

Zach snorted. "We did kind of go overboard, didn't we?"

Riley flipped her hair. "It's what we do."

As she put away the cleaning supplies, Riley asked, "Where have you been?"

Zach narrowed his eyes. "Mitch told me you would probably understand. If you don't, I can't explain. I went with Mitch and Hector to Atlanta because Mitch didn't want to be away from Hector. I tagged along to care for Hector while Mitch talked to one of his IT buddies about reports. Mitch showed him two sets of reports.

The Atlanta IT guy created a new report, which matched Mitch's, not the official report."

"Wow." Riley's eyes widened. "Were Mitch and the IT..."

Zach interrupted her. "I've told you what I know. Mitch dropped me off at home before he and Hector went to a friend's place. He said I'd be safe because I don't know anything; he isn't safe, and you obviously aren't either."

Riley frowned. "I need to find out who is behind all this."

"I'll help you any way I can; I'm smart, stronger than I look, and a master at keeping quiet." Zach smiled as he left the room.

When Ben stepped out of the surgical room and into the trauma room, he said, "We have talented vets. Toby will be out of the surgical room in a few minutes."

Riley furrowed her brow, and her lower lip quivered. Her breathing became ragged, then rapidly escalated to hyperventilation. Ben strode across the room and pulled her close. "Slow down, honey, Toby's fine. Breathe in. Hold it. Breathe out through your mouth."

Ben stroked her hair and whispered, "You're okay; I've got you."

Riley relaxed at the calmness of his voice; when she leaned against his chest, she mumbled, "You're holding me too tight."

"Am not." He squeezed her tighter and kissed the top of her head, and Riley smiled as she snuggled against him.

Zach opened the door. "Toby's stirring, Riley."

Ben followed Riley as she rushed to the surgical room, and Doc Thad met them in the hallway. "Toby did great," Doc Thad said. "A bullet grazed his neck; we cleaned his wound, then put in a few stitches. We removed the bullet from his shoulder. It didn't hit any major blood vessels or bone, but he'll be out of commission for a while."

When Riley opened the door, Doc Julie Rae smiled. "She's here, Toby."

Toby whimpered, and Riley stroked his back. "I'm fine. Thank you for telling me to run."

Pia cleared her throat, and Doc Julie Rae said, "Let's take Toby to an exam room, Riley, so these folks can straighten up."

After Riley and Ben rolled Toby to exam room one, Ben asked, "Will you be okay with Toby? I'm going to clean up your car."

Riley nodded, and Ben left. Doc Julie Rae dragged her visitor's chair into the exam room from her office. "Here you go, Riley. You and Toby can hang out here while George and I fix the large crate for Toby."

Riley stroked Toby's back and whispered to calm him as he struggled with his restlessness from the anesthesia. "I'm right here, and both of us are safe. Doc Julie Rae and Doc Thad patched you up, and you'll be fine soon."

Toby relaxed, and Riley leaned against the table with her hand on Toby's back and closed her eyes.

Zach came into the room. "Can I get you anything, Riley?"

Riley narrowed her eyes. "A glass of water, then I need to know who generates the so-called official inventory reports."

"Got it. I'll be right back with the water. It might take me a little longer on the reports."

"Don't call any attention to yourself," she said.

"Never." Zach winked as he left.

Toby whined.

"I know what I'm doing; you don't have to lecture me, but I suppose if it makes you feel better, go ahead," Riley said.

Toby yipped, and Riley smiled. "I'm not surprised you plan to take full advantage of your injuries."

Pia entered the exam room and cooed, "How are you doing, Toby?"

Toby whimpered.

"Poor guy," Pia said.

Riley rolled her eyes. "You're overdoing it, Toby."

Toby wiggled his expressive eyebrows, and Riley giggled as she rubbed his ear. "As soon as Doc Julie Rae and George have your crate ready, we'll let you rest. I'll be back in the morning."

"Ready for Toby," George called out.

Riley and Pia rolled Toby to the kennel.

Doc Thad and Doc Julie Rae eased Toby into the crate; after Doc Julie Rae draped a warmed blanket over Toby, he sighed as he closed his eyes.

George smiled. "He's settled in. You all can get out of our hair now."

Riley and Pia strolled together to the breakroom.

"How ya doing, girlfriend?" Pia asked.

"Not bad: my car's back window is shattered, I've got bullet holes in the side of my car, my Toby took two bullets that were intended for me, and the ice cream I bought earlier at the grocery store is probably melted, but other than that, I might have lost two pounds in that sprint I did to my car in the parking lot."

Pia snickered. "You have such a twisted sense of humor; I love it."

Riley smiled. "What about you?"

"My husband's missing, and Jackson and Jordy are too ornery to let me mope, but no one has shot at me today, so there's that."

Riley rolled her eyes. "We're a mess, aren't we? I need to give Ben a ride to the sheriff's department so he can get back to work."

"Zach and Ben took your car to the gas station for repairs; Zach gave Ben a ride to work." Doc Julie Rae joined them in the breakroom. "I'll give you a ride home, Riley, and pick you up in the morning."

Doc Thad stood in the doorway. "Claire just called me. You're invited to our house for dinner, Pia. She and Jackson made an extra enchilada casserole for you and Ben, Riley. I'm the delivery guy. Tips are appreciated."

"Are you ready to go home?" Doc Julie Rae asked.

"I need to go by the gas station for my backpack and house key," Riley said as they strolled to the back door.

"Ben gave me your backpack and house key before he left. Your backpack is in my truck."

On the way to Riley's house, Doc Julie Rae asked, "Are you going to be okay by yourself? You can go home with me, or I'll drop you off at Claire's if you like."

"I'll be fine. I have some reading I'd like to do, and maybe I'll take a soaking bath."

When she pulled into the driveway, Doc said, "Call me if you need me."

"Will do. I'll see you in the morning." Riley hopped out of the truck and hurried inside.

She rushed to the bathroom, turned on the shower before she stripped, and stepped into the hot, soothing stream of water. After scrubbing and washing her hair, she climbed out of the shower, wrapped herself with a towel, and carried her soiled clothes to the washer.

She dressed in a T-shirt, soft flannel pants, and fleecy socks, combed out the tangles in her hair, and pulled out the manuscript from her backpack. She sat on the sofa with her feet propped up, starting with page one. She raised her eyebrows. "This is revised."

When she reached the point where the earlier document stopped, she flipped through the pages. "I'm only a third of the way through." She made a cup of tea and then resumed reading.

After a half hour of reading, she slammed down the manuscript and stormed to the refrigerator for ice cream. "A short, red-headed gunslinger from a rodeo show named Rita? I'm not sure I like this story after all, Tom."

Riley searched the freezer but couldn't find any ice cream. She sighed as she returned to the sofa. "Rita must have finished it off."

While she read, Ben's truck pulled into the driveway. She hurried to the door and opened it as Doc Thad parked at the curb. Ben strode to Doc Thad's car, and

Doc Thad handed him a box. *Wish they'd talk louder, so I could hear them.* Riley shivered. *And faster; I'm freezing.*

Ben stopped by his truck, pulled out a sack, and rushed to the house.

"What are you doing? It's cold out here," Ben said.

"Hi, honey, you're home," Riley smirked.

Ben chuckled. "Thanks for noticing. Do you want wine, beer, or hot tea with your supper?" He sat the box and sack on the dining table and then hurried to light the fireplace.

"That's a hard choice. How about hot tea with supper, then wine with dessert? What did you get?"

"Butter pecan." He placed the ice cream in the freezer. "How did you know I got dessert?"

I'm not sure he'd understand if I told him that Joe, the young deputy in Tom's story, gave gunslinger Rita a piece of rock candy before he arrested her.

Riley padded to the kitchen and put plates and forks on the table while Ben brewed her hot tea and poured a tall glass of iced tea for himself.

While they ate, Riley asked, "How was being in surgery?"

"I'd helped my uncle with a few, so it wasn't new to me, but I'd forgotten the thrill of watching a talented veterinarian make a difference for a patient. The way Doc Julie Rae and Doc Thad worked together was inspiring; it was like they'd been partners for years. I'm warming up to the idea of veterinary college because we'll be training together."

Riley smiled while Ben talked about what Doc Julie Rae did and what Doc Thad did throughout the surgery.

"I hate to do this, but I have to go back to work for a few more hours," Ben said while they ate their ice cream. "Will you be okay?"

"I'll be fine. I'll take care of the dishes, put up my feet, and read."

Ben smiled and then kissed her butter pecan mouth. "You're sweet."

Riley giggled. "You're funny."

He chuckled as he headed out the door.

Riley jumped up from the table, quickly cleared the dishes, put them into the dishwasher, and dashed to the sofa to read.

While she read, her phone rang. *Should I ignore it?* She peeked at her phone and then quickly answered.

"Hi, Mom," she said.

"Is now a good time to talk? Are you eating?"

"No, we just finished, and Ben has returned to work."

"We heard about Toby. Is he okay? Ben's uncle is on standby if you need him."

"Doc Julie Rae and Doc Thad removed the bullet in his shoulder and took care of a graze wound on the side of his neck. He's resting at the animal hospital. A retired animal control officer stays with our overnight patients and is very fond of Toby. Toby has celebrity status at the clinic."

"I would think so," Melissa said. "Why did Ben go back to work?"

"They're short-handed right now."

"That's nice."

Riley furrowed her brow. *Maybe she didn't understand what I said.*

Melissa cleared her throat. "You got a letter from the veterinary college. Jake told me not to bother you about it because you'd probably be here this weekend, but since we're talking about veterinarians, you'll want to stay close to Toby..."

Riley rolled her eyes. "Would you open it for me?"

"Oh, really? I could mail it to you; after all, it is addressed to you, and only the addressee should open a letter delivered by the US Postal Service. Is that enough protesting, do you think? I'll open it."

Riley smirked at the sound of an envelope being ripped apart.

Melissa squealed. "You're off the waitlist."

"Oh." Riley sighed.

"Aren't you excited? I'm excited," Melissa said.

Riley bit her lip. "It's great to have the waiting over."

"Wait a minute. I just realized I left out the part where you've been accepted. That's why you are no longer on the waitlist. I read it all in one swoop but didn't quite get everything out when I told you."

"Wow. Now, I'm excited." Riley jumped up to tell Toby. *Dang it. Toby needs to know, too.*

"Shall I send you the letter?"

"Why don't you keep it? Could you scan it and email it to me?"

"Excellent idea. I'll do that as soon as we get off the phone. What are you going to wear on your first day of class?"

Riley laughed. "Most of my clothes are scrubs. I guess I need to decide what my civilian self wears other than flannel shirts when it's cold or T-shirts when it's hot with my jeans and boots."

"It sounds like you have the perfect wardrobe. I have a million more trivial questions, but I'll save them so I can scan your letter immediately. Congratulations, Riley Erin." Melissa disconnected.

I'll wait to get my copy of the letter before saying anything to anyone, but I have to tell Ben first.

Riley stared at her phone. *He's working. This is not an emergency. I'd scare him if I called him.*

She picked up the manuscript and resumed reading.

After a half hour, her eyes widened. *I'm not sure Blair should be leering at Novalee like that. She's going to deck him if he isn't careful.*

Riley checked her email, read the letter Melissa had scanned in, and then read it three more times. She giggled. *This is so awesome.*

Her phone rang as she headed to the kitchen to brew another cup of tea. *Pia.*

"I heard Ben went back to work; got a few minutes?" Pia asked.

"Sure. Something going on?"

"Jackson, Jordy, and I visited the clinic to see Toby. It was Jackson's idea. He said Jordy wanted to stay with Toby tonight. I wasn't sure it was a good idea, but George agreed with Jackson. We're leaving Jordy with Toby for the weekend."

"That is so thoughtful."

"Toby has cared for so many of our patients, it seemed only right to let Jordy be with him. When we got there,

Zach was there. George sent Zach home with a promise to call him if George got tired."

"Does George know he'd have a full house if he doesn't put his foot down?"

Pia giggled. "No kidding."

"How's your evening going?" Riley asked.

"Really quiet. Jackson's had his shower, and he's watching the old-time cartoons that he loves so much, and I can't stand. I got a call from a cousin."

Chapter Seven

"It's nice to hear from family," Riley said. *Pia's selecting her words carefully.*

"It really is. He called to see how Jackson and I were doing, and we chatted. He said Blair misses me," Pia said.

Riley's eyes widened. *She heard from Tom.* "Aw, that's sweet."

"I thought so, too. I was almost weepy. Blair's always been my favorite niece. He said maybe I could visit them some time; I might go tomorrow."

"We'll be fine at work. Family really makes a difference, doesn't it?" Riley wiped away an errant tear.

"Truly. I might call Doc Julie Rae to see if it's okay with her."

"Be safe. Let me know if you need me to do anything. I'll be working and hovering around Toby."

Pia chuckled. "I know you will."

After they hung up, Riley hugged herself. "Wow. What awesome news." *I sure wish Ben or Toby were here.* She frowned. *Should I say anything to Ben?*

She returned to the 'Phantom Cattle'. *Why do I feel I should cover my eyes?* She smiled as Novalee continued to flirt with Blair.

Her eyes widened as Blair paid Rita's bond and hired her on behalf of the ranchers to track down the cattle rustlers. 'Blair said, "Missy, you're the only one those rustlers fear. Bring 'em back to Justice.'"

Riley reread the last sentence. *Why didn't he say, 'Bring them to justice'?*

She rolled her eyes. "I get it: Justice is the name of the town. Well done, Tom."

She finished the chapter and giggled. *If I read much more, I will start swaggering, and my drawl will slow to a crawl. Y'all.*

Riley flipped back a few pages and narrowed her eyes as she reread a section. "Blair said Rita is the only one the rustlers fear. I think Tom was telling me to find the criminal." *I need Toby, so I'm not talking to myself.* Riley shrugged. "Maybe Blair will have some ideas on how to do that."

Riley picked up the manuscript and resumed reading.

When she heard Ben's truck in the driveway, she flipped ahead. *Four more pages until the end of the chapter.* She sighed and placed the manuscript on the table next to her before she hurried to the door.

"Are you exhausted?" she asked as Ben slowly climbed out of his truck.

"You know it, babe. I'm dragging."

"Take a shower; you'll feel better," she said.

"I haven't trained for this job; sitting all day is hard work," Ben said. "My back hates it."

"A shower might help."

After his shower, Ben came to the living room in sweats. "I hadn't noticed it before, but the shower head is dripping a steady stream. I tried to tighten it, but it might need a new one."

"I'll call Helen tomorrow," Riley said. "Mom called me."

Ben picked up the book he'd been reading and flopped beside Riley.

"Really? What did she have to say?"

"Do you want a quick answer or a full of suspense answer? She gave me the full of suspense version."

Ben frowned and set his book on the sofa. "This doesn't sound good; I'll take the quick answer."

"I've been accepted into the veterinary college program."

"Yes!" Ben shouted, picking her up and swinging her in a circle. "I knew it; I told you so."

Riley laughed. "Are you gloating?"

"You got it, babe. I know you said you'd go with me while I went to school, but this is perfect. I can cheat off you."

Riley's eyes widened. "Ben!"

He smirked. "Just kidding."

Riley wiggled. "You can put me down now."

"Never."

When Ben released her, Riley pulled him closer and kissed him, and he matched her passion. After their long kiss, Riley sighed as she sat down.

Ben sat close to her and pointed to the manuscript. "What are you reading?"

"An unpublished work. It's actually pretty good."

Ben nodded and found his place, and Riley smiled.

After she read another chapter, Riley closed her eyes. When her head jerked, she woke. *Ben's asleep.*

"Honey. Ben." Riley raised her voice. "Honey."

Ben opened his eyes. "Fell asleep," he mumbled.

"I know. Go to bed, and I'll turn off the fireplace and the lights."

He leaned over and kissed her before he stumbled to bed.

Riley turned off the fireplace before she walked to the back door to check the lock. *Habit. I was going to call Toby to come inside.*

She locked the deadbolt on the front door, turned off the lights, and strolled to bed. As she relaxed, she thought about the rustlers, who had no idea Rita was chasing them. *That's exactly what I need to do: chase the rustler.*

* * *

The next morning, the familiar aroma of coffee woke Riley. She hurried to the kitchen and frowned. *No Ben.* She read the note on the dining table. "Had to leave early. Your lunch is in the fridge. Love you."

She poured a cup of coffee and left it to cool while she dressed. On her way back to the kitchen, she picked up 'Phantom Cattle,' sipped her coffee, and read.

The bartender stepped out of the saloon and cleared his throat to catch Rita's attention as she strolled by on her way to the corral for her horse. He spoke in a low, raspy voice. "Ranger went after them thieving rustlers, but according to one of the drifters, Ranger is in cahoots with the rustlers and helped 'em carve out a few cattle from each ranch's herd before they left. Watch yerself."

The bartender glanced around nervously. "You didn't hear nothin' from me."

Riley's phone startled her when it buzzed a text from Doc Julie Rae.

"Five minutes."

She stuck the manuscript and her lunch into her backpack and put on her warm coat before she stepped outside to wait for Doc.

On the way to the animal hospital, Doc said, "Pia asked for the day off today and won't be coming in. I'm glad she and Jackson can get away for the weekend, and I love the idea of Jordy staying with Toby."

"If you release Toby early, Jordy can spend the weekend with us." Riley side-glanced at Doc.

"That was subtle." Doc chuckled. "I don't think Toby will be ready to leave before Tuesday, but we'll see how he does over the weekend. Doc Thad and I will take turns Sunday checking on him, and Zach will relieve George early Sunday morning."

"I'll stay today until George comes this evening," Riley said.

"That'll work. Zach offered, but I told him you'd want a turn too."

"I'm really glad we have Zach," Riley said.

"We really have the best team in the world, don't we?" Doc Julie Rae pulled into her spot and parked. When they went inside to the breakroom, Doc Julie Rae started the coffee, and Riley put her lunch in the refrigerator before she hurried to the kennel.

"Hi, how's everybody doing?" Riley asked.

George waved as he gathered his things, and Jordy wiggled on his way to Riley. Riley rubbed Jordy's face and smiled at Toby, who whined as his tail thudded against the crate.

"I'm happy to see you, too," Riley said. "You're looking good."

"He ate most of his breakfast, and we've been outside for a break. He did well with the dog wagon and the sling I built, and Jordy was a tremendous help." George turned to Toby and Jordy. "See you this evening, gentlemen."

After George left, Doc Julie Rae brought Riley a cup of coffee and rubbed Jordy's chest. "How are Toby and Jordy?" she asked.

"George said Toby had a good night, and Jordy was very helpful," Riley said.

"After Doc Thad arrives, we'll check the wounds and apply new dressings. I'll be in my office to catch up on paperwork," Doc said. "Tell him to come get me if you see him before I do."

"Too late." Riley smiled when Jordy yipped. "Doc Thad and Claire just pulled into the parking lot."

Doc Julie Rae's eyes twinkled as she hurried to the hallway to greet the Faradays. "Tell Pia this is for her."

"About time you showed up, Thad," Doc Julie Rae said. "We were just about to leave for lunch."

Claire giggled as she hurried into the breakroom while Doc Thad sputtered, "We're not any...did Pia put you up to that?"

Doc Julie Rae tittered. "I'm an independent thinker. Ready to check Toby and change the dressings?"

Doc Thad chuckled. "I'll hang up my coat and be right there."

When Riley approached Claire's desk, Claire smiled as she handed Riley the patient folder as the front door opened. "This one's yours, Riley."

A petite four-year-old girl struggled with an oversized, soft-sided carrier as she came into the reception area in her long, green princess dress with a sparkly pale green overskirt. She stopped near the door and set down the carrier.

"Hello, Ms. Riley. Sir Cedwick is sick," she said, and the orange cat inside the carrier, Sir Cedwick, yowled.

"Hello, Allison. I'm sorry, Sir Cedwick," Riley said.

"He's having trouble..." Allison stepped close to Riley, and Riley leaned down as Allison glanced around the room, then cupped her hands around her mouth and whispered, "Going pee-pee."

Riley nodded as she picked up the carrier. "Let's go into an exam room, and we'll have Doc Thad look at him. You remember Doc Thad, don't you?"

Sir Cedwick purred.

"Sir Cedwick said he likes Doc Thad, and so do I," Allison said.

As they went to the exam room, Allison said, "Sir Cedwick has had trouble for four days, but it was worse yesterday."

Sir Cedwick mewed.

"Sir Cedwick said much worse, but Doc Thad will make him better, won't he?" Allison asked.

"Yes, he will. Sir Cedwick, I'll weigh you and take your temperature." Riley set the carrier on the exam table, and Allison stood next to Riley so she could watch.

"Do you need more space to work, Riley? Allison might be too close, but she wants to see and learn everything," Allison's mother said.

"We're fine. Allison, I have a small stool you can stand on so you can see better."

"Yes, please. That would be stupendous."

Riley's eyes widened, and she glanced at Allison's mother, who said, "That's our new word this week."

"What a stupendous word," Riley said, and Allison applauded. "Good job, Ms. Riley."

"Thank you, Allison." Riley placed the small stool beside the table, and Allison stepped up.

"Much better; thank you, Ms. Riley."

"We're working on manners and being polite," Allison's mother said.

"You're welcome, Allison, and you are doing very well with your manners." Riley gently lifted Sir Cedwick from the carrier and placed him on the scale. "Two extra pounds. He may be retaining urine," Riley said.

"Urine?" Allison asked.

Riley whispered, "It's the doctor word for pee-pee."

"Urine," Allison repeated. "Stupendous word."

Allison's mother rolled her eyes. "Welcome to my world, Ms. Riley."

Riley smiled. "It is a catchy word. Sorry in advance, Sir Cedwick, but I'll have to take your temperature now."

Sir Cedwick meowed, and Allison said, "He knows you're fast. Go ahead."

"Elevated temperature," Riley said. "That means he has a fever."

"Elevated temshure?" Allison asked.

"Temperature," her mother said.

"Elevated tempashure. I'll say fever because it's easier."

When Doc Thad entered the exam room, he said, "Hello, everyone."

Sir Cedwick yowled.

"Sorry you don't feel good, Sir Cedwick. What's going on?"

"He has two extra pounds and a fever, and he's having trouble going urine," Allison said.

Doc Thad glanced at Riley, who nodded and pointed to the file with Allison's name printed in large letters.

"Thank you, Allison. We have good medicine to help Sir Cedwick feel better and more medicine to fix his urine problem. Is it okay if I examine you, Sir Cedwick?"

Sir Cedwick mewed.

"He said yes," Allison said.

After Doc examined Sir Cedwick, he wrote the prescriptions. "Sir Cedwick should be more comfortable by this evening, and should have less urine trouble by Monday morning, but don't forget to give him the medicine until it's all gone and make sure he has access to plenty of fresh water."

"We can do that, Doc Thad. Thank you," Allison's mother said.

"You are stupendous, Doc Thad," Allison added.

"Thank you very much, Allison." Doc beamed as he left the room.

"I'll meet you at Ms. Claire's desk with the medicine." Riley lifted Sir Cedwick back into the carrier and zipped it up.

"Mommy can carry Sir Cedwick. I already made my arms tired when we came inside."

After Allison and her mother left the clinic with Sir Cedwick and the medicine, Claire said, "I understand I'm married to a stupendous doctor."

Riley grinned. "It's Allison's word for this week."

"Well, she certainly made Thad's day, but I think he's adopted the word himself."

"That's stupendous." Riley giggled.

Claire rolled her eyes. "It's going to get old stupendously fast, isn't it?"

Zach joined them at the desk. "You're staying this afternoon, Riley?"

"Ben's working. I could go home and do laundry, clean house, or mope around because Toby's not there, or I could stay here with Toby, and that reminds me: I need to call my landlady about our leaking showerhead."

"Let me know if you'll need to be home for the plumber," Zach said.

"Will do, but I don't think I will because Helen's my landlady." Riley hurried to the breakroom to call Helen.

After Riley told her about the leaky showerhead, Helen asked, "Are you sure it's leaking into the tub and not down the wall?"

"Just into the tub, so there's no water damage," Riley said.

"That's good. I have an appointment with Bethany Buchanan this afternoon to show her some homes for her daughter, and I'd hate to cancel on her. Have you met Bethany? Nice, but awfully quiet and nothing like her husband. Ezra Buchanan doesn't really fit in here. Have you met him? He is really brash. I saw him having coffee with Marc from the GBI. It made me wonder if Marc was investigating Buchanan because the usually congenial Marc had quite a dark look on his face. Wouldn't surprise me one lick."

"Bethany and Regina came to the clinic to get acquainted," Riley said.

"Isn't Regina a beauty? I asked Bethany if Ezra was settling in as well as she was in our small town, and she told me it was more of an adjustment for him because Barton is the smallest facility he's ever managed. I got the impression we must be beneath Mr. Buchanan, and if he leaves here for the city, Bethany would be perfectly content to stay. I still have a few more phone calls to make before I'll have the houses lined up for Bethany and Regina." Helen chuckled. "Bethany told me Regina knows what the children would like. Isn't that cute? I'll get to that leak later today if I can or on Monday, for sure."

When Riley returned to Claire's desk, Zach was waiting for her.

"Helen's showing some properties this afternoon. She'll look at the shower later today or on Monday," Riley said.

Zach nodded. "Let me know if anything changes."

"Helen's amazing, isn't she?" Claire asked after Zach left. "It must save her a ton of money since she's so handy with repairs."

Riley nodded. "Amanda told me her mother said if you wanted something fixed right, invite Ms. Helen to dinner, but my cooking skills will need to improve stupendously to match Ms. Helen's handyperson skills."

Claire rolled her eyes. "Thank goodness we aren't working all day. I hope you and Thad get bored with the remarkably annoying word before Monday. Oh no, I just remembered I go home with Thad."

"Don't you feel sorry for Allison's mother? Wonder what the next word of the week will be?"

"If you find out," Claire said as Riley headed down the hallway, "do not tell my husband."

While Riley cleaned Sir Cedwick's exam room, Zach joined her.

"I've been thinking about the reports," he said. "Have you considered that there may be more than one bad character involved? One who is inside the distribution company, and a second one who is outside the company?"

"I've half-entertained the idea but have nothing to back it up. What are you thinking?"

"The insider would know what to show on the report from the business standpoint, and the outsider could provide the technical expertise. Mitch and I talked about it a bit, and he said he could recreate the phony reports, but he couldn't have created them without guidance because he doesn't have the business knowledge to hide the thefts or create nonexistent inventory."

Riley narrowed her eyes. *Cattle rustlers and Ranger.* "We're saying insider business knowledge and technical knowledge; do we also need a shield to divert any potential investigations?"

"Seems like it could quickly become unstable with three top bad guys."

"You're right; would it be possible for the shield to also bring the technical knowledge?" Riley asked.

"If the technical is contracted out, there might not be a reason for a third top bad guy, but then you've brought in smart guys who could easily figure out what's happening."

Riley rubbed her forehead. "If the smart guys are good guys, they'd turn them in; if they're bad guys, they'd want their cut. This criminal stuff is hard."

"We might be headed in the wrong direction, but the answer is there somewhere," Zach said. "We'll keep brainstorming."

"Back to your original idea, I'm convinced there could easily be more than one bad guy involved, but I wonder if there is only one killer or two."

"Ouch. I didn't think about that; maybe that's contracted out," Zach said.

"We are definitely creating a complex criminal organization. Isn't simple better?"

"Yes. Let's stick with one killer unless we find something that points to two," Zach said.

"I really want to stop the killer; maybe we've narrowed it down to just two possibilities?"

"Maybe. I'm going to see if my patient's here. More later?"

"Absolutely." *Who is the killer, Tom? The cattle rustler or the Ranger?* Riley put away the cleaning supplies and headed to the kennel to visit Toby.

While she told Toby and Jordy about the cattle rustler and the Ranger, Claire stood in the hallway and motioned for Riley to join her.

"Toby has a visitor," she whispered. "I didn't know whether he was up to seeing anyone. It's Regina. Ezra Buchanan brought her. He's the new general manager at the distribution center. What do you think?"

"I'll check," Riley whispered. "I'll come to your desk."

"Thanks."

Riley hurried to Toby's crate. "Regina is here and wants to visit with you. Is that okay?" Toby whined, and Jordy yipped.

Riley nodded. "I understand. You'd rather be stronger when she sees you. I'll ask her to come back Monday. You should be feeling a lot stronger by then."

Riley strolled to Claire's desk. "Hi, Regina. Hello, Mr. Buchanan, I'm Riley Malloy."

"I've heard a lot about you in the short time I've been here. It's nice to meet you, Ms. Malloy."

"You too." Riley turned her attention to Regina. "I know you'd like to visit with Toby today, but he's still under sedation and can't have any visitors. If you could come back on Monday, I know he'd really appreciate seeing you."

Regina licked Riley's hand in agreement.

"Thank you."

"I've heard you understand animals, but I've never seen a dog whisperer in action before. It was obvious that Regina knew what you were saying."

Riley smiled.

Ezra glanced down the hallway toward the exam rooms. "I was under the impression Mrs. Grant worked here too. Everyone at the center is concerned about Tom."

"As we all are, but she isn't here today; we work only a half day on Saturdays, and the Grants have a school-age child."

"Oh, of course. I'd heard Doc Julie Rae was particularly accommodating to her staff, but I assumed it was a local myth. Quaint practice, but I assume the purpose is to build a strong bond in a small operation."

Riley nodded, and Claire picked up a file and stormed to the back hallway.

"Will Mrs. Grant be here on Monday? I may bring Regina myself to convey the entire corporation's concerns."

Riley smiled. "Of course. Monday is a regularly scheduled workday for all of us. You're very kind."

"I won't take up any more of your time, Ms. Malloy." He smiled, but his smile was cold and didn't reach his eyes. "Come, Regina." He tugged Regina's leash, and she strained against the leash and yipped, but after he jerked the leash with more force, she followed him.

Riley smiled as Claire returned from the hallway.

"I want to be you when I grow up," Claire said. "I was ready to smash his patronizing face with my clipboard when he said Doc Julie Rae was 'accommodating' in that demeaning tone and then had the nerve to drool his patronizing slime all over our nice, clean floor. So, what did Regina say right before she left?"

Riley chuckled. "That little vixen knew I was lying about Toby, and she told him to get well soon."

Claire laughed. "Oh, my. Good thing nobody else knew you were busted, except for Toby and Jordy. So what was with all the questions Mr. Pompous Pants had about Pia?"

"I don't know. Maybe it was just his awkward version of social skills to show his attempt at compassion for a distribution center employee's family."

Claire guffawed. "Love it." After she settled down, she wiped her eyes. "This has been an absolutely stupendous morning, and you can't tell Thad I said that."

"Oh no, with everything that's gone on this morning, I completely forgot. We need an emergency staff meeting as soon as Zach's patient leaves. I have to go tell Doc Julie Rae. Bring Zach to the breakroom."

Riley hurried to the kennel. "Toby, did you hear Regina? Wasn't that nice? I think it was wise to ask her to come see you on Monday when you're stronger. I have something to tell you."

Toby whined.

"Of course, it's good news. Ready?" Riley whispered, "I was accepted into the veterinary college at UGA."

Toby and Jordy howled, and Riley laughed. Doc Julie Rae raced to the kennel and was out of breath when she arrived. "What's wrong?"

"Toby and Jordy were celebrating with me. We need to have an emergency staff meeting in the breakroom. Can you tell Doc Thad? Claire will bring Zach."

Doc Julie Rae narrowed her eyes. "Are you...never mind. You wouldn't call a staff meeting for that; we'd all know."

Riley tilted her head and furrowed her brow. "What?"

"The meeting is not to tell us that you and Ben eloped because we'd all have been a part of planning it. So, never mind. See you in the breakroom in two minutes, and this better be worth that howl." Doc Julie Rae headed to Doc Thad's office.

"I'm staying this afternoon until George comes back. We'll talk more later." Riley rushed to the breakroom.

When everyone was in the breakroom, Riley said, "The UGA veterinary college accepted me. I'm not on the wait list anymore."

"No wonder Toby and Jordy howled. It's totally howl-worthy." Doc Julie Rae threw back her head and howled, and everyone laughed.

"When do classes start?" Zach asked.

"Ben and I start classes together next fall," Riley said.

"You'll be a stupendous veterinarian," Doc Thad said.

"What?" Doc Julie Rae stared at Doc Thad.

Riley told Doc Julie Rae and Zach about Allison and her word of the week.

"Is there anything else that will make Doc Julie Rae howl?" Claire asked. "Because, if not, I'll return to my desk before Doc Thad uses his new word of the week again."

Riley followed Claire and picked up the patient folder.

"The puppy got into an anthill on Tuesday, but the bites may be infected," Claire said. "The ants weren't fire ants, so the family wasn't too concerned at first. It's another case of a working family that can't afford to take off work during the week."

"Do we know when most of the folks get off work?" Riley asked.

Claire smiled. "I've been asking, and most of them get home by five thirty or six."

"Would it be worth staying open until eight or so one night a week?"

"It would benefit our patients and clients and relieve our Saturday crush. We'll need to ask Doc Julie Rae what she thinks."

"I think chocolate is good. What are we talking about?" Doc Julie Rae joined them at the desk as Riley's patient and client came inside.

"Riley will tell you later, Doc," Claire said. "This patient's yours, Riley."

After their patient left, Riley and Doc Julie Rae cleaned the exam room together while Riley summarized the discussion about working families waiting until Saturday for an appointment. "Claire has talked to our Saturday clients; she learned most of them are home from work by six on weekdays. We would benefit our clients and patients and may alleviate our Saturday workload if we are here one day a week in the evening."

Doc Julie Rae furrowed her brow. "I couldn't handle on-demand, after-hours appointments because my home life would suffer, but an extra three hours one day a week that we share might help everyone. We'll talk on Monday when the entire staff is here. Speaking of which, are you sure you should be here by yourself all afternoon?"

"I brought my lunch and will let Ben know where I am."

"I could beat anyone to the clinic except Ben, so if you can't reach him, call me."

Claire, Doc Thad, and Zach joined Riley in the breakroom as Riley pulled her lunch from the refrigerator.

"We can stay with you until George gets here, or if you want some quiet time with Toby, we can sit in the car in the parking lot," Claire said.

"I promised Amanda I'd help her with a few things this afternoon, but after we finish her list, I can come back," Zach said.

"I appreciate the offers, everyone, but Toby, Jordy, and I will be fine. I suspect George will be here by the middle of the afternoon or earlier, anyway."

When the three of them didn't move, Riley said, "Please go so I can eat lunch with Toby and Jordy."

Riley locked the door behind Zach, who was the last to leave, and then made a pot of coffee before she carried her cup and lunch to the kennel. After she ate, Riley told Toby and Jordy about Sir Cedwick's Allison and her word of the week. Toby and Jordy grinned when she told them how much Doc Thad liked his new word.

"Honestly, I think he liked it so much because he could tease Claire."

Jordy growled softly.

"I heard a tap at the front door, too," Riley whispered.

She stepped into the dark hallway with Jordy by her side as she peered at the front door. *What is Eli doing here?*

Jordy whined.

"It's okay; he can't see us."

After he left, Riley's phone buzzed with a text from Claire.

"Eli is at the back door."

Riley replied, "Find out what he wants. Tell him I'm at Doc Julie Rae's."

"Got it."

Jordy growled again at a knock at the back door.

"Claire will find out what he wants. Let's tell Toby what's going on. He's probably worried."

When Riley and Jordy reached the kennel, Toby stood in his crate.

"Toby, it's okay; you can relax," Riley said. "Eli was at the front door then went to the back; Claire and probably Doc Thad will ask him what he's doing."

Toby moaned as he slowly lay down.

"Are you okay?" Riley asked.

When Toby whimpered, Riley said, "I'm sorry you hurt. It's probably time for your pain medicine; I'll check."

While Riley gave Toby his medication, Doc Thad unlocked the back door and followed Claire to the kennel after he locked it.

"How's Toby?" Doc Thad asked.

"I just gave him his meds. He stood after Jordy and I left him to see who was at the front door."

Claire sat on the floor next to Toby's crate and cooed while she stroked his back, and Toby relaxed then closed his eyes.

"Let's go into the breakroom." Doc Thad helped Claire up.

"I brought dessert." Claire opened her backpack, pulled out a large sack of cookies, and placed them on the table.

Riley smiled. "Coffee's fresh."

While Doc Thad refilled Riley's cup and filled two cups, Claire said, "I added coconut to my chocolate chip recipe. What do you think?"

Riley bit into her cookie. "Yum, excellent."

Doc Thad jammed a cookie into his mouth, and Claire said, "When he saw us pull into the lot, he smiled and hurried to us. He told us he drove by and saw your car, so he stopped to say hello, but no one answered the door when he knocked. He was worried, so he went to the back door. He seemed genuinely relieved to see us."

Doc Thad added, "Emphasis on the seemed. I'm not quite as generous as Claire regarding Agent Reeves."

Claire nodded. "Thad and Zach don't trust Eli. I told him your future mother-in-law picked you up to go shopping. I know you said to tell him you'd gone to Julie Rae's, but I didn't want him to go to her house."

Riley smiled. "Good thinking."

Doc Thad snorted. "Claire surprised Reeves with the 'future mother-in-law.' He sighed very dramatically before he said, 'Oh, Ben.' When Claire tucked her chin, raised her eyebrows, and peered at him with that look she has that withers the most wayward sixth-grade boy, it took everything I had to keep from laughing at his hangdog expression." Doc Thad mimicked Eli's sad face.

Riley giggled, and Claire said, "I prefer to think of it as my 'did you hear what you just said?' look, but back to why Eli was here in the first place: I asked him why he was looking for you, and he implied you were in danger, so I asked him what gave him that idea, and he said, 'scuttlebutt.'"

"I might be reading too much into his word selection, but to me, 'scuttlebutt' is found in a more exclusive group than gossip, which is more widespread," Doc Thad said.

Riley frowned as she rubbed the back of her neck. "Eli's exclusive group is the GBI."

"That's what I thought too." Claire rose and then checked the coffee pot. "Anyone care for more coffee?" She poured out the coffee and continued, "Would it be worth asking Marc, Riley?"

"I've been very reluctant to talk about anything outside our small group."

Doc Thad narrowed his eyes. "Why?"

"Mrs. Smythe referred to the ranger in Tom's story as 'secretive.' I don't know how she knew about Tom's novel, but I took what she said as a serious warning. I haven't finished reading Tom's novel yet, but I intend to this afternoon," Riley said.

"Mrs. Smythe is spooky sometimes, but she's never wrong, as far as I'm concerned. You read, and we'll stay here to greet visitors." Doc Thad grabbed the last cookie, took a large bite, and wiped off the crumbs from the table before crumpled the sack and tossed it into the trash can. "Are you going to read at the kennel? We've got your back."

"Thanks." Riley smiled as she headed down the hallway.

"Hi, Toby. Claire and Doc Thad are staying to babysit us while I read." Riley sat on the floor next to the crate and pulled out the manuscript from her backpack before she leaned against the wall and read.

After an hour, she finished the manuscript, slammed it on the floor, and screamed. "Agggh!"

Her shout woke Toby and startled Jordy; Doc Thad and Claire raced down the hallway.

Riley fumed. "Tom didn't finish his story. He just ends it." She picked up the manuscript, flipped to the last page, and read the last sentence. "It's all up to Rita."

She threw the manuscript against the wall.

Claire softly asked, "Riley, who's Rita?"

"The gunslinger. Me," Riley said. "The bad guy ordered his gang to kill Blair; they were unsuccessful but lied to the bad guy. After the bad guy thought Blair was dead, he shifted to target the fiery Novalee because she held the documents with proof of the crime and the gunslinger, Rita, because she was on his trail and would expose him. Blair devised a plan to hide Novalee and to send a warning to Rita."

Doc Thad furrowed his brow. "Does Blair know who the bad guy is?"

Riley's eyes widened. "I was so focused on the story that I didn't think about that." Riley rubbed her forehead. "He might because the story hints at his identity."

"Maybe that's what Rita's supposed to do: identify the bad guy," Doc Thad said.

"And not get killed," Claire added.

"I think you're right, Doc Thad. I'll go back through and read what Blair thinks of the bad guy."

After forty-five minutes, Riley joined Doc Thad and Claire in the breakroom as they played a board game.

"I'm happy you're here, Riley. Thad's winning, but he cheats," Claire said.

"Do not; you say that every time you're losing. So, what did you learn, Riley?"

"The bad guy is a respected authority in his organization. In the story, the bad guy is either the local banker or the senior ranger who is in charge of investigating the cattle rustling."

"That's terrible news," Doc Thad said. "That completely leaves Agent Reeves in the clear. He's definitely not a respected authority in anything."

"You don't know that," Claire said.

Riley smiled. "I think I found Eli. The local barber wants to be the first to know so he can show off. The bad guy takes advantage of the barber who is inadvertently tracking the comings and goings of Novalee and Rita for the bad guy."

"There's your Eli. Does the barber ever realize who the bad guy is?" Doc Thad asked.

"Not in the incomplete version that I have," Riley said

"Well, we can't just ask Eli who is interested in what he says he knows about Riley," Claire said.

Riley shrugged. "Maybe we can."

Chapter Eight

"Can I join this party?" George chuckled as he continued to the kennel.

"I was so focused on what you were saying that I didn't hear George enter the building. I'm not much of a guard." Claire sighed. "What's our plan?"

"I need to talk to Ben first. If Ben doesn't like it, there is no plan," Riley said.

"Do I talk to him if you can't break him down?" Claire asked.

"Of course," Riley said.

"Good." Claire grabbed her coat and backpack. "Ready, Thad?"

"I'll be right there. I have some things in the office..."

"If you'll give me the keys, I'll warm the engine," Claire said.

"Would it help if I talked to Ben?" Doc Thad asked after Claire left.

Riley bit her lip. "I'd really like to talk to the sheriff, but I don't know if that's possible."

"I'll work it for you." Doc Thad swaggered out of the room.

Riley cocked her head. *Did those two double-team me? Doc Thad sure was proud of himself.*

George smiled when Riley joined them. "We're going for a walk; care to join us?"

Toby rose to his feet and grinned as George opened his crate. George slipped the wide support band under Toby's belly. Jordy led the way to the back door, and Riley followed George and Toby.

"See how well he's doing? He's bearing most of his weight himself with only a little assistance from me," George said.

"That's outstanding," Riley said.

After their short walk, George gave Toby and Jordy a treat.

"What are your plans for the rest of the day?" George asked.

"I thought I'd just relax here," she said.

When Toby whined, she said, "I don't need to take a break."

"We don't agree," George said. "We're ready to settle in for a lazy night and don't need anyone to tell us we snore when we nap. Wouldn't hurt for you to get off your feet, too."

Riley sighed. "Okay, but call me if you need a break."

After Riley started her car, her phone buzzed with a text from Ben.

"Call me when you can talk."

She called him immediately while her engine warmed up.

"Hey, babe," Ben said. "I don't really have anything special to talk about. I just wanted to hear your voice."

"I'm sitting in my car at the parking lot at work while my engine warms up. Toby and George insisted that I go home."

"I heard you and Mom were out shopping. What did you get me?" Ben chuckled.

Riley snickered. "That's excellent that the rumor is making the rounds; Claire told Eli that's where I was when he came by the clinic after everyone had left except for me and them. Doc Thad and Claire were my self-assigned perimeter guards."

"I don't like it; why is he stalking you?" Ben growled.

"He may be the unknowing stooge for the bad guy." Riley told Ben about the barber in Tom's unfinished manuscript. "How did you hear?"

"Some guys at the gas station ribbed me about you and Mom going shopping for a dress," Ben said.

"A dress? That's a twist I didn't expect. Why would Mom and I shop for a dress? Why not a pair of boots?"

Ben snorted. "A wedding dress, babe; although, I could see you and Mom finding boots and then shopping for a dress to go with the boots."

"Where did that come from?" Riley rolled her eyes. "I'll have to tell Claire that her rumor took on a life of its own. It was supposed to help expose the bad guy, not fuel the gas station gossip mill and embarrass you."

Ben cleared his throat. "It didn't embarrass me. Are you embarrassed?"

"Only if you are, because that was not the intent."

"We can talk more about that later. Sheriff was much better this morning and claimed he's going home tomorrow; he was a little vague about what his doctors said. I'll drop by the hospital and talk to him about Reeves and the barber." Ben sighed. "I have some things to do before going to the hospital. Be safe, babe."

After Ben hung up, Riley frowned. *What is it that we'll talk about later?*

On the way home, Riley drummed her fingers on the steering wheel while waiting for the traffic light to change. *Are we moving too fast with Toby? Should he be walking this soon after his injury?*

Riley drove past her house and continued around the block as she headed toward the clinic. *George is going to think I'm checking up on him.* She glanced in the rearview mirror. *That car has followed me through each turn since I left the clinic.*

Riley pulled into the gas station and filled up, went inside the store, went straight to the ice cream cooler, picked up two vanilla ice cream cones covered with chocolate and nuts, and stood in line to pay.

When the mechanic entered the store, one of the men in line said, "You're putting in a lot of extra hours these days, Isaac. Why don't you get yourself some help?"

"It's hard to find anyone willing to work in a small town, but I've got a couple of guys coming next week. Y'all have to stop scaring off these young guys just because you have good-lookin' daughters."

The men grumbled as they headed out the door.

When Riley placed the two cones on the counter, Isaac frowned. "What's the fight about? Is it you or Ben who has the pre-wedding jitters?"

"Fight? No, this is dessert." Riley chuckled. "Don't you have to have a wedding scheduled before you can have pre-wedding anything? There's no wedding planned that I know of. Where'd you hear that?"

"That fella sitting right out there in the parking lot, Agent Reeves."

"That's interesting. I wonder where he heard it."

Isaac shrugged. "Why don't you ask him?"

"Guess I better." Riley paid for the ice cream and then strolled to Eli's car.

Eli's eyes widened as Riley approached his car. He reached to put it into gear, then visibly sighed and lowered his window.

"Hey, Eli." Riley smiled. "I haven't seen you in a while. What's going on?"

Eli's face softened as he returned her smile. "Not much; you know, just working. What about you?"

"Same. I just heard the funniest thing. Isaac told me I'm getting married." She giggled. "News to me. Have you heard that? I can't imagine how it got started."

Eli raised his eyebrows. "You mean it's not true? Well, that's good news. I mean, you know it's good to know it's not true when it isn't. People should be careful about repeating things that they don't know if they're true."

Doing lots of stumbling for words for a slick talker, Eli. Riley nodded, then smiled. "I better get going; my ice cream is melting. Nice to see you, Eli."

"Yeah, you too."

When Riley reached her car, her eyes narrowed as Eli pulled away from the gas station. *Eli is our barber.*

After Riley put away the ice cream, she read the note from Helen that she found on the dining table and smiled. *Our awesome landlady fixed the shower.*

She pulled out her phone from her back pocket and texted Doc Thad. "Ran into Eli at the gas station. He is the barber."

Doc Thad replied, "Ok."

Riley chuckled as she read his text. *That's Doc; straight to the point.*

After she started a load of laundry and unloaded the dishwasher, she stared at the contents in the refrigerator and then the freezer. *I could quick-thaw some chicken and make a chicken and rice casserole.*

As she reached for the chicken, her phone buzzed with a text from Ben.

"Leaving in ten min. Will order pizza and pick it up on my way."

Riley smiled as she replied, "I got ice cream."

While she waited for Ben, she swept the floor and set the table. When she heard the crunch of his tires on the driveway, she rushed to open the door, and Ben grinned as he carried in the pizza box and a large grocery sack.

"Hi, honey, I'm home."

Riley took the pizza box from him and smiled. "Never gets old."

Ben leaned down for a kiss. "Sure doesn't."

While Riley placed the pizza on the table, her phone buzzed a text as Ben asked, "Beer or wine? I'm officially off duty until six tomorrow morning, and so are you."

"Beer with pizza, but I haven't been on duty."

Ben snorted as he set two bottles on the table and placed the rest in the refrigerator while she read her text.

"That's odd," she said. "It's from Zach."

She read it to Ben. "I have Hector. Be there soon. Tell Ben."

Riley narrowed her eyes at Ben. "Why do you want to know where Zach is?"

Ben shrugged. "Tell me about your day."

While they ate, Riley told him the rest of Tom's story, including Rita and the barber. After they finished eating, she wrapped the leftover pizza, and Ben loaded the dishwasher.

"Another beer with our ice cream or wait?" Ben asked.

"Let's wait." Riley pulled out the cones, and they sat together on the sofa.

"Brain freeze." Riley clutched her forehead.

"I'm immune." Ben wiggled his eyebrows, and Riley snickered.

After they finished their dessert, Riley told Ben about Eli showing up at the clinic and Claire's interception.

Ben's face reddened, and his nostrils flared as he growled, "That's it; he's done. I'm calling the sheriff." Ben rose, but Riley grabbed onto his arm.

"Wait, honey, Eli's our barber."

Ben sighed as he sat close to Riley, wrapped his arms around her, and nuzzled her neck. "Explain."

"Mmm," Riley moaned. "I've missed snuggling."

"So have I," Ben mumbled as he nibbled on her neck. "I'm listening."

Riley giggled as she raised her shoulder to protect her neck. "You'll have to stop tickling first."

Ben kissed her cheek and then leaned back. "Two minutes. Go."

Riley sat up straight, then turned sideways on the sofa to face Ben. "The bad guy is getting information from Eli, so we tell Eli what we want the bad guy to believe."

"Hmm, what do we want the bad guy to know?"

Riley furrowed her brow. "I haven't quite filled in the details yet."

Ben snorted. "Reeves can have a short reprieve, but his career is toast. Let's talk about something more pleasant. Where are we going on vacation?"

"That's definitely something more pleasant, but I didn't know we were going on vacation. When is that?"

"We have to go on vacation before we start veterinary college."

"That sounds great." Riley smiled. "Do we know where we're going?"

"I asked you first; we'll go wherever you want. You decide, and we'll have a combo vacation."

"I never heard of a combo vacation. Is that like a working vacation?" Riley asked.

Ben smiled as he leaned forward and lightly kissed Riley. "I love you."

She wrapped her arms around his neck and pulled him closer to her, then kissed him with longing, and he moaned as he matched her passionate kiss and entwined his fingers in her hair.

Riley sighed as they reluctantly parted. "I love you so much."

Ben gazed intently at her, then gently brushed her hair away from her face as he tucked it behind her ear. "If we have a wedding, we can combine our vacation with a honeymoon."

Riley smiled as she met his gaze. "You always have the best plans."

Ben smirked. "I do, don't I? So, is that a yes?"

"Yes."

After Ben lifted Riley up into a hug, she leaned against his chest and listened to his heartbeat.

"I'll listen to your chest for the rest of your life. Does that give you pre-wedding jitters?"

"What?" Ben frowned as he tilted his head and set Riley down.

Riley told him about Isaac and the pre-wedding jitters and confronting Eli.

"You just walked right up to his car?" Ben chuckled. "I'll bet that threw him for a loop."

"I don't expect he'll change his ways, though."

"I agree, but it won't take him long to get the word out that he knew all along that there wasn't any wedding planned." Ben mused, "if we wait a couple of days, he'll look like an unreliable witness."

"We could call Mom and Dad tonight or tomorrow night, then tell everyone else on Monday that we're engaged," Riley said.

Ben furrowed his brow. "We don't have an engagement ring for you."

"I couldn't wear a fancy engagement ring at work, and it doesn't make sense to have a ring to put on after work. I don't think we need one."

"I don't know; it doesn't feel right."

"An engagement ring makes no sense to me; it seems to be a waste of money, but I obviously don't understand why it's important. Maybe Mom can explain it to me. Ready to call the folks?"

"I'm too excited to sit still; let's go for a walk," Ben said. "You set the pace."

"I'd like to run and walk, but I can't run very fast."

"Set your own pace. I'll stay with you whether you walk or run."

After Riley ran to the corner of their street, she shifted to a fast walk with Ben at her side while they continued around the block.

"I'm whipped, but it felt good because I ran farther than when Toby told me to run," she said when they went inside. "My goal is to be able to run around the block."

"We can go for a run or a walk whenever you like. Ready for a beer and a phone call?"

"Sure am. Are we asking Mom her opinion about a ring?"

"Nope; that's our call, and you're right. You dazzled me with your brilliant logic and ice cream."

Riley giggled as Ben strutted to the refrigerator and grabbed two beers. After sitting beside her, Ben said, "Before I met you, Mom would always ask me if I was okay first thing when I called her; now, she asks if you're okay every single time."

"You're exaggerating." Riley rolled her eyes.

"Am not." Ben called his mom's phone.

"Is Riley okay?" Melissa asked when she answered the phone, and Ben grinned as he nudged Riley with his elbow.

"She's fine, and we have you on speakerphone. Is Dad around?"

"He's right here, and I have you on speakerphone too."

Ben winked at Riley. "Riley doesn't want an engagement ring."

Riley snorted and punched Ben's arm, and he smirked.

"What?" Melissa asked.

"Good call, Riley, and congratulations to you both," Jake said.

"That is just about the sneakiest...I'm sure there's a story, and you can tell me later. I won't forget to remind you. So, when's the wedding? And where?" Melissa asked.

Ben glanced at Riley, and she shrugged.

"We know we want to be married before we start school, but that's all we've decided so far," Ben said.

"You're more than welcome to have the wedding here, and it can be as small or large, formal or informal as you like."

"You have plenty of time to decide," Jake said. "How's Toby doing?"

"He's doing very well. He'd hobble home if he thought he could get away with it, but Doc Thad plans to release him on Monday or Tuesday, depending on his condition," Riley said.

"All good news," Jake said. "Anything else?"

"That's it," Ben said.

"It was fantastic news. Is this public information?" Melissa asked.

"Not quite yet," Riley said. "We'll give ourselves a little time to enjoy our news and discuss our plans first. We'll probably tell my office early next week, but I'll let you know."

"Thank you so much for calling. You've certainly made our weekend," Melissa said.

After they hung up, Riley snuggled closer to Ben. "I'm glad we called. I'm sure I'll get the same questions at the clinic when we tell them, so I'll be ready with my answer that we haven't decided."

Ben tilted Riley's chin up and gazed at her. "I'm going to marry the prettiest girl I've ever seen." After they kissed, he sighed and held her, and she relaxed as she rested her head on his chest and listened to the comforting rhythm of his heartbeat.

Chapter Nine

Mitch glanced in his rearview mirror as he sped north on the interstate. "We're less than two hours from Atlanta. When we're closer, I'll call my friend; he found someone we can trust at the Georgia Bureau of Investigation. I've sent copies of the reports to Riley; she'll see the fraud immediately and will find the notes from Tom that I added about the traitor."

He narrowed his eyes as he checked the mirror again. "The car behind us has been pacing us for the past thirty minutes."

Mitch frowned and drummed his fingers on the steering wheel. "Fuel's getting low, and Hector's been fidgeting; he's ready for a break. I have to take the next exit and fill up."

Zach glanced at Hector in the backseat. "I'll walk Hector while you pump the gas."

As Mitch approached the truck stop, he pointed to the large, grassy field next to the entrance, "Long line at the car pumps. I'll pull over and let you and Hector out, then you two can join me after Hector's ready."

When Mitch stopped, Zach grabbed his backpack, jacket, and Hector's leash before he opened the back door; Hector hopped out and trotted to the field.

Mitch chuckled. "See you in a few minutes."

Zach hurried to catch up with Hector. "I wish I had boots instead of my running shoes. You'll tell me if there are any snakes, won't you?"

Hector yipped and wandered the field with his nose to the ground for the perfect spot to relieve himself. While Hector cruised, Zach noticed his backpack was wide open. *Hope I didn't lose anything.* He glanced around the field and at the truck stop, then noticed a car that blocked Mitch's car at the pump. The driver scanned the area while two men jumped out and approached Mitch.

Zach's eyes widened in horror as one man shoved a pistol into Mitch's side and then pushed him into their car. The second man finished refueling Mitch's car and then followed the abductors to the south ramp on the interstate. Zach whistled for Hector and attached the leash to his collar.

"We have to find Mitch, boy." He ran with Hector to the south ramp and continued down the ramp to the interstate, then stopped as cars and trucks whizzed past them.

"I can't even see them," Zach moaned. He led Hector back up the ramp and pulled out his phone. "Oh, great!" he fumed. "My battery's down to eight percent."

Hector barked, and Zach inhaled, then exhaled. "Right, so what can I do with my failing phone? Riley."

He sent a text to Riley then searched his backpack. "Now what, Hector? I've lost my wallet."

They headed back up the ramp to the intersection; a heavy-duty, four-door pickup truck that pulled an empty three-horse slant trailer slowed then stopped, and the woman in the passenger's seat lowered her window. "Me and Pop saw your friend leave with those other guys without you. You two going south? We'll leave the interstate and head toward Alabama on the back roads sixty or so miles down the road, but you're welcome to catch a ride with us that far. You two don't look like you'll take up much room."

This is crazy, but I have Hector. Zach helped Hector into the truck's back seat next to a large picnic cooler.

As they rolled down the interstate, the woman told Zach of their adventures on their farm raising and training horses, growing hay, and selling horses and hay in their forty-three years together.

"I haven't seen many horse trailers, but I don't think I've ever seen one like yours," Zach said.

"It's a three-horse slant trailer. The slant trailer allows the horse to walk out of the trailer headfirst. It's not appropriate for the large horses that need the extra width the straight sides allow, but the horse has to be backed out of a straight trailer. I can't tell you how many horses I've seen get spooked or balky when they were unloaded back end first from a straight side after a trip." She shook her head.

After Zach told her he was a vet tech, she handed him the business card for their farm. "Call us if you're ever out of work or just looking for a change. Us and our neighbors run our poor vet ragged. He's always moaning that he'd give anything for a good vet tech."

When the farmer slowed to drop Zach and Hector off at the westward route exit, the woman said, "Reach in that cooler and grab yourself a sandwich. Pull out two and give ole Hector there the meat out of one."

Before Zach and Hector jumped out of the truck, Zach said, "Thanks for the ride, sandwiches, and stories."

The man chuckled. "You two just saved me from having to listen to the stories I've heard a hundred times."

The woman smacked his arm and giggled. "Oh, g'wan with you."

Zach waved, and Hector barked as the truck turned west on the road, then they headed south on the frontage road toward Barton.

Chapter Ten

Riley woke before dawn the next morning, hurried to the kitchen, and sighed. *He's already left.*

The coffee pot was hot, so she poured a cup before she noticed the note on the dining table. "Be safe. Love you."

After drinking her coffee, she dressed before she stripped the linens from both beds, started the first load of sheets in the washer, and made the beds with clean sheets. When the washer finished, she tossed the sheets into the dryer and started a second load of laundry. She checked the time on the stove: *Eight o'clock. I'll leave to see Toby after I grab a bite.*

Riley dropped a slice of bread into the toaster and pulled out the butter. While she waited for her toast, she picked up her phone as the toaster popped. *I missed this text from yesterday. I don't recognize the number; I'll check it later.*

She smeared butter on her toast and then sat at the table to enjoy breakfast. After Riley finished her coffee and straightened the kitchen, she zipped up her coat and slipped her computer into her backpack.

When she pulled into the parking lot behind the building, she frowned. *George's car is here, but I thought Zach's would be here too.*

As she climbed out of her car, George, Toby, and Jordy came outside.

George smiled. "Should have known you were here; these two scoundrels were raising a ruckus to come outside. Toby's doing great, isn't he?"

Toby ambled slowly toward Riley, and she rushed to him. "You're amazing, but aren't you overdoing it just a bit?"

Toby yipped, and Riley smiled. "You're right; I always overdo too. Let's go inside; it's cold out here."

After he helped Toby into his crate, George asked, "Have you heard from Zach? I thought he would have been here by now."

"I was surprised he wasn't here when I drove up. You don't need to wait. Ben's at work, and I'm at loose ends for the day anyway. I'm sure I'll hear something from Zach soon."

"Thanks for the offer; I want to get in a quick catnap before my granddaughter's birthday party this afternoon. There's a fresh pot of coffee; I made it right before we went outside."

"We'll be fine. Have a great time at that party."

After George left, Riley poured a cup of coffee and carried it to the kennel. When Toby yipped, Riley said, "I'll send Amanda a text to ask her if she's heard from Zach this morning."

Riley sent texts to Amanda and Zach while she sipped her coffee and then sent a text to Ben.

"I'm with T&J. Zach is not here yet. Take a lunch break with us? We can tell T&J our news."

Ben replied, "Ok."

Riley's phone rang; she smiled as she answered.

"Is Ben there? Are you busy?" Melissa asked.

"He's at work. I'm hanging out with Toby and Jordy until Zach shows up. Toby had a good night."

"That's great news. Are you excited? I had trouble sleeping."

"I'm not sure it's sunk in yet."

Riley told Melissa about the wedding gossip that started when Claire told Eli about the two of them going shopping.

Melissa laughed. "Do you think your friend Claire will take credit for nudging Ben into proposing? Tell me about the engagement ring."

"I never wore rings or any jewelry as a kid because Dad and I were always working on machinery or I was helping Grandma at her cabin. When I started vet tech school, it was a real advantage not to have to keep track of a ring during our lab sessions. It was always so sad when someone lost one, especially an engagement ring. Ben didn't really understand, but he's willing to support my decision."

"I blame Pamela Suzanne," Melissa said.

Riley giggled. "I'll go with that."

After chatting for another thirty minutes, Melissa said, "I have to pop the cinnamon rolls into the oven before Jake comes home from his hardware store trip. Call me anytime."

Riley smiled at Toby, who had fallen asleep while she was on the phone. She slipped his water dish from his crate and carried it to the breakroom. She washed and rinsed Toby's water bowl, then returned it to the kennel.

After returning Toby's water to his crate, she remembered the unknown text and pulled out her phone to check to see if it was important.

"From Hector: ck email. Do not reply."

"This is strange. I got a text that says it's from someone named Hector. I don't..."

Toby barked, and Riley's eyes widened. "Of course; the text is from Mitch. I'll check my email."

Riley pulled out her laptop and logged into her email. "Nothing, but I forgot Mitch wouldn't have my email address. I'll check the office email."

Riley hurried to Claire's desk, turned on the computer, and logged into the office email. She scrolled through the emails and then snickered when she found an email from Hector Pitt. *Well played, Mitch.* Subject: Your Accounting Data for Comparison.

She opened and read the email: "Attached are four files. #1 is Regional, as reported to HQ. #2 is Regional duplicated at HQ. #3 is HQ actual. #4 is an analysis of differences. Of particular note is the regional inventory overage that offsets the cash shortage."

Riley narrowed her eyes. *The result on the total assets on the balance sheet would be zero. Wouldn't an audit find that?*

After she copied the files to the office computer, she inserted her flash drive into the computer slot, copied the files and the email to her flash drive, and then deleted the email. Riley deleted the files in the download folder and renamed the files she had saved on the computer before emptying the recycle bin. She bit her lip and drummed her fingers on the desk. *A techie could still recover the files, but they'd have to know what to look for.*

She returned to Toby and Jordy at the kennel and reviewed the files on her flash drive. "Thanks to Mitch, we have the evidence of inventory fraud at the distribution center, but why hasn't an audit found it, and who designed the regional report for the contracting company? Who is behind the murders is still our critical unanswered question."

Riley exhaled in exasperation and slammed her computer shut. She leaned back and closed her eyes. *Where is Zach?*

Chapter Eleven

He glowered as he pushed aside the paperwork he'd been reviewing, then asked, "Have we heard anything from Buchanan?"

"No, boss."

He sighed and then picked up his phone. When Ezra answered, he said, "I expected to hear from you by now. What's the status?"

"We found him and have his computer. The files are there, just like we thought. College boy must have had a heart condition or something because after one of the guys put him into a choke hold for just a few minutes, he quit breathing," Ezra said.

"Criminy, what's wrong with you?" he shouted. "First, you have your goons shoot at the sheriff, and now you let them kill a guy? Was this before or after he told you who else knew about the reports?"

"It was after. I was in the room with my hands tied when the guys tossed him in, just like you said. I told him I knew a way for both of us to get away. He told me nobody else had copies of the reports."

He sneered. "He just got up from the floor and told you no one else had copies."

Ezra snorted. "I was giving you the executive summary. We talked, and I told him they asked me about the reports. I asked him what he knew, and he told me he had a copy of the report. I asked him to run for me." Ezra's voice had an edge of disdain. "The guys came in and said my story checked out, and I was released; I left the room. The guys said he told them the same thing, but I guess they got a little rough."

"You call killing a guy before he can talk being a little rough? I call it a whole lot of stupid. When did this happen?"

Ezra's tone of boredom deepened. "How do I know? I don't carry a watch. It was sometime late last night."

"What about Riley?" he asked.

"She's harmless. I'll get to her later," Ezra said.

Buchanan's an idiot. Riley is anything but harmless. He hung up and fumed, "I'm done with Buchanan. Get him out of my face."

"Yes, boss."

I'll call Eli. He'll know the current news on Riley.

Chapter Twelve

When Jordy barked, Riley jumped to her feet. "I'll be right back, Toby; I'll unlock the door for Ben." She rushed to the back door with Jordy at her side.

Ben grinned as he waved a large white sack as he came into the building. "How did you know I rushed out without making my sandwich this morning? I picked up subs and sweet tea for us. How's Toby?"

"Doing great. We can drop off our lunch in the breakroom. He'll be excited to see you."

Jordy barked, and Ben chuckled. "I'm happy to see you too."

Toby barked as they headed toward the kennel, and Ben sprinted to the kennel with Jordy on his heels. Riley smiled as she followed them.

When she reached the kennel, Ben had opened Toby's crate door and sat on the floor as he stroked Toby's face and murmured comforting words.

"Riley and I have news," Ben said, and Toby lifted his head, and his ears perked up.

Ben grinned. "You tell them, babe."

Riley giggled. "Good punt."

She crowded next to Ben and put her arm around Toby, and Jordy put his head on her knee. "Ben and I are going to be married."

Toby barked while Jordy howled, and then Toby howled, too. Ben laughed and hugged Riley.

After Toby and Jordy settled down, Riley said, "I'll tell the staff on Monday, but we couldn't wait to tell you."

When Toby whined, Riley smiled and glanced at Ben.

"What did he say?" Ben asked.

"He asked, what took you so long?"

"I'm shy," Ben said, and Toby yipped while Jordy shook his head.

"They don't believe—" Riley was interrupted by the buzz of a text on Ben's phone.

After he read it, he said, "I have to run; I'll grab my sandwich. Sorry, babe." He kissed her cheek before he raced to the breakroom and then dashed to the back door.

"Lock this," he called out as he left.

Riley locked the back door before she went to the breakroom to eat her sandwich.

After she finished her lunch, she joined Toby and Jordy then dozed off as she leaned against Toby's crate.

She jerked awake when her phone rang. *Ben.* She smiled and answered it.

"Meet me at the back door in five minutes." Ben hung up before she could say anything.

"Since when did Ben become so mysterious?"

Toby whined.

"Yes, but if it is so all-fired important, why couldn't he just tell me?" she grumbled as she headed to the back door.

When she stepped outside, Jordy joined her and remained close beside her while Ben pulled his cruiser into the lot. As Ben strode to her, she searched his somber face for a clue and shuddered with dread.

Ben hugged her and then kept one arm around her shoulder. "Let's go inside."

After he locked the door behind them, he continued to hold her. "Babe, Mitch was murdered last night. A Florida state trooper found his body at an interstate rest area north of here; there was no sign of his car."

"Mitch? They killed Mitch?" Riley's knees buckled, and Ben tightened his hold. "He was smart and kind, and Hector..."

Jordy whined; tears rolled down Riley's cheeks as she sobbed, "Hector must be heartbroken."

"I know." Ben gently stroked her hair while she cried for Mitch and Hector; Riley inhaled and exhaled slowly when her tears slowed.

"It's almost too much," she said.

"I agree, but now Zach's text makes more sense. I haven't shared that Zach contacted you with anyone because I wanted to talk to him first; let me know when you hear from him again." Ben sighed. "I have to go."

Ben kissed Riley and left; Riley dragged her feet as she and Jordy headed down the hallway to tell Toby about Mitch.

After Riley talked about Hector and Mitch, Jordy told them about waiting for Dr. Witmer inside the van after the doc parked it on the side of the road.

Riley nodded. "He left the windows down for you."

Jordy told them Dr. Witmer said he wouldn't be long, but after Doc didn't return, Jordy said he decided something was wrong. After he jumped out and raced down the road, he couldn't find him and was scared. When he ran across the road to check the other side, he forgot to check for traffic, and the truck hit him. Jordy whimpered as he told them how sad he was when Riley said Dr. Witmer wouldn't come to get him.

Riley hugged him. "We're so sorry, Jordy. Thanks for telling us."

Riley hummed quietly until her phone buzzed with a text from Claire. "On our way there."

The lock at the back door clicked, and Claire called out, "It's us."

Riley snickered. *She must have sent the text while they pulled into the parking lot.*

Claire and Doc Thad came from the hallway to the kennel, and Hector trotted along behind them.

Riley's eyes widened. "Where is..."

Claire interrupted Riley as she cleared her throat and put an index finger over her lips.

Jordy and Toby whined, and Hector flopped down next to Toby's crate; Jordy moved close to Hector and methodically groomed his face and ears while Riley knelt next to them.

She stroked Hector's back while she whispered, "We're so sorry; Mitch won't be coming to get you. He loved you very much and would be here if he could."

Hector's mournful whimper tugged at Riley's heart, and tears welled in her eyes. When Toby and Jordy joined in with their sorrowful whines, she bit her lip to keep from sobbing.

"George is on his way here," Doc Thad said. "I'll stay with him until everyone is settled."

"Go home with me," Claire said. "Ben can pick you up there."

"If you'll give me your keys, Riley, I'll have transportation home."

Riley grabbed her backpack and jacket and then followed Claire to the car.

After she fastened her seatbelt, Riley asked, "Now?"

Claire shook her head, and they rode in silence to Claire's house.

Claire parked in her driveway and grabbed a full shopping bag from the back seat, and then they went inside.

After Claire closed the front door, she leaned against it and exhaled. "I've been holding my breath to keep from saying anything. Zach's in the shower. I picked up clothes for him to wear while we washed his. Make yourself comfortable. I'll be right back."

Claire hurried down the hallway and then tapped on a door. "I have a sack with clothes and antibiotic cream. I'll drop in the sack inside the door."

When Claire opened the door, Riley heard the water spray of a shower before Claire joined her in the living room.

"It's normally too early for wine, but today is an exception. I made a fresh pot of coffee. Would you like wine, coffee, sweet tea, or hot tea? I'll have whatever you're having."

"Hot tea sounds great." Riley followed Claire to the kitchen.

While the tea steeped, Claire said, "Zach called Thad and asked him to pick him up at a convenience store about fifteen miles from here. I rode along and was surprised by how dirty and scratched up Zach was but even more surprised when I saw Hector."

Zach wore gray sweatpants and a green long-sleeved T-shirt when he joined them. "Thanks for the clean clothes, Claire. I must have looked like a bum in my dirty shirt and pants. Hector and I did a little backwoods hiking, which was my first. My phone was useless because my battery ran down yesterday. One of the local farmers loaned me his phone so I could call Thad. The farmer told me any kid with a dog deserved a hand up and bought me a cup of coffee and jerky for Hector, and the store clerk gave Hector some water." Zach sighed as he rubbed his hand through his wet hair. "Nice people."

"I'll make you a snack. Coffee or hot tea?" Claire asked.

"Anything hot." Zach joined Riley at the kitchen table while Claire poured him a cup of coffee, then opened the refrigerator and pulled out eggs, grated cheese, and sliced ham.

Zach sipped his coffee. "I need to talk to Ben, but nobody can know I'm here."

"That's easy." Claire served Zach an omelet. "Riley, you and Ben are invited to have supper with us. What time can we plan on Ben being here?"

"I'll check." Riley sent Ben a text.

Ben replied, and Riley said, "About an hour. He'll let me know if he's delayed."

"That's good." Zach ate his last bite and then tried to hide his yawn.

Claire narrowed her eyes. "Zach, I'll show you the guest room, and you can put up your feet and maybe nap until Ben gets here."

After Claire returned to the kitchen, she said, "An hour is great. I'll throw together a large pan of lasagna and pop it into the oven, and then we can make a salad when Ben's on his way."

Riley watched as Claire browned the ground turkey, made a sauce, and started the water boiling for the noodles.

"Your kitchen is magical," Riley said. "You open the refrigerator or a cupboard door and pull out exactly what you need."

Claire chuckled. "Not to ruin the mystique, but I shopped yesterday for our weekly groceries. I like to make a large casserole or a big pot of chili that I can warm up or freeze for premade meals when we come home from work."

"Will Doc Thad be here for supper?" Riley asked.

"He will when I tell him what we're having." Claire smiled.

Ben texted Riley. "On my way."

Riley showed Claire the text, and Claire said, "I'll let Thad know if you'll tap on Zach's door."

Before Riley reached the bedroom, Zach met her in the hallway. "I think I'm still on high alert; I'm exhausted, but I couldn't sleep," he said. "Where's Hector?"

"He's at the clinic with Doc Thad, George, Toby, and Jordy," Riley said as they went to the kitchen.

"I'll ask Ben to give me a ride after supper so I can stay at the clinic too."

"You need to rest," Claire said. "Thad is bringing Hector here to be with you."

Zach nodded. "Hector and I belong together until we find Mitch."

Claire's eyes misted, and she turned her back to peek in the oven.

Riley picked up the placemats and silverware that Claire had placed in the middle of the table and set the table for five. *Claire heard what I told Hector.*

After Ben parked in front of the house, Riley rushed to the door, met him on the sidewalk, and threw her arms around him. He hugged her, and she raised her head for a kiss.

"Thanks for my smooch." Ben smiled and kept his arm around her waist as they strolled to the house.

"Anytime you're hankering for a smooch, cowboy, I'm your gal." Riley returned his smile.

"How's Zach?" he asked.

"Too exhausted to think straight and too wired to rest. I didn't say anything about Mitch, but I did tell Hector at the clinic. Doc Thad will bring him here."

"I'd like to hear what Zach says before I tell him about Mitch."

After they went inside, Ben and Zach shook hands and headed to the living room.

Riley hurried to the kitchen and asked, "Do we have a little time to talk before we eat?"

"All you need," Claire said. "The lasagna needs time to rest, and I'm just now pulling it out of the oven."

As Riley joined Ben on the sofa, he said, "Tell me what happened."

Zach sighed. "I went with Mitch to Atlanta to take care of Hector while he talked to a trusted friend about the discrepancies in the reports Dylan found and Mitch had recreated. Mitch was concerned that someone in the GBI was involved."

Zach continued as he told Ben about the car following them and the two men forcing Mitch into their car by gunpoint and taking Mitch's car.

"Hector and I were in a field beside the truck stop." Zach exhaled. "It all happened so fast. The two cars headed to the interstate southbound ramp, and Hector and I ran after them. I don't know how I thought we'd catch up, but we'd have been right there if they tossed Mitch out of the car."

Zach told Ben about catching rides, shortcuts through the woods that weren't easy after all, and the kindness at the small town convenience store.

"Mitch told me something I didn't fully understand on our trip north. He told me he'd sent copies of the reports to Riley, and she would understand them, then he added that he left hints in the reports or his notes based on Tom's story..." He rubbed his face and then shook his head. "I'm sorry, but my head's fuzzy, and I'm not sure about the details; anyway, he said Riley would figure it out."

His smile was weak as he shrugged. "Sorry, Riley; no pressure."

Riley smiled. "You know me: I thrive on pressure."

Ben grumbled, "I can confirm that."

Riley rose. "I'm going to help Claire in the kitchen."

As she left, Ben said, "I have sad news about Mitch."

While Riley cut the tomatoes for the salad, she said, "Ben is telling Zach the bad news about Mitch."

Claire tried in vain to sniff back her tears. "I heard you tell Hector. Thad and I were afraid that was what happened."

When Doc Thad and Hector came into the house, Hector scrambled across the wood floor to Zach, who braced himself for the enthusiastic greeting. Hector leaped up, put his paws on Zach's chest, and whimpered as he kissed Zach's neck and chin.

"Good boy, Hector, good boy." Zach laughed and turned his head from side to side to avoid the slobbery kisses on his mouth and nose.

"Supper's on the table," Claire said. Doc Thad washed his hands at the kitchen sink and then took drink orders.

While everyone ate, Claire said, "Zach, we'd love it if you and Hector would stay with us for a couple of days."

"Thanks, but we'll be fine at home, and I'll sleep better in my own bed."

"Can't argue with that, honey," Doc Thad said. "Zach, I'll give you a ride home when you're ready."

"I'm leaving; why don't I take you home, Zach? Riley's car is here, and she'll want to take her car home," Ben said.

"Sure, Ben, makes sense," Zach said, and Doc Thad nodded.

Riley cleared the table while Claire wrapped the leftovers.

Claire placed a covered aluminum pan in front of Zach and snickered. "You can't turn down leftovers. This should hold you for a couple of days."

Zach smiled. "No way would I turn down leftovers."

He picked up the pan and yawned. "Ready, Ben?"

Claire handed Zach a large paper sack at the door. "I washed and dried your clothes."

Zach blushed and cleared his throat. "Thanks."

Riley glanced at Claire, and they exchanged smiles. *Zach was a little embarrassed.*

After Ben, Zach, and Hector left, Riley asked, "Is there anything I can do before I leave?"

"Everything is done," Claire said. "See you tomorrow."

Riley dropped her backpack on the passenger's seat, but her phone rang before she started the engine. *Ben.*

"I'll be a while. We've stopped at the grocery store to pick up a few things for Hector. Do we need anything?"

"Not that I can think of; take your time."

After Riley parked in her driveway and went inside, she kicked off her boots and hung up her coat before she pulled her laptop out of her backpack.

She scoured each document for the hint left by Mitch, then rubbed her eyes. *I have to give my eyes a rest. I didn't see a thing.*

Ben parked his truck in the driveway, then came inside and held Riley. "Zach had a key to Mitch's place, so we gathered Hector's things. I could tell by how Hector moped when we were there that he knew Mitch was gone. Zach took one of Mitch's shirts for Hector to have. It was really sad to see Hector mourning Mitch."

"Did you come across anything useful?" she asked.

"You know me so well." Ben smiled. "The only interesting thing I found was nothing. Zach had a key, and there was no sign of forced entry. When we went inside, Zach was shocked and told me he'd never seen Mitch's place so clean. There was no clutter and no trash. Nothing was in his desk drawers, and his file cabinet was completely empty. A professional stripped the place of any potential evidence without disturbing any personal items. Zach checked Mitch's pockets and found a spare set of car keys in a jacket pocket."

"Do you think they found what they were looking for?"

"I think their motive was to take everything so no one else could find anything. What have you found?"

"Nothing new. The documents Mitch sent me clearly show inventory fraud and a significant diversion of cash. I don't know who performs their financial audits, but they would have to be in on it."

Ben's face hardened. "I heard that Marc owns an auditing company; it's not unusual for law enforcement personnel to have a supplementary income as long as there's no conflict of interest, and an auditing firm would be a good fit for an accountant."

Riley stared at him. "Dylan told me that after GBI took Tom's computer, Mitch told him there had to be a cover-up, and I should beware of anyone involved in the investigation of Tom's disappearance. Marc took Tom's computer and is very much involved in the investigation."

"Let's be off duty because I need to think. Wine or beer?" Ben strode to the refrigerator. "We need brain food. Do we have ice cream?"

"Wine and ice cream for me," Riley joined him in the kitchen.

Ben's phone rang, and he shook his head. "Our off-duty mode may be canceled. It's the sheriff."

"Hello, Sheriff." Ben glanced at Riley. "We're home and were just about to go off duty. Are you still in the hospital?"

Ben raised his eyebrows. "Wine, beer, and ice cream." He nodded. "See you in a few."

After he disconnected, Ben chuckled. "Sheriff left the hospital and is on his way here. He said he needs to talk to us unofficially because he's sure there's a cover-up, and he'd appreciate an informal chat. He said he could have ice cream, but we should crack a few before he arrives, so it'll all be off duty. What do you think?"

"Does a glass of wine count as a crack a few?"

"Absolutely."

"What about root beer? We have two bottles left in the refrigerator if the sheriff would like to crack one, too," Riley said. "I've never heard of crack a few before now. It sounds super cool."

Ben chuckled as he poured Riley's glass of wine and opened a bottle of beer. "I'll dish up ice cream after the sheriff's here."

When the sheriff arrived, Ben welcomed him inside.

"Sheriff, we have some root beer if you'd like to join us in a crack a few," Riley said.

The sheriff laughed as he sat on the chair in the living room. "I'd love a root beer with my ice cream."

"We have vanilla and butter pecan. What would you like?" Ben asked.

"Butter pecan," the sheriff said.

"Three butter pecans coming up." Ben flourished the ice cream scoop and then dug into the carton.

Riley opened the root beer for the sheriff, carried the root beer and her wine to the living room, picked up two bowls of ice cream, and gave the sheriff his bowl.

"Sheriff, is there anyone in GBI you would trust unconditionally?" Riley asked before she popped a spoonful of ice cream into her mouth.

The sheriff frowned. "At one time, I would have said Marc, but I'm starting to hear some things that are unsettling. Why?"

"Zach said Mitch had a good friend in Atlanta who had a trusted contact at GBI."

"Mitch was an IT guy, so his friend is probably IT and knows the GBI IT team in Atlanta. I hadn't thought about that. I've got some retired folks I can ask without stirring up any interest."

"Riley has copies of Mitch's reports and the official reports that detail the inventory fraud and diversion of cash," Ben said.

Riley added, "I would have expected an audit to have found the fraud, but I just realized that I don't know who performed the audit because there's no record of an audit expense."

"Cash, do you suppose?" Ben asked.

Riley shrugged. "Or I just missed it. I'll look again."

Riley's fingers twitched as she glanced at her computer, and Ben smiled. "Go ahead. Sheriff and I will talk unless that will distract you."

"I'll be fine." Riley carried her wine to her computer and was soon immersed in the documents.

"I hear you're doing a bang-up job at the department," Sheriff said. "I'm getting pressure to promote you and send you to Macon for some GBI classes. You've really proven you're a talented leader. Let me know if you're interested."

Ben rubbed his face. "I'm really torn."

"I can understand that," the sheriff said. "Talk it over with Riley."

Ben audibly exhaled. "I need to think about it first."

The sheriff raised his eyebrows and then shook his head. "I'll rephrase that: let me know after you talk to Riley."

"I've been through all the expense records." Riley snapped her laptop closed. "I found a miscellaneous audit report expense, but it was less than one hundred dollars. I'd be interested in seeing the detailed audit report. Wouldn't that go to the stockholders?"

"Summary report, not necessarily the detailed, but I don't think the distribution company has stockholders," Sheriff said.

"Easy to check." Riley turned back to her computer.

Ben smiled. "We've lost her again."

"Have y'all heard anything about Tom or Dylan?" Sheriff asked.

"Not a word, and if Riley or anyone else at the clinic, other than Doc Julie Rae, had heard anything, I'd know."

Sheriff nodded. "You'd be surprised how many people don't realize how tight-lipped Doc can be when it's necessary. We have a strong trust relationship, so I asked her, and she hasn't. That's good. Eli's been keeping me up-to-date on Riley, and I'm sure I'm not the only one. It's too bad Riley had to cancel the wedding. So, what's the name of this new girlfriend you have?"

Ben laughed. "I'd love to be listening when Eli asks Riley or Claire about my new girlfriend. He definitely gets wrapped up in his personal version of Riley's life, doesn't he?"

"It will catch up with him. I'd like to tell him that Riley's lost interest in finding Tom now that she's been accepted into veterinary school because she's busy with her online pre-vet courses. What do you think?" Sheriff asked.

"Hey, honey," Ben called out, and Riley turned her attention from the screen to him and smiled.

Ben returned her smile and continued, "Sheriff plans to tell Eli you're taking online pre-vet courses and have lost interest in finding Tom. What do you think?"

"It's worth a shot. Eli will add his own spin, of course. I expect he'll add that he's tutoring me because he's so much smarter than I am." Riley furrowed her brow. "Why don't we have Claire tell him? She's been his source, and Sheriff can tell us what version of the story gets out."

"I like that," the sheriff said.

While Riley called Claire to tell her the latest rumor for Eli, the sheriff and Ben continued their discussion.

"The GBI training center and UGA are only five miles apart," the sheriff said. "You could do all your training and field assignments close to the university while Riley completes her studies. You definitely have the opportunity to take either path."

After Riley told Claire her latest Eli assignment, she returned to scouring the reports.

Ben furrowed his brow. "Riley has two university classes to pick up before she begins veterinary college. She was planning to take them online, but it would be better to take them on campus because of the opportunity to adjust before she's attending full time."

"Let me know what you and Riley decide."

"I found something," Riley said. "What are we going to decide?"

"We'll talk," Ben said. "What did you find?"

"Mitch included a copy of the Barton sales reports for the past six months, and there was a sudden gap in the inventory four months ago. I'll bet Angie discovered it through her sales records." Riley exhaled as she turned away from her computer. "Ranger is the bad guy, just like we thought."

"Do we know what Ranger's name is?" Ben asked.

"It's in the journal."

"I give up." The sheriff rolled his eyes. "Is this some kind of young folks code?"

Riley giggled, and Ben told the sheriff about Tom's story.

"But I don't remember anything about a journal," Ben said.

"Pia gave me Tom's writing journal before Marc searched her house," Riley said. "It's partly a diary, a weather tracker, snippets of his story, some calculations, and most importantly, details about the characters in Tom's novel. I didn't read all of it earlier because I didn't know what to look for."

"Show me where you found that in the reports." Ben pulled up a chair next to her.

Riley scrolled to the bottom of a report and pointed as the sheriff peered over her shoulder. "It's only on this one page."

"Looks like dots or a printer smudge," the sheriff said.

"My exact thoughts," Riley said, "until I remembered these are the reports that Mitch generated; they weren't printed. Watch this." She magnified the page to four hundred percent.

Ben frowned as he read the footnote. "Looks like it's the path for the report source. How is that telling us anything?"

Riley giggled. "Pick out words you recognize."

"I see phantom and silver," Ben said.

"I see horse and journal, except it's jo, dot, ur, dollar sign, nal," the sheriff added.

"That's it." Riley beamed. "Journal is what initially caught my eye because the dollar sign was an unusual symbol to see in a source path."

"I understand why you said journal, but Tom's book has no silver horse." Ben frowned.

"Is there a phantom?" Sheriff asked.

"I forgot to tell you 'Phantom Cattle' is the name of the book," Ben said.

"How did you know about the horse named Silver? Aren't you too young to remember Old West stuff like that?" Sheriff asked.

Ben chuckled. "Riley and I are super fans of Old West stories."

"What about Mitch? How did he know about Ranger and the journal?" Sheriff asked.

"Dylan or Tom must have told him before they disappeared," Riley said. "Tom's journal is in my backpack."

After she pulled out the journal, she glanced at Ben, who raised his eyebrows and side-glanced at the sheriff.

Riley smiled and nodded as she set the journal down. "Sheriff, Ben has something to tell you."

Ben burst out laughing and then wiped his eyes while the sheriff stared at him. "Well done, babe. Sheriff, I asked Riley to marry me. We haven't set the date, but it will be before we go to school."

The sheriff grinned, then hugged Riley and shook Ben's hand. "Best news I've had in ages. What took you so long?"

Ben rolled his eyes, and Riley laughed. "That's what Toby said."

"So, who all have you told?"

Riley counted on her fingers. "You, Toby, Jordy, and Ben's folks."

"I'm honored to be included in such illustrious company. When do you plan to share your news with the community?"

"We had planned to tell Riley's office tomorrow, but our new gossip kind of changes things, doesn't it?" Ben asked.

"We can wait." Riley searched Tom's journal for character descriptions. "Found it. Ranger's name is G.B., and Tom added a note: 'I marked G.B. for follow up.'"

"Mitch was a really creative guy. What a loss." Ben ran his fingers through his hair. "Even I understand that 'I marked G.B.' shuffles to 'GBI Mark.' We know what the crime is and who the criminal is, but we don't have any real proof."

"We're missing a piece," Riley said.

Ben and the sheriff glanced at each other; the sheriff shook his head. Ben frowned and then gazed at Riley, who met his gaze.

"I think I've got it," Ben said, "We're missing the inside piece: someone in the company high enough to pick the auditor, direct the contracting company in the design of the phony reports, and identify any staff member who was a threat."

"Yes, and Ezra is my choice, but I have nothing to back it up except for my dislike of him as a human being," Riley said.

"I'd go with your instincts any day, babe. How do we determine whether Ezra is involved and what his tie to Marc is?" Ben asked.

Riley dropped the journal into the backpack. "The easy answer is to ask Dylan or Tom."

The sheriff nodded. "I think I can take care of that, and I'll find us someone higher than Marc at GBI who we can trust."

After the sheriff left, Riley asked, "What will we decide?"

"You sure you aren't too tired?" Ben bit his lip.

"No such luck." Riley narrowed her eyes and moved to the sofa.

Ben sighed as he joined her. "Babe, I'm a good cop and love it."

"Your heart's not really in veterinary medicine, is it?" she asked as he put his arm around her. "I don't want to go to UGA without you."

"I could attend GBI training and start with the next spring class." Ben smiled. "The sheriff reminded me the training center is five miles from UGA."

Riley raised her eyebrows. "I didn't know the training center was so close. That takes care of my spring classes, but I have four years of veterinary school after that."

"I have options. I could work at the nearby GBI regional office or take additional specialized classes, and then after you graduate, you could support me so I don't have to take a side job." Ben grinned.

Riley giggled. "You got me there; every girl dreams of supporting her sexy cowboy husband."

Ben's eyes widened. "I'm sexy?"

Riley fluttered her eyelashes and whispered in a raspy voice, "Oh yeah, baby."

Ben kissed her, then buried his face in her hair and moaned. "Can we get married tomorrow?"

"It would have to be a secret wedding," she said, "and lots of people will be mad at us."

"Let's sleep on it." Ben helped Riley to her feet and kissed her good night before he locked up.

Riley's thoughts raced as she went to her bedroom and undressed for bed. *Ben would be happier at GBI. Maybe we could get married this weekend.*

She pulled up the covers and sighed. *He only applied to UGA, so I would apply. Did Marc or Ezra kill Mitch? Who could I talk to about a wedding? How could we get married with a killer still free? Wouldn't our wedding bring together the people the killer wants to silence? Will Mom be hurt if we get married in Barton?*

Riley flopped from one side to the other and stared at the ceiling. *I can't sleep.* She rolled to turn on her light and check the time. *Midnight. I wonder if Ben's asleep.*

She padded to his bedroom door and stood in the hallway while she listened to him breathe, then his bed creaked.

"You can't sleep either, babe?" Ben turned on the lamp next to his bed.

She gazed at his muscular arms and bare back and shivered with delight at the sight of his bare bottom when he reached for his jeans on the floor then slipped them on. *My sexy cowboy.* She glanced down at her flannel pajamas and rolled her eyes. *Not very alluring, even for a gunslinger.*

Ben put his arm around her. "You're shivering. I'll turn on the fire, and we can talk."

Riley smiled. "You make me shiver, but a fire sounds nice."

She sat on the sofa while Ben lit the fire in their gas fireplace. "I think I just need more cuddle time," she said.

When he joined her, Ben wrapped his arm around her shoulder and pulled her close, then kissed her neck, and she moaned.

Riley turned to face him and stroked his cheek with her fingertips before he bent forward and kissed her lightly. While she gazed at his face, she unbuttoned her pajama top and smiled when he grinned, then leered at her bare chest.

She pulled him into a passionate kiss, and he slipped his hand under her pajama top in the back and across her shoulder, and her pajama top slid down.

As their passion intensified, Riley leaned back her head and moaned. Ben nibbled her ear, then kissed her neck at her throat. "My place or yours, babe?"

"My place is bigger. Turn off the fireplace, and I'll pick up our clothes, then we can make a run for it."

Ben grinned and kissed her forehead. After he rose, Riley grabbed their clothes off the floor and dashed to her bed. She jumped under the covers and shivered in anticipation as Ben climbed next to her and pulled her close.

"I love you, Riley Erin." Ben moaned.

"I love you, Benjamin Jacob." Riley turned off her bedside lamp.

Riley smiled when she woke with Ben's arm draped across her. *Four thirty; if I can slip out quietly, I can make coffee, cinnamon rolls, and sandwiches before he wakes up for a change.*

She slowly slid out from under Ben's arm and cautiously slipped out of bed before she snatched her pajamas from the floor. She crept to the hall, then hurried to the kitchen and dressed. After she mixed the dough to rise and started a pot of coffee, Riley made three sandwiches and washed two apples. She checked the dryer and smiled at the small load of dry clothes. She pulled out underwear, a shirt, and jeans and hurried to the main bathroom for a quick shower.

When she returned to the kitchen, she rolled out the dough and spread on the cinnamon, sugar, and butter before she rolled the dough into a pinwheel log and cut it into buns. After she slid the rolls into the oven, she heard Ben in the shower and smiled. *Perfect timing. The aroma of baking cinnamon rolls will surprise him.*

When the bathroom door opened, Riley poured two cups of coffee while Ben hurried to the kitchen in his deputy uniform and wet hair.

"When did you get up, babe? I smelled cinnamon rolls. Does this mean we're getting married today?" He leaned over for a kiss before he grabbed his coffee and then turned to the refrigerator.

"I already made our lunch sandwiches," she said.

"When will the cinnamon rolls be done? I have enough time to fry some eggs to go with our cinnamon rolls for our wedding breakfast." Ben grinned his big, lop-sided grin.

"Three more minutes. Maybe we could have the wedding this weekend; I need to talk to somebody about that, but I don't know who. I know Mom offered to do everything. Maybe she'd like to host a family reception at her house, but I think I want the wedding to be where all our friends are."

Ben set the skillet on the stove and then opened the refrigerator. "Maybe you could talk to Doc Julie Rae, and she'll say to get married today; Sheriff said he trusted her."

Riley pulled out the cinnamon rolls from the oven while Ben fried their eggs.

After Ben plated their eggs and sat at the table, he bit into his cinnamon roll. "Mmm, babe. This is really good; will you marry me?"

Riley giggled. "You are such a goof. I heard you already had a fiancée."

"Fine, then, will you be my wife?" He peered at her over his cinnamon bun.

Riley laughed at his serious face that didn't hide his smirk then refilled both cups. "You are so sharp in the morning."

"Thanks." Ben sipped his coffee while Riley loaded all the dishes into the dishwasher and started it.

"I've got another idea," Ben said. "If Doc Thad releases Toby today, let's all go to your cabin for the rest of the week. It will be romantic there, and we'll have the actual fireplace."

"Okay. I'll work on a meal plan and a shopping list. Wait. That sounded very practical and not romantic at all. I might need you to pick up the slack for me."

"Sure, babe. Can I pick you up during lunch break to get our marriage license?"

"Now, that's romantic. I don't see why not. Do I need anything besides my birth certificate and my driver's license?"

"I think that's all; I guess we'll find out. So, can I tell the sheriff he can submit my name for the GBI training?"

"Yes."

"I love how you say yes." Ben kissed her, then snatched up his lunch sack and dropped in an extra cinnamon roll as he headed toward the door.

"Just one minute, mister." Riley grabbed his arm. "You can be all business-like with your polite hugs and run-out-the-door kisses, but I'm hankering for a real fiancé kiss from my sexy cowboy."

Ben's eyes twinkled. "Challenge accepted, ma'am."

He dropped the lunch sack on the floor, took her into his arms, and kissed her as he held her tight, then swung her backward until her hair touched the floor. Riley returned his deeply passionate kisses until she tapped his back twice.

"You absolutely took away my breath; you win." Riley giggled when he righted her.

Ben grinned. "I once saw that in an old movie when I wandered into the living room while Mom was watching TV. I was twelve and almost threw up."

Riley's eyes gleamed as she fanned her face with her hand. "You definitely caught the full spirit of a sexy cowboy, fiancé kiss."

She followed him outside for one more quick kiss, then grinned and waved at the neighbors who peeked through their window blinds when he shouted, "I love you!" while he opened his truck door.

She slid her computer into her backpack, wrapped the cinnamon rolls to take to the clinic, and grabbed her lunch from the refrigerator before she put on her heavy coat and dashed out to her car.

She frowned while she sat at an intersection and waited for the light to change. *I'll see how to change my online spring registration to on-campus classes and work on meal planning for the week. Maybe Claire can help me with meals; I have to talk to Doc Julie Rae about a wedding.*

The driver in the car behind her tapped his horn lightly once; Riley jumped and glanced at the green light, waved her thanks, and accelerated through the intersection.

After she pulled into her favorite spot in the staff parking lot, she exhaled and scolded herself. *You go heads down into your details and forget to be aware of your surroundings. The cabin's perfect until the sheriff's friend arrests Marc. You'll be safe with Ben, Jordy, and Toby.*

She scanned the parking lot and the street before she gathered her things and climbed out of her car. *Much better.*

Chapter Thirteen

Riley continued to scan her surroundings as she hurried inside to the breakroom. *I wonder if the rush to get married is because Ben thinks I might change my mind or something because I'm not very romantic and get too immersed in trying to figure out crimes and criminals. I need to work on that.*

Before starting a fresh coffee pot, she put her lunch in the refrigerator and the cinnamon rolls on the table. While she watched the coffee drip into the pot, she smiled. *But I am playful.*

She sent Ben a text. "We still share tonight, right, S.C.?"

While she waited for him to see and decode her message, she rushed down the hallway to see Toby and Jordy and to relieve George.

When she reached the kennel, Toby and Jordy barked, and George smiled. "We were fixing to go outside for a break. Care to tag along?"

"I'd love to."

Riley squealed when Toby stepped out of his open crate and trotted down the hall to the back door. "You're doing great, Toby. You'll definitely be going home today."

While Toby and Jordy investigated the grassy area surrounding the parking lot and took care of their morning business, Riley said, "If you'd like to go inside, George, we'll be fine. I made a fresh pot of coffee and brought cinnamon rolls."

"I'm happy to be outside in this crisp, fresh air, but you got me with the cinnamon rolls." George grinned, then went inside.

Riley's phone buzzed with a text from Ben. "Got you covered."

He understood my romantic reminder that we'd sleep together at the cabin. Riley smiled and then replied, "Yes."

After Toby and Jordy trotted to the back door, Riley let them inside, then raked and picked up the grassy area. As she put away the rake, she narrowed her eyes at the car that was partially hidden in the trees behind the clinic parking lot. *Must be Eli because nobody has shot me.*

Riley headed toward the door, but as she approached the dumpster, she spotted a quarter half-hidden in the gravel and leaned over to pick it up when a shot rang out. She clutched the quarter as she dived behind the dumpster onto her stomach, and the car from the trees roared past the clinic parking lot. Riley raised herself on one elbow but was too slow to get more than a quick look at the driver.

She sighed. *I spoke too soon. Big guy and I'm pretty sure it wasn't Eli.* Riley brushed the dirt and small rocks off her jeans and jacket then stuck her lucky quarter into her jeans' front pocket and went inside to wash her hands to clean off the dirt from the scratches on her left palm and the knuckles on her right hand.

While Riley texted Ben, Claire and Doc Thad came inside.

"Hi, Riley, there's a fresh bullet hole in the dumpster; did you see it? Oh, sorry; didn't notice that you were busy," Claire said.

Riley sent the text and stuck her phone into her pocket. "I'm done; I sent Ben a text. I brought our Monday cinnamon rolls and made fresh coffee."

While Doc Thad rushed to the breakroom for a cinnamon roll, Claire narrowed her eyes at the scrapes on Riley's hands. "Did someone shoot at you?"

Riley told her about picking up the area and her lucky quarter.

"That's awful. Do you want us to call Ben?" Claire asked.

"I don't think it will be necessary," Riley said as Ben burst into the back door, snatched Riley into his arms, and hugged her tightly.

Claire shook her head as she hurried to the breakroom.

"Babe," Ben sighed as he held her tighter. "What happened? Did you see who it was?"

She told him about picking up after the dogs, the car parked in the woods, and her lucky quarter. "The car sped past the clinic," she added. "The driver was a big guy, but I didn't get a good enough look to tell who it was; the car was a new model and dark, maybe black."

Ben narrowed his eyes. "Who knows about the shooting? Do you think it's possible he thought he was successful?"

Riley smiled. *He definitely has the soul of a cop.* "Doc Thad, Claire, and maybe George would know because they are here. It might have looked like he got me because I leaned over just as he shot, then immediately hit the dirt."

"Go with me to the breakroom; I want to talk to Thad and Claire, then call the sheriff."

After Riley and Ben joined Doc Thad and Claire at the table, Doc Julie Rae came in. "What's going on?" she asked.

"Coffee and cinnamon rolls," Claire said, "and we're about to receive instructions from Deputy Carter because someone shot at Riley this morning."

"And missed," Riley added.

Doc Julie Rae stared at Riley before she sat at the table, reached for a napkin, and selected a cinnamon roll. "What a way to start off the week; at least he missed."

Ben nodded. "It's possible the shooter thought he was successful because Riley bent over..."

Claire interrupted Ben, "to pick up a quarter that is her lucky quarter; oops, sorry." Claire blushed and pursed her lips.

Ben's mouth twitched as he suppressed a smile. "Yes, her lucky quarter, and she dove for the ground when she heard the shot. I'd like to keep this quiet and Riley out of sight. Is it possible to claim Riley took a vacation day, except be a little sad because you might be hiding that she was fatally shot?"

"Of course," Doc Julie Rae said. "Zach and Hector will be here today; we'll be fine."

"I'll fill in Zach," Doc Thad said.

"This cancels the Eli story, right?" Claire asked.

"Good point," Ben said. "Yes. I'll call the sheriff, then Riley and I will leave. I'll pick up Jordy and Toby at the end of the day."

After Ben left the breakroom, Doc Julie Rae said, "Let's see that lucky quarter, Riley. It might be the one I lost."

Riley pulled out the quarter while Doc Thad and Claire laughed.

Doc Julie Rae examined the coin and then handed it back to Riley. "Might be a sister to mine, but this one is definitely yours. Today will be especially wonderful for you because you have found your lucky quarter. Thank you for our Monday cinnamon rolls. Now, what was the Eli story that is now canceled?"

After Claire told Doc Julie Rae the story with the additional Claire embellishments, Riley said, "I'm kind of sad we won't get to hear Eli's version."

Claire nodded. "I'm absolutely certain it would top mine."

"You'll come up with something later for him, honey," Doc Thad said.

Claire frowned. "As long as he doesn't get himself fired first."

Doc Julie Rae rose. "I'll stop by and let George know we're all here so he can leave, then I'll be in my office. Come get me if there are any more instructions."

Claire sighed. "I have to get busy too. Talk to you later, Riley."

After they left, Doc Thad said, "Let me know if you need me to do any legwork for you while you're lying low."

Riley sipped her coffee while she thought. "There is one thing. If Ezra brings in Regina, take her to see Toby. I'll talk to Toby before I leave."

"I can do that." Doc Thad grinned. "No one outside this clinic would understand, but it makes total sense to me."

After he left for his office, Riley hurried to the kennel to talk to Toby. She told Jordy and Toby about someone shooting at her, and they growled. She said she wouldn't be at the clinic the rest of the day, then explained she'd asked Doc Thad to bring Regina back to talk to them if she came to the clinic. "Ask Regina if Ezra was home this morning, if he has a gun, and if he's a good shot."

Toby yipped, and Riley nodded. "Asking whether she trusts him is excellent; whatever you think might help. Ben will pick you up at the end of the day, so I'll see you later."

Riley strolled to Doc Julie Rae's office and tapped on her door as she walked in.

"More deputy instructions?" Doc asked.

"No, something personal."

"Close the door, sit down, and let's talk." Doc Julie Rae closed her laptop.

"Ben wants to get married today, but I don't see how to pull anything together before this weekend."

"Does he know that?"

"Yes, I've told him, but he still wants to get married today. He told me I should talk to you."

"Sounds like you aren't actually averse to being married today, so I think it's okay for you to relax. If he can pull it off, go for it. If you want a wedding this weekend, let me know. Either way, I'll put Charlie on notice for a wedding reception this weekend."

Tears slipped down Riley's cheek. "Thank you so much. I'll let you know, or Ben will; this takes off so much pressure."

Doc Julie Rae handed her a tissue. "You're entitled to cry on your wedding day. My money's on Ben, by the way. You may discover that he's as resourceful as you are."

Riley blew her nose, then cried again, and Doc handed her another tissue. Riley blew her nose one last time. "I'm done. I guess I needed that."

"It's your wedding week; you're entitled to act like a bride. When were you going to tell the rest of the staff?"

Riley's eyes widened. "Originally, we were going to keep our engagement quiet because of the Eli rumor, but there's no need now to keep it quiet." She frowned. "Except for the shooter."

Doc Julie Rae nodded. "I got all caught up in the excitement. Ben wants the shooter to think he might have been successful."

"Right, so we'll continue with Ben's plan."

"And keep our failsafe alternate plan in our back pockets," Doc Julie Rae added, and Riley snickered as she left the office for Claire's desk.

"I need help with a supper menu for this week so I can give Ben a grocery shopping list. Do you have some ideas or recipes for me?" Riley asked.

"Give me five minutes, and I'll have a ten-day menu and shopping list for you. I'll email you the recipes, including some of Thad's specialties. You and Ben will be great home cooks in no time."

"Thank you so much." Riley smiled. "My grilled cheese and frozen pizza diet got old four years ago."

Claire smiled. "My specialties before Thad and I were married were box macaroni and cheese and hot dogs; my mom always added vitamins to my birthday and Christmas presents." Claire motioned for Riley to leave. "You aren't supposed to be here; our first patient is in exam room three with Zach, and our next one will be here any time. I'll bring the lists to you."

After Riley returned to the breakroom, Ben called. "I'm picking up things for us to take to the cabin. I've packed all your clothes and everything from your bathroom. Can you think of anything else?"

"It wouldn't hurt to have two extra bath towels, and we'll need a food bowl for Jordy. Claire will give me a menu and grocery list in a few minutes."

"Perfect. Text me the shopping list, and I'll take care of it. Then I'll pick you up, and we'll go to the county building. Love you, babe."

Ben hung up, and Riley felt a twinge of panic. *I forgot to research the waiting requirements to be married in Georgia.*

She inhaled deeply through her nose and then held her breath before slowly exhaling through her pursed lips. *Okay, sexy cowboy, I'll relax and go for it.*

Claire brought her the meal suggestions and the shopping list. "I'll send you the recipes before lunch. Call or text me anytime if you have any questions."

Riley texted the shopping list to Ben. When Ben breezed into the break room an hour later, he grinned. "You ready, babe?"

She picked up her backpack and grabbed her sandwich from the refrigerator while Ben reached for the lone cinnamon roll on the table.

She hugged him. "I'm with you." He put his arm around her shoulders, and Doc Julie Rae smiled as they passed her in the hallway on their way out.

"Charlie plans to go with a cowboy theme at the boys' request," Doc whispered.

"Perfect," Riley said.

After they were on their way to the county building, Riley said, "I talked to Doc Julie Rae, and I'm ready for a wedding whenever we can be married. Our wedding consultants are planning a cowboy theme for the reception this weekend."

Ben raised his eyebrows and then smirked. "Kenny and Freddy, right? I'm impressed; you hired the most exclusive planners in town."

"I knew you'd approve. So, are we getting married today?"

"Yep. We'll go to the sheriff's office."

A tear slid down Riley's cheek. "Ben, that's wonderful. It will almost be like Dad is there."

Ben glanced at her. "Are you okay?"

"I'm fine except for my leaking eyes. It's a bride thing, according to Doc Julie Rae."

Ben paled. "I wasn't thinking. Did you want a big wedding and a bridal gown?"

Riley wiped away her tears and laughed. "Did you hear what you just said? Do you have groom jitters or something? Can you imagine me in a dress so fancy that it would be called a gown? What would our wedding consultants think?"

Ben chuckled. "I'd be run out of town by the cowhand club. To keep my secret, I'll have to bribe you with yellow flowers."

As he parked, Ben said, "Leave your backpack and carry piece in the truck, but bring your driver's license. Georgia verified your ID the last time you renewed your license, so you won't need your birth certificate after all."

Riley scanned the parking lot as they hurried through the cold to the building. "Eli just pulled into the parking lot and parked near the exit."

Ben grumbled as he called the sheriff. "Eli is parked in the county building parking lot." Ben nodded while he listened, then hung up.

"The sheriff said he'd send somebody to keep Agent Reeves busy for the next few days."

When they stepped into the building, Ben signed in as a county deputy, and then they headed to the Probate Office. There was no line, and the clerk guided them through their application. When she said, "Check this," Ben checked where she indicated. They presented their Georgia driver's licenses, signed the form, and were done.

She slid their license across the counter, and her eyes twinkled. "I love being the first to say, 'Congratulations.'"

When they stepped into the sheriff's office, Sheriff beamed, and Doc Julie Rae smiled as she handed Riley a small bouquet of white roses tied with a yellow ribbon. "I called the sheriff after we talked, Riley, and offered to be the second witness. I hope it's okay."

"It's more than okay; it's absolutely perfect," Riley said, and Ben smiled.

When the spry, wizened pastor came into the office, he said, "Thanks for the call, Ben. It's certainly a pleasure to meet you, Riley."

"You too, Pastor." *Ben thought of everything.*

The pastor's pale blue eyes twinkled as he smiled. "May I see your license?"

Ben handed him the license, and the pastor put on his reading glasses and nodded before he set the paper on the sheriff's desk and turned to face Riley and Ben. "No surprise; everything's in order. Doc, would you stand next to our bride? Sheriff, stand next to our groom?"

After everyone was in place, the pastor bowed his head and briefly closed his eyes, then asked, "Now, do you want the quick y'all kiss version or the long version that includes my most eloquent hour-long sermon?"

He scanned the four wide-eyed faces and then laughed. "I'm happy to see that I have your complete attention. The Lord and I thought we'd proceed with y'all kiss and go straight to the vows; by the book, okay, or have you written your own?"

Riley stared at Ben. *If he's written his vows, he better have written mine, too.*

Doc stepped closer to Riley. "By the book."

Pastor nodded, then asked, "May I have the ring?"

When Ben's face paled, the sheriff pulled out a ring from the chest pocket of his shirt. "This was my wife's engagement ring that a good friend of mine handcrafted for me, but she never wore it because we ran off to be married the day after she said yes. She saved it for the daughter we never had. It would be an honor if you would accept it, Riley. It's simple because she never cared for fancy jewelry."

When Sheriff handed the ring to the pastor, Doc said, "The two intertwined hearts are beautiful."

The pastor nodded, then blessed the ring and gave it back to the sheriff, who waited for the signal to give it to Ben.

"Take the left hand of your bride and repeat after me, Ben."

After Ben and Riley said their vows and Ben slipped the ring on Riley's finger, Pastor's eyes twinkled again. "You may kiss the groom."

Riley giggled, Ben grinned then leaned down, and she kissed him while Doc and Sheriff applauded.

"Paperwork, people." Pastor showed Riley and Doc, then Ben and Sheriff, where to sign.

"I'll take the license to my office and record it in the church records so I can get my holy credit for another successful wedding, then our office manager will run it over to be registered by the county in the morning. You'll get your certified copy in a couple of weeks. Meanwhile, the church record is legally binding."

The pastor left, and Doc hugged Riley and then Ben. "I have to run back to work. Thank you so much for letting me be a part of your special day."

Doc carefully returned Riley's bouquet to its box and left, while Sheriff hugged Riley and shook Ben's hand.

"Stay safe." Sheriff handed the bouquet box to Riley before she and Ben left.

As they drove out of town on their way to the cabin, Riley said, "That was the most awesome wedding I could have imagined, but I should have worn a gown."

Ben laughed. "You aren't going to let me forget that, are you?"

"Nope." Riley held out her left hand. "The ring fits my finger perfectly, and there aren't any sharp edges to catch on anything. It would be very easy to wear under gloves at work. Is it okay with you if I wear it as my wedding ring, or did you have something else in mind?"

"Obviously, I had nothing in mind." Ben smiled. "If you decide you'd like something later, we could always pick out a ring together, but your ring is almost like a family heirloom, isn't it?"

When they reached the cabin, Ben said, "After we put away the groceries and eat our sandwiches, I have to return to work. I'm really sorry about that, and I feel like such a jerk, but I have a few loose ends to take care of before the end of the day."

"Just means more stories to tell our children." Riley carried a duffel bag and her backpack to the front door and then set them on the porch while she unlocked the door. When she walked inside, Riley smiled at the cabin's signature aroma of cinnamon and the familiar smell of lingering wood smoke from the fireplace. *We're home.*

Ben brought in the cooler he'd filled with their refrigerated items, and while Riley emptied the cooler into the refrigerator and the freezer, he returned with both of their duffel bags and his uniforms that were still on hangers. After he carried the bags to the bedroom and hung up his uniforms in the closet, Ben said, "Ready for lunch? I'll unpack the rest of my clothes after Toby, Jordy, and I return later this afternoon."

While they ate lunch, Ben frowned. "Will you be okay by yourself out here? I'm not so sure I should leave you alone. Maybe you could spend the afternoon at Doc Julie Rae's house with Charlie, the boys, and Chuck."

"I'll be fine; you won't be gone that long, and I have a lot to do. I'm very familiar with the property. If someone came up the driveway or even tried to hike through the trees and brush, I'd hear them; I could disappear before they were within sight of the cabin. Finish your lunch, and kiss the bride."

Ben stuffed the rest of his sandwich into his mouth and, with his cheeks bulging with food, puckered his lips for a kiss; Riley spewed her sweet tea and sputtered. "Warn me next time."

Ben wiggled his eyebrows, then after he chewed and swallowed, he rose from his chair, crammed on his ballcap, and tapped the brim with two fingers. "Beware of my romantic side, ma'am."

She laughed. "I'll keep that in mind, cowboy."

Ben pulled Riley to her feet and hugged her. "Be safe, babe."

She pulled him into a sweet kiss; then they walked to his truck with their arms around each other.

"I love you, honey," she said as he climbed into the truck.

"Isn't that great?" Ben waved as he backed out and headed down the lane to the driveway.

After she put away the rest of the groceries and unpacked her clothes, Riley sat at the dining table with her laptop and opened her email to check for the email from Claire. She read the recipes. *I can do this.*

She scanned the rest of her emails and stared at an email as it popped up. *It's from Hector Pitt.*

"Call work. Woof."

She giggled. *Has to be Zach.*

Claire answered. "Good afternoon, ma'am. Please hold."

Riley narrowed her eyes. *Someone must have been standing at Claire's desk. Wonder if it's Eli.*

When Zach picked up the phone, Riley raised an eyebrow. *The background noise is gone. He's in one of the docs' offices.*

"I have information from our writer friend," Zach said. "The reports are new in the Barton distribution center but were used in Atlanta last year and in Augusta the year before that. E was charged with fraud in Augusta, but the charges were dropped after all the witnesses and the critical evidence disappeared."

"That doesn't sound good at all. Do we have any evidence of the other reports? Does the sheriff know about this?" Riley asked.

"I knew you'd want proof, so I asked, and the writer said to check the store numbers on the reports; as far as the sheriff is concerned, that's your job." Zach chuckled as he hung up.

Riley opened one of the reports on her computer, furrowed her brow as she carefully scanned it, then leaned back and exhaled. *I don't know what I'm looking for. I'll see if I can find the regional distribution center identification numbers on their website.*

While she searched the company's website for the locations of their regional offices, her phone rang.

When she answered, Claire said, "Sorry about sounding so weird when you called earlier; Eli stopped by to pump me for information. Of course, it took him forever to get to his point because he had to tell me about his big, fancy promotion and relocation to Savannah. He said he heard there was a shooting in this area and wanted to know if everyone was okay. After I told him we hadn't heard anything, he wanted to know where you were so he could tell you goodbye. I asked him questions about the shooting, and he ignored me; instead, he told me how desperately they needed him in Savannah because he starts tomorrow. Thankfully, a patient and client came in, and he left."

"I thought someone must have been there. I'm not really surprised it was Eli."

After their call ended, Riley found a map and a list of the distribution centers, including plant numbers, physical and mailing addresses, county, and phone numbers. She wrote the plant numbers for Atlanta and Augusta in her notebook and then frowned. *Barton isn't listed.* She examined the map. It would be in the same region as Columbus, which is Region 05. Armed with her new information, Riley reviewed all the reports and divided them into three distribution centers by plant numbers.

This confirms that they skimmed cash and covered up the shortage with the overstated inventory on their reports in the three locations where Ezra was General Manager. The audit reports from Marc's firm validated the fraudulent reports.

Riley sent Ben a text. "I've found the evidence for cattle rustler and Ranger."

Ben replied, "Will pick you up in 30 min."

While Riley organized her notes and the computer files, she heard a vehicle barreling up the driveway. *It isn't Ben's truck.*

She stuffed her computer and notes into her backpack and grabbed her coat before she locked the door and dashed into the brush behind the tool shed. Riley raced east along the narrow deer path toward the stream, then diverted to the south into the thickened brush before she stopped near an old ground blind. *This is the best spot to hear everything said at the cabin. It's like a sound funnel.* After Riley zipped up her coat and pulled the brown hood over her head, she crouched in the thicket, silenced her phone, and listened.

The vehicle skidded to a stop on the driveway gravel; Riley's eyes widened when three car doors slammed. She held her breath at the loud banging on the cabin door and flinched at the sound of the splintering door.

She bit her lip. *I have my carry piece, but I should have grabbed my rifle.*

"Go find her, girl. Go find Riley." Ezra's loud command echoed in the low section where she hid.

"I told you to keep your voice down," Marc growled.

Riley sent a text to Ben. "Marc and Ezra just broke into the cabin. May be a third man. I'm safe."

Ben replied, "On the way. Stay hidden."

While Marc and Ezra argued, the sound of an animal moved through the brush toward Riley, and then Regina licked Riley's cheek.

Riley swallowed hard before she pointed west and whispered, "They want to hurt me. Run to the driveway, then go away from the road and bark."

After Riley hugged her, Regina quietly made her way west. Riley exhaled as Regina raced north on the driveway and barked to announce she was hot on the trail.

"Let's take the car," Ezra said.

"Why don't you wait here," Marc said.

"Now, boss?" the third man asked.

"Now," Marc said, and a shot rang out.

"See what the dog's got, but I don't think Riley's in the woods," Marc said. "I think she's hiding in the house. I'll take care of Riley."

Riley sent another text. "Ezra shot. Marc is searching the cabin. Third man is searching north on foot. Be careful."

Riley's phone flashed a notice of an incoming call, and she shuddered. *Marc is calling me and listening for my phone.*

Marc hung up, and then she received a text from him. "Ben's at the ER. I can give you a ride. Where are you?"

If I don't answer, will he know I'm onto him?

Riley shrugged and left her backpack behind as she crept toward the cabin.

"Ran into some poison ivy or something, Boss. No sign of the dog," the man said as he approached the cabin.

Riley heard Marc step out of the cabin and onto the porch, "Thanks for your help; I'll take it from here."

The shot startled Riley, and she shuddered at the cruelty in Marc's voice as she crept toward the tool shed. When she heard Ben's truck roaring up the driveway, she clenched her teeth and texted, "Beware! Ambush!"

Ben's truck didn't slow down, and when Riley reached the back of the shed, she pulled out her pistol and peered around the corner. Marc faced the lane that led from the driveway to the cabin; he stood casually behind the car with his pistol drawn. As the truck tore down the lane, Marc clenched and unclenched his left fist, then brought it up to steady the pistol he held in his right hand.

Riley stepped away from the shed and assumed a shooting stance as she held her gun with two hands and pointed it at Marc. She slowed her breathing and waited.

Ben's truck stopped abruptly in the lane out of sight from the cabin, and Riley's mouth quivered into a weak smile. *He read my text.*

"Hey, Riley! Are you here? I've got a flat tire," Ben shouted.

Marc hesitated before he lowered his gun out of sight. "That you, Ben? Riley's not here, but I found two fatalities."

"Perp still around?" Ben called out between grunts.

Marc leaned to peer down the lane, lowered his gun, and rubbed his forehead. "Long gone."

He put his pistol behind his back and casually strolled toward the lane. "You know where Riley is?"

"Thought she was here." Ben groaned. "Been a while since I've changed a tire."

Marc continued his cautious pace in the middle of the lane, and Riley stepped into the trees on the south side and crept along, staying parallel to him to keep him in her gun sights. Her eyes widened as Regina appeared in the pine trees on the north side across from her.

"That's far enough, Marc. Drop your weapon," Ben growled. "We've got you covered."

Marc sneered. "With what? You and your tire iron?"

"And me," Riley said, and Regina snarled.

Chapter Fourteen

Marc hesitated before he turned his head from side to side to look for Riley and Regina, then, in one swift motion, raised his gun, pivoted, and fired at Riley. The three shots were indistinguishable as Marc collapsed.

Riley kept her weapon trained on Marc.

Ben called out, "You okay, babe?"

"Not a scratch."

When Ben reached Marc, Riley stepped out of the trees, and Regina bounded to her while Ben checked Marc.

"Two wounds: one on the side of his head and one on the left side of his chest." Ben strode to Riley and hugged her then pulled out his cell phone while he held onto her. "I'll call the sheriff."

While Ben was on the phone, Riley reached out for Regina and stroked her face. "You were awesome; thank you so much for your help. You saved me, you know."

After Ben hung up, he grinned. "I'm on administrative leave for two weeks. Shall we honeymoon at the beach after we have the receptions here and at Mom and Dad's this weekend?"

"Beach sounds great, but it will be cold." Riley shivered as a blast of cold wind blew off her hood and chilled her.

"Let's wait inside the cabin," Ben said, and they walked arm in arm as Regina trotted alongside them.

While Ben stoked the fire, Riley heated water for hot tea and started a fresh pot of coffee in the old, blue-speckled campfire pot, and the sirens that wailed in the distance grew closer.

When the sheriff burst into the cabin, Regina growled and leaned against Riley.

"Sheriff's one of the good guys," Riley whispered.

Regina trotted to the sheriff and welcomed him when he offered his hand to sniff.

"Coffee?" Ben poured two cups and handed one to the sheriff.

After Ben and the sheriff sat at the dining table, the sheriff said, "Tell me what happened."

When Riley joined them at the table with her hot tea, Ben had moved her chair close to his. He wrapped his arm around her shoulder and held onto her tightly.

She began her story by telling them about hiding in the woods after she heard the car speeding up the driveway with the three men inside. When she explained that Regina found her and then diverted the men's attention to the north, Regina sat up and proudly raised her head while Ben scratched her ears and said, "Good girl."

"Who busted down the door?" the sheriff asked.

"I'm not positive, but I think it was Marc because he searched the cabin after he said I was hiding inside."

The sheriff slammed his fist on the table, grabbed the coffee pot from the stove, and refilled the two cups. After he returned the pot to the burner, he stood at the kitchen window with his steaming cup and stared outside.

"Marc was a good friend and a trusted colleague for a long time." His voice was soft.

"I had twinges of doubt..." He shook his head as he resumed his seat. "Who shot Ezra?"

"Marc gave the order, and the other man fired. Marc shot the other man." Riley's voice cracked. "I guess the guy had outlived his usefulness."

"These are the texts Riley sent me." Ben handed his phone to the sheriff.

"Marc called me, and he sent this after I didn't answer." Riley slid her phone to Ben.

After Ben read it, he gave Riley's phone to the sheriff.

The sheriff's face reddened as he read Marc's text. "Show me your evidence, Riley."

"I left my backpack in the woods. I'll be right back." She put on her heavy coat.

"I'm going too," Ben said, and Regina waited at the door.

While Ben followed Riley down the deer path, Regina disappeared into the trees.

"Why did you leave your backpack?" Ben asked as he scanned the thick brush.

"I had to move fast, and if Marc survived me, I didn't want him to have the evidence."

"Sorry I asked," Ben mumbled.

After Riley picked up her backpack, Ben whispered, "I can hear the crew on the lane talking, and their voices are very clear. Can they hear us?"

"Not at all. Grandma showed me this a long time ago. I was the only one that knew about her listening spot."

"This is totally awesome. The slope must channel the sound."

After they returned to the cabin, Riley powered on her computer and explained how she found the plant numbers then showed the two hovering men the reports and explained the discrepancies.

"Give me your notes and copies of those reports, and I'll give them to the right GBI team," the sheriff said.

While Riley copied the electronic files to a flash drive, the sheriff said, "Tom will be rejoining his family soon, and Dylan and his family will return to town. One of the retired sheriffs in our old guys' network found both of them and orchestrated Tom's move to a safe house in our network and Dylan's move to a safe campground where Marc couldn't find either one of them. Old sheriffs stick together."

A tear slid down Riley's cheek as she gave Sheriff the flash drive and the folder with all her notes. "You are truly awesome."

"The protect and serve never stops, Riley. Ben and a few of his trusted peers will most likely continue our legacy in the years ahead. Are you ready for that?" the sheriff asked.

"Absolutely; that's who he is," Riley said.

Ben blushed and cleared his throat as he shifted his attention to Regina. He raised his eyebrows at Regina's coat matted with burrs and her muddy feet. "You look like you had a great time, but you'll need an emergency appointment with your groomer."

"When can we leave, Sheriff?" Riley asked.

"Any time. I'll go to tell Mrs. Buchanan about her husband's demise."

"Thanks," Riley said. "I'd like to return Regina to Bethany."

"I could take Regina with me when I see Mrs. Buchanan," the sheriff said. "Ready to go, Regina?"

Regina bounded to the door and grinned.

"You are a really smart girl," the sheriff said as they left.

"We still need to pick up Toby and Jordy," Riley said. "I'll call Mom to let her know the wedding isn't a secret anymore, and we can have our reception this weekend."

Ben nodded. "I'll fix the front door."

While Ben gathered tools and wood and repaired the door and the latch, Riley called Melissa and then Doc Julie Rae.

When Riley hung up after her calls, Ben had finished the repairs and picked up his tools and scraps.

"That didn't take long. Ready to go?" he asked.

Riley giggled. "Mom told me she needed to get busy and practically hung up on me. Doc Julie Rae said Charlie has already started his preparations for Saturday; Pia heard about Ezra, so she and Jackson will pick up Jordy at the clinic this afternoon. The sheriff called Doc Julie Rae and offered to pick up Toby at the end of the day and bring him here. I wasn't terribly surprised; it's a small town."

Ben grinned, swooped Riley into his arms, and carried her to their bedroom. "Babe, finally, our honeymoon officially begins."

Next to read:

STALKED BY DEATH, RILEY MALLOY MYSTERY, Book 4

Riley Malloy, vet tech and dog whisperer, is the only one left alive who believes her father's death was not an accident and can expose the crimes of an international ring. Her enemy watches and waits for an opportunity to kill Riley.

BarrettBookShop.com

Subscribe and Save

About the Author

Judith A. Barrett is an award-winning author of thriller, mystery, and science fiction stories with a twist to spark the reader's imagination. Her unusual main characters are brilliant, talented, and down-to-earth folks who solve difficult cases and stop killers. Her novels take place in small towns and rural areas in the southern states of the US.

Judith lives on a small farm in rural Georgia with her husband, two rescue dogs, TJ and Toby, and sassy chickens. When she isn't writing, Judith is busy working on the farm, camping with her FarmerMan, TJ, and Toby (but still writing), or relaxing on her front porch while she watches the sunset and wonders what will happen next in her latest book she is writing.

You keep reading; I'll keep writing!

Also by Judith A. Barrett

RILEY MALLOY THRILLER SERIES
WREN AND RASCAL MYSTERY SERIES
GRID DOWN SURVIVAL SERIES
MAGGIE SLOAN THRILLER SERIES
DONUT LADY MYSTERY SERIES

Interested in more information about her books?
Check Barrett Book Shop: BarrettBookShop.com
Browse, shop, read, enjoy!

www.ingramcontent.com/pod-product-compliance
Lightning Source LLC
Chambersburg PA
CBHW030633030726
47497CB00006B/1762